#CassiNova

About the Author

Lori G. Matthews lives outside of Philadelphia with her wife and two cats. Her first brush with literary fame came at the age of thirteen when her composition, an amusing tale told from the perspective of a soccer ball, was the only one read aloud by her teacher. To this day, she still loves to write lighthearted comedies because laughter truly is the best medicine. When not writing, you can find her in the woods hiking, bird watching, or looking for her golf ball.

#CassiNova

Lori G. Matthews

BELLA
BOOKS
2020

Bella Books, Inc.
P.O. Box 10543
Tallahassee, FL 32302

Printed in the United States of America on acid-free paper.

First Bella Books Edition 2020

Editor: Alissa McGowan
Cover Designer: Kayla Mancuso

ISBN: 978-1-64247-165-6

Acknowledgment

This book has been a wonderful journey for me. What started out as a fanfiction, morphed into a debut novel, and it would not have been possible without the help of a few good women. I first have to give a big thank-you to my publishers, Linda and Jessica Hill of Bella Books, who saw potential and took a chance on me.

Thank you to my editor, Alissa McGowan, whose steady guidance made my first editing process a breeze.

Where would I be without my three beta readers? Ana Wootten, who was and still is my biggest cheerleader. Any time I had doubts about my ability, she would offer words of encouragement, then tell me she was going to go back and read it again. I think she read the manuscript more than I did. Lisa Magnum, who was more than a beta, she was my wingman. She purchased the Chicago Manual of Style for both of us, and when we each received our copy, she said, "It's a big book." And I said, "I ain't reading that." Patsy R., my friend of twenty years, who read the first version of this manuscript and told me it was great, even though it was an overly wordy, head hopping mess.

A big shout-out to all the friends I met online these past few years. E, my adopted pseudo-daughter, who showed me that an Internet connection can turn into a wonderful friendship. Regina, who bet me three years ago that I could turn this story into a published novel. Guess what? I had to pay up. Aliza M., who insisted I was good enough to get published and helped get me started. All the crazies I affectionately dubbed my Misfit Toys, who commented on my fan fictions and blew up my first Facebook post with a thousand gifs. Thanks to you I had days and days of notifications on my phone. And I would be remiss if I didn't mention The Purple Chicken Cook-Off, which remains one of the highlights of the last few years. Thank you, Misfits. I am honored to call you friends.

Lastly, my partner and wife of twenty years, whose patience and support enabled me to see this through. She spent countless hours reading chapters, with me hanging over her shoulder, yelling, "Why aren't you laughing?" Thank you, T. I love you.

One last shout-out, to our beautiful dog Everette, who was the inspiration for Yogi. Our Evi Bear crossed the rainbow bridge last year, but he'll live on in this story. And that's pretty damn cool.

CHAPTER ONE

West Hollywood

It was a crime scene.

Flecks covered the cabinets. Dots peppered the ceiling. The spatter had made it clear across the room. The only thing missing was the chalk outline of the avocado that had met its untimely end in the Cuisinart Pro food processor. And in the middle of it all stood Samantha Cassidy, Emmy-award-winning actress, nibbling on her bottom lip. Chunks of green goo perched in her blond hair, and pea-colored fragments stuck to her cheeks. "Shit."

The front door slammed. "Sami! Where you at?" Jade called.

"In the kitchen."

"What's cooking in there? Hopefully not your cookbook."

In the annals of kitchen disasters, the cookbook incident ranked right at the top. Sam's Emeril Lagasse recipe book had gone up in flames during the maiden voyage of the Viking gas stove a few months ago. It had been propped on the back burner, making it easier to read while sautéing on the front burner. The wrong knob was turned, and poof!

As Jade walked into the kitchen, Sam hopped up from the floor, sponge in hand. "Hey." She wiped her forehead, smearing green goop through her dark brows.

"Huh." Jade stood with hands on hips. "Forget the lid?"

"Gah. Can you believe it?"

"Yes, Sami. Yes, I can believe it."

Jade placed her car keys on the counter and tiptoed around puddles of gunk to grab a beer from the fridge. "I'm gonna pitch an idea to the network. It'll be a cooking show called *What Not to Do in the Kitchen*. Starring you, of course. We'll bill it as a comedy."

Sam grimaced. "I'm not that bad."

"Well, you almost burned the place down with your little cookbook adventure."

"Oh please. It was just a small fire."

"Tell that to the fire department. Now, c'mon. Clean that shit up later. Your show's coming on." She hurried into the living room.

Sam spent every Sunday night from February through April with her best friend and manager, Jade Ramos, watching her hit sci-fi series, *Gemini*. Well, Jade watched. Sam usually had her earbuds in listening to music and checking fans' reactions on social media. Neither she nor their friend Emma, who also starred on the show, could stomach watching themselves on-screen. However, tonight was the season finale, and a quick peek may not be out of the question. Sam's character, Commander Calleah "Callie" Jenkins, was consummating her relationship with fan-favorite Ophelia Beck. #Calliope had been trending for a season and a half.

Jade grabbed the TV remote. "I think a lot of people are going to lose their shit tonight, my friend."

Sam hunkered down on the couch next to Jade. "I don't think it'll be that bad."

"Ten bucks says it's a shitstorm."

"You're on. Jackson and the other writers think everyone will love the fact that they hook up."

"Oh, they'll love the hookup. They ain't gonna love what comes next. The fan base is gonna go fucking ballistic."

"I'm getting you a swear jar," Sam threatened, "and it's gonna be a buck for every f-bomb. And then I'm donating it to charity."

"A buck? What happened to a quarter?"

"Inflation."

As the opening credits started to roll, Sam's phone rang. "It's Emma." She hit the speaker button. "Hey, E."

"Hey, bitches, I'm at the gate. Open up."

Jade hustled over to push the gate button and returned to the couch. "After six months, you'd think she'd remember the damn code."

"I love her, but she barely remembers her lines."

A minute later the door flew open, and a breathless Emma ran in. "Did I miss the sex?"

Jade cocked an eyebrow. "Well, somebody's excited. Hurry. It's starting."

"I need a drink." Emma jogged into the kitchen and froze. "Whoa! What happened in here?"

"Sam made dip."

"Why's it on the ceiling?"

"Because *Sam* made dip."

Pasadena

"I think this is it!" Alex Novato sat on the floor in front of the couch with her dog, Yogi, nestled in beside her. "You guys are gonna miss it." She cranked the volume on the remote.

Alex's older sister, Lenna, and her wife, Sophia, hustled in from the kitchen and plopped onto the sofa behind Alex.

"Finally, after two seasons," Lenna said.

All eyes locked on the screen as Ophelia tugged Callie closer and kissed her softly on the lips. They ripped at each other's clothing, and soon their naked bodies pressed against each other on the hard ground inside the cave.

"Yeah, baby!" Alex and Lenna shared a high five as the show went to commercial.

Sophia sighed. "The actresses have such great chemistry. You don't see that much with two women on TV."

"Sam Cassidy is my favorite actress," Lenna gushed. "Goddamn, she's hot."

"I wouldn't kick her out of bed," Alex agreed.

"I guess not. She's just your type. All blond haired and blue eyed."

"And she's got curves in all the right places—"

"Okay, you two, stop drooling," Sophia said. "And stop objectifying her. Now, be quiet. It's coming back on."

The sisters exchanged a sheepish look.

"Sorry, babe, you're right," Lenna said.

The mood at the Novato house changed dramatically as the next scene unfolded, their euphoria over the kiss short-lived. Lenna and Sophia gawped at the screen as the ending credits rolled.

"Wow, no more shipping Calliope," was all Alex could manage.

Sophia finally found her voice. "They had sex, and then they killed her? How could they do that?"

Alex slumped against the couch. "Assholes. 'Bury the gays' trope strikes again."

West Hollywood

As the episode ended, Sam and Emma sniffled and wiped their eyes while a stoic Jade checked her phone.

"Well?" Sam asked.

"Holy hell, it's Armageddon. Twitter's blowing up. Would you like to hear from your fans?"

"Oh God. Go ahead." Sam's stomach muscles clenched.

"Let's see. @calliopeforever says, 'What the hell was that?' And @calliopeshipper wrote, 'Why are they always killing the lesbians?' @ishipcalliope tweeted, 'I will never watch this show again!' It goes on and on and on. You owe me ten bucks."

Sam slapped the arm of the couch. "I knew it! I told them not to kill her off. I begged them not to do it." She collapsed against the back of the sofa and pinched the bridge of her nose as uneasiness settled in her gut. The next few weeks would be challenging. An angry fan base could damage the show.

Jade continued to scroll. "What a fucking nightmare."

Sam cleared her throat and extended a hand.

Glaring, Jade sat back with crossed arms. "Fuck that."

Sam put both hands out and wiggled her fingers.

Jade sighed as she reached into a pocket and grabbed a five-dollar bill. "Change?"

"No. I'll keep a tab."

"Why does she owe money?" Emma asked.

"I'm charging a buck for every f-bomb," Sam said.

"Oh. She's gonna need more than a five-dollar bill."

CHAPTER TWO

Jade, Emma, and Sam took turns hosting girl's night, where they would *usually* enjoy a nice, home-cooked meal. But this week, it was Sam's turn.

"Thanks for stopping at Maggio's to pick this up," she said to Jade as they relaxed on the patio, their bellies full. Maggio's was Sam's go-to place whenever disaster struck in the kitchen.

"No problem. I figured it's better than eating cookbook à la mode."

"So what happened in there tonight?" Emma asked.

"Well, I'm not quite used to the temperature of the oven—"

"Sami," Jade interrupted.

"What?"

"Four hundred degrees is the same in every oven, buddy."

"No, I think it's hotter in this oven."

"I'm sure that's it," Jade mumbled.

"What?"

"Nothing."

Sam surveyed the jungle that was her backyard. "I can't wait to get all this cleaned up. I think I'm gonna hire someone to do it."

"That would be wise," Jade said.

Sam had purchased the fixer-upper in West Hollywood about six months earlier. The kitchen and bathroom renovations had topped her to-do list, and the contractors had arrived shortly after closing. But the outside landscaping was a horror show. And that was being kind. Potential existed, and with imagination and effort, it could be a peaceful retreat. A quaint and wonderful space to share with a special someone.

Sam grabbed her sketchbook and walked to the pool. She yanked at the weeds growing between the cracks in the concrete.

Emma's eyes were glued to her phone. "One good thing about all the hubbub with the show these past few weeks, the fan fiction is lot more interesting."

"You got that right," Jade said. "Some juicy shit out there."

"You read that stuff?" Sam asked. She breathed in the scent of the honeysuckle growing over the crumbling retaining wall on the far side of the pool. Honeysuckle was one of her favorite smells. Her father had introduced it to her when she was six years old. Sam had delighted in watching the hummingbirds stream into their backyard to drink the nectar from the flowers.

"Hell yeah. Most of them are rewriting the last episode, giving it a happy ending," Jade said.

Emma smirked. "You just like the sex scenes."

"Guilty."

Sam began sketching a pond with a waterfall and flowers surrounding it. When she finished drawing, she collapsed on a chaise.

"What's up?" Jade asked. "You've been down the last few weeks. Have you seen Brian lately?"

"No. I'm so over that."

"He serves a purpose, you know."

"I know, he's my cover. I get it. But he can be an ass. I don't think it's gonna last much longer."

"What's bothering you?"

"I don't know. Ever since the episode aired, it's stirred stuff up, like I'm betraying everyone by hiding in the closet. And I think about how much I miss being with a woman. You know how long it's been since I kissed a girl?"

"Who are you? Katy Perry?"

"I'm serious! It's been since college. Maggie, remember? That's six or seven years ago. I've been feeling lonely lately." Sam gazed into the distance. "I think I…I just wanna fall in love again."

"You know what I think? I think you think too much." Jade stood and grabbed some dishes to take inside.

"I miss being with a woman!" Sam picked up the rest of the dishes and followed Jade into the house. She was out to family and close friends, but to the rest of the world she was Samantha Cassidy, heterosexual Hollywood starlet. And she hated it.

Jade stopped in the dining room and turned to Sam. "Hey, who's that on the mantel?"

Sam glanced at the gold statuette sitting on the shelf. "Mr. Emmy."

"Exactly. And why is there an empty spot next to him?"

"Because he needs a friend."

Jade continued to the kitchen. "Exactly. He needs Mr. Oscar. Whose childhood dream is it to win an Oscar?"

"Mine."

"Exactly. See how agreeable you can be?" Jade loaded the dishwasher. "The chances of you getting Oscar-worthy scripts are a lot slimmer if you're an out lesbian in Hollywood. I mean, it's not impossible, but tougher." Jade put a hand on each of Sam's shoulders. "So listen. You lay low. You win an Oscar, and in your acceptance speech, you flip them all the bird and tell them you would like to thank your lover, Susie so-and-so."

"But there's *not* a Susie so-and-so to thank. I don't even have discreet affairs. I want a fucking girlfriend!"

Jade grabbed the swear jar and shook it. "If I have to pay, everyone pays."

After cleaning the kitchen, they all headed to the living room. Two couches and two overstuffed, comfy chairs with ottomans surrounded the 55-inch LED television. A large square coffee table sat in the middle like an anchor. Blues and soft yellows were the colors du jour. Sam had a weakness for throw pillows—a multitude of them littered every sitting surface. When she was home alone, she liked nothing better than to curl up on the couch and immerse herself in pillows.

Sam chilled in one of the oversized chairs as she put the finishing touches on her backyard dream space.

Jade stood next to the sofa and began tossing pillows in the air. "Where's the damn couch? I swear you are banned from buying any more pillows." She finally cleared a spot and nestled in. "What movie should we watch tonight? How about that new comedy with Sandy Bullock? It's on HBO."

Sam fiddled with her pencil, lost in thought.

"All right, you know what? You need to get laid. Hey, E, we need to get Sami laid."

"Okay."

Sam pressed her lips together. "I don't think that's what I need."

Jade bounced up and paced around the room. "Find someone for her to bang."

"I really don't want that."

Her friends ignored her.

"Tap that," Emma added, hopping off the ottoman to follow Jade around the room.

"Hit it and quit it. Get your freak on. Ride her hard and put her away wet." Jade's voice changed with each expression as she danced around the room. "Git jiggy with it."

"Yeah! Get jiggy!" Emma waved a hand in the air, shaking her bottom to an imaginary beat.

Exasperated, Sam chucked a throw pillow at each of their heads. "You both suck." She laid her head back against the chair and groaned. "I'm destined to be alone."

Jade tossed a pillow back in Sam's direction. "Oh, c'mon. You can have any woman you want because you are that gorgeous. But you're too much of a romantic. You gotta be *in love*. God forbid you have a little promiscuous sex."

"Promiscuous sex can be healthy," Emma suggested.

"Healthy? Being a vegan's healthy," Jade said. "She needs more than black bean burgers. She needs some mind-blowing orgasms."

While her besties kept going on about her sex life, Sam's mind drifted to Jade's earlier statement. If she wanted the best chance at good scripts, she had to stay in the closet.

Memories of childhood floated back to her. When she was young, Sam had often performed for her parents. She would sing and dance, and they'd always clap, lauding her talent. Dad was the biggest fan of all. He'd made an Oscar from an old glass bottle and aluminum foil, presenting it to Sam after every performance. But despite all the acting at home, she hadn't taken it any further.

Then one gloomy Tuesday morning when Sam was fourteen, her mom had arrived at school with crushing news. Dad had died from a massive heart attack. In the blink of an eye, Sam's life changed forever.

After his death, she was inconsolable. A teacher at school pushed Sam toward theater, thinking she could channel all those emotions into performing, and that's when Sam had gotten hooked on acting for good. High school plays, musicals, community theater—she'd done it all. She was determined to win an Oscar for her dad and dedicate it to him.

So for now, the status quo. No soft lips to kiss. No silky-smooth skin to caress. No deep emotional connections.

Miss Right would have to wait. For now.

CHAPTER THREE

Alex arrived home from work on Saturday exhausted. A nice warm soak was just what the doctor ordered to soothe her aching muscles. She slipped into the water, inhaling the scent of lavender bubbles, and the stress of the day melted away.

Tonight she had a hot date with Cynthia, a real looker with stylish blond hair and legs for days. They'd hooked up last Saturday, and the sex had been good enough for a repeat performance—a rare event for Alex's current lifestyle.

She toweled off, dressed, and headed downstairs.

Lenna and Sophia were staring at the computer when Alex entered the kitchen. They made a striking couple, both usually the tallest women in a room. But the similarities ended there. Lenna's short, dark hair swept away from her face, and her wide shoulders tapered down to narrow hips. Sophia was all soft curves and smiles, and had long reddish brown ringlets that cascaded down her back. Their personalities were also at opposite ends of the spectrum. Lenna, a black belt in Taekwondo, tended to be crass and would just as soon hug you as punch you. Sophia was a psychiatrist, and her soft, caring demeanor drew people to her. If Alex needed an emotional pick-me-up, Soph was her go-to gal.

"What are you two birds doing?"

"Reading some fan fiction on our favorite show. Everyone is writing happy endings for Calliope," Lenna said.

"And there's lots of sex," Sophia added.

Alex cocked one eyebrow. "So you're basically reading porn."

Lenna scoffed. "It's not porn. It's love. Is that what you're wearing for your date?"

Alex checked herself out: old, weathered jeans, black boots, tight-fitting tank, and a baseball hat. "Yeah, what's wrong with it?"

"You look like a slob."

"It doesn't matter. It's coming off in a couple of hours anyway."

"You're such a player. Who's the flavor of the week tonight?"

"Same girl as last weekend."

"Oh, wow, that's a first. A second date." Sophia chuckled.

"Why can't you find a nice girl and settle down?" The creases in her forehead deepened. "You're thirty, for God's sake. I worry about you."

Alex rolled her eyes and playfully flipped her sister the bird on the way to the door. "Later, bitches. Have fun reading about sex, while I'll actually be having it."

"Oh, we'll be having it," Sophia called after her.

"Yeah, if you come home and there's a sock on the door, it means do not disturb," Lenna added.

Alex waved a hand in the air. "Right. Don't wait up."

* * *

Alex woke early the next morning, disoriented, and it took a moment to adjust to her surroundings. Cynthia's arms were wrapped around her like tentacles, clinging and squeezing the life from her. With as much stealth as possible, she tried to disentangle herself. She wasn't surreptitious enough, apparently, because the arms tightened.

"Mmm. You feel good," Cynthia purred. "I hope you're staying this time. I'll make breakfast."

Panic rose in Alex's chest. She tried to let Cynthia down as gently as possible. "I can't. I have some work I have to finish today."

"It's Sunday. We can lounge around all day if you want."

Alex jolted from the bed just in time to avoid Cynthia's searching lips. Time to make a swift getaway before any more talk of future plans. She hunted through the clothes on the floor and started getting dressed.

"You're really leaving?"

Alex silently cursed. This was why she didn't do second dates. "I can't stay. I'm sorry." She bent down, gave Cynthia a peck on the lips, and hurried from the room.

"Call me!" echoed down the steps as Alex closed the front door.

When she made it home and stepped onto the front porch, Alex laughed. It wasn't a sock. It was underwear. Of the pink lacey variety. Taking it off the doorknob, she quietly entered the house. Yogi greeted her with a furiously wagging tail.

"Hey, Yogi Bear, how's my boy? Anybody up yet? C'mon, let's go outside." As soon as the back door opened, he shot into the yard.

Alex still had the underwear, so she put it on her head and went to the bottom of the steps, where she yelled, "Get your asses up if you want some of my world-famous eggs." She listened, smiling when footsteps pattered on the floorboards above.

Ten minutes later, two sleepyheads came downstairs, still in their pajamas, yawning.

"Did someone say eggs by Alex?" Sophia asked.

"You know that underwear is dirty," Lenna said.

"Gross. Who puts dirty underwear on the door?" Alex threw the offending panties across the room.

"I forgot to do laundry."

Alex scooped eggs onto plates. She let Yogi back in and put food in his bowl.

As everyone quietly enjoyed their breakfast, Alex looked around the table, realizing how lucky she was to be a part of this quirky family.

"You never opened your mail from yesterday," Lenna said between bites.

Alex had forgotten all about it. In fact, she didn't even have to read the letter.

"Who wants to guess what this one says?" Alex asked, ripping it open.

"Who's it from?" Sophia asked.

"Premier Books."

"Oh, let me," Lenna said. "Ah, Dear Miss Novato—"

"Eeehhh." Alex imitated a buzzer. "Wrong. It says, 'Dear Author, we regret to inform you we will not be publishing your manuscript *The Seekers* blah blah blah…' I'll just add this one to my growing stack."

"It's gonna happen someday." Sophia squeezed Alex's hand.

"It's been two years," Alex said, dejected. She imagined the manuscript languishing on some editor's hard drive. Buried in a folder with a thousand other submissions.

"These things take time. Stay positive," Sophia said.

"So how was your date?" Lenna asked.

"I probably won't be seeing her again. She got clingy this morning."

"God forbid she likes you." Lenna rolled her eyes.

Alex changed the subject. "How was your porn reading last night?"

"Fun, but I was telling Soph about *your* porn. Remember you had that creative writing class in college where you spent a week learning how to write a love scene?"

"I do remember. And I have the porn to prove it." Alex had graduated from Arizona State University with a major in English and minor in astronomy. To some, the two disciplines were an odd couple, but Alex's dream was to write science fiction, so they made perfect sense for her.

"Alex was instructed to read her scene out loud in class," Lenna told Sophia. "She got halfway through, and the teacher told her to stop."

Alex pretended to be wounded. "Evidently, my lesbian sex was too explicit."

Sophia laughed. "That's funny. You should write fanfic then. Bet you'd write some good sex scenes."

"What a great idea! Write a fanfic. Do it, do it," Lenna begged.

"I am not writing a fanfic."

"Why not? You've had writer's block on the sequel to your novel. Maybe if you write something else, it'll get those creative juices flowing."

Alex didn't immediately dismiss the idea, because she did need a jump-start of sorts. "What would I write about?"

"Our show," Sophia said. "Give Calliope a happy ending."

Both Lenna and Sophia stared at Alex with hopeful eyes.

The wheels started to turn in Alex's head. Plotlines and character arcs started to develop and evolve. "All right, maybe I will."

"Yeah, baby!" Lenna jumped up and pulled Alex into one of her patented headlocks. "We're gonna get you a following, and then we're gonna get that book of yours published."

Alex gasped for air and slapped at Lenna's arm until Lenna relented and sat back down.

"You're getting ahead of yourself, chief." Alex rubbed her throat.

"Sorry, guess I got carried away. But we will get you a following."

* * *

Over the next few weeks, Alex spent her spare time writing. When chapter one was ready, they all sat around the computer.

Lenna had fingers poised above the keyboard. "Okay, it's ready to go. Now, I'm gonna need your pseud."

"My pseud? Like a pen name? Crap, what should I call myself?"

"I have an idea." Lenna smirked. "Remember the nickname you had in high school?"

Alex groaned. "Oh, no."

"Yes."

"What was it?" Sophia asked.

"Hearteyes." Lenna laughed wickedly.

Sophia's eyebrows shot up. "You're kidding. Hearteyes? You?"

Alex felt color rise in her cheeks. "I had a serious crush on a senior. My friends said I looked at her with hearteyes."

"Aw, how cute."

"Not really. It's stupid." Why, after all this time, would Lenna pull that one out of her ass?

"Hearteyes. Done." Lenna hit enter before Alex could stop her.

Alex blew out a frustrated breath, thinking she'd left that sorry little nickname in the rearview mirror years ago. Big sisters sucked sometimes.

Lenna's hand hovered over the mouse. "We ready to post?"

Alex nodded.

Lenna pushed the button.

"Now what?"

Lenna shrugged. "Now, we wait for kudos and comments."

"What if we don't get any?"

Sophia put an arm around Alex. "Honey, we read it. You have some grade-A sex scenes in there. You're gonna get some comments. Trust me."

* * *

Sam stretched out on the couch with three new scripts from Zach. Her feet rested in Jade's lap.

"Oh, goodie, a new fanfic," Jade said as she scrolled through her iPad.

"Are you still reading those?"

"Yes. Go read your scripts."

Sam stuck her tongue out and opened the first one. "Do I want to do a rom-com?"

Jade was too engrossed in a story to answer.

Sam chuckled. "Maybe you should read an actual book occasionally. You know, expand your horizons."

"Fu..." Jade hesitated, glancing at the jar, already out over twenty bucks. "No, I wanna read smutty fan fiction. This one is by someone called Hearteyes."

"Must be a hopeless romantic, like me." Sam closed her eyes and briefly fantasized about falling in love with a beautiful stranger. If life were only like the movies. Where was her *Notting Hill*? With a resigned sigh, she pushed aside all thoughts of fairy-tale endings.

Thirty pages into the script, Sam decided there was no com in the rom-com. Tossing it on the floor, she glanced at Jade, whose brow was furrowed in concentration. She took her foot and its fuzzy sock and nudged Jade's ear.

"Please remove your toes from my ear. I have no idea where they've been."

"My toes? They were just in the shower. Now the sock? I cannot vouch for the sock. I found it in the back of the closet."

"Gross!" Jade pushed Sam's foot down.

"Whatcha reading?"

"A well-written story."

"By Hearteyes, my future wife?"

"Yeah. I'm not shitting you. It's super creative. Better than the writing on your show."

"Oh, c'mon. It can't be that good."

"I'm serious. You should read this."

"We're not supposed to read fan fiction related to the show. You know that."

"Who cares? This is good and you need to read it."

Sam glanced at the stack of boring scripts. "All right, send me the link."

An hour and a half later, Jade and Sam had finished reading. Both of their heart rates were elevated, and a flush was present on their cheeks.

"You should comment." Sam shoved Jade's shoulder.

"What should I say?"

"I don't know. Just say it was a fucking awesome sex scene."

Jade nodded. "Okay, but it's your dollar."

Sam slapped the back of Jade's head. "Comment!"

"Ow. Calm yourself. *Dude, that was a fucking awesome sex scene.*' Done."

"I'm going to bed." Sam jumped off the couch.

"Which really means, I'm gonna go find my vibrator," Jade teased.

"Ha! I was just gonna use the showerhead." Sam paused. "We have to find the woman who wrote this."

"Yeah, I'd like to meet her. She's probably hot as hell," Jade said.

"You think? I bet ten bucks she's some middle-aged housewife with three kids. Writing it in a bathrobe and curlers."

"I don't think so."

"Hmm, maybe it is some unbelievably hot lesbian I can marry and have babies with. How we gonna find her?"

There was no response.

"Are you reading chapter six again? Jade? You can stay the night if you're too sexually hungover to drive."

"Babies, yes, have some."

Sam tossed a pillow in Jade's direction and headed for the stairs.

* * *

The next morning when Alex came downstairs in her boxers and tank, Lenna and Sophia were sitting at the table eating breakfast, huge smiles plastered to their faces.

"Why are you two so happy?" She opened the fridge and grabbed an apple.

"Do you wanna see?" Lenna turned the laptop around.

Alex's eyes widened. "Does that say five hundred and seven hits, one hundred and fifty-six kudos, and seventy comments?"

"It sure does!" Lenna high-fived her.

Sophia refilled her coffee mug. "Looks like you have a lot of new fans."

Alex clicked on chapter six to check the comments and laughed. "There's my fav right there, *'Dude, that was a fucking awesome sex scene.'* Short and to the point. I'm gonna go get ready for a run, then I'm going to the gym. I should be at work by nine."

"We need more chapters," Lenna said.

Alex headed up the steps, a little extra pep in her step. "Way ahead of you. I have three more ready!"

CHAPTER FOUR

Sam sat home on a quiet Thursday night catching up on emails. Most of them were from Jade, who kept sending photos of lesbians, asking, "How about this one?" or "Here's a cutie, want me to call?" Sam had no idea how Jade convinced these women to pose for pictures, and quite frankly, she didn't want to know.

The evening wasn't so quiet anymore as the buzzer on the front gate sounded.

Sam set the laptop on the coffee table and went to the intercom, knowing exactly who it was. Jade liked to buzz a little song, just to be a pain in the ass. "Who dat?"

"I gotta pee."

"Yeah, so? You know the code."

"I know, I just wanted to make sure you weren't in the bathroom."

"All clear. See you in five, four, three…"

Jade burst into the house and headed straight for the bathroom, not bothering to shut the door. "The final chapters are done!"

Sam perked up. "Really?"

"Yeah, and in her comments, she says there's smut."

"Oh, good. I'm going to my bedroom." Sam grabbed the laptop and hopped up the steps two at a time, almost face planting at the top step. Almost. That would've been hard to live down.

Finishing up in the powder room, Jade yelled, "You're disgusting... Can I use the spare bedroom?"

An hour later, Sam's phone rang. It was Jade, calling from the spare bedroom.

"Hello?" Sam asked innocently.

"Did you see the comments?"

"I'm sorry, who's this?"

"Read the comments."

"Okay, okay. What am I reading?"

"Go down to the bottom. A friend mentions her name— Alexa—and spills the beans about where she works."

Sam was busy not paying attention because she was rereading the sex scene. "Uh-huh."

"We need to take a trip to Pasadena tomorrow."

"Why?"

"Because we need some landscaping done."

* * *

"This seems wrong on so many levels," Sam said, as they slouched in Jade's car in the parking lot of Novato's Landscape and Hardscape. Both wore sunglasses, and a wide-brimmed, floppy beach hat perched atop Sam's head. The only things missing were a nose and mustache.

"We're just having a little fun, doing a little sleuthing."

"You call it sleuthing. The rest of the world calls it stalking. I'm the actress. I'm the one who's supposed to be stalked—the stalkee, not the stalker."

"Quiet. Do you see anybody who looks like they could write a lusty sex scene?"

"No." Sam fanned herself with a magazine. The heat from the blacktop filtered through the open windows, and the absence of a breeze added to the stuffiness.

"Hand me those pretzels. Sleuthing makes me hungry."

Sam passed the pretzels to Jade. After taking off her sandals, she put her feet up on the dashboard and moved them around like she was practicing dance moves.

"What the hell happened to your toes? It looks like they were gnawed on by some animal."

Sam studied them. The red polish had mostly flaked off. The nails were varying lengths, some chipped and jagged. *God, when did this happen?* Her toes were usually so cute. Now look at them. She self-consciously put her feet back on the floor, blaming this lack of personal hygiene on her "offness" since season three had ended.

"I guess I'm due for a pedi."

"You think? They look like Fred Flintstone feet."

"They're not *that* bad."

"Put your shoes back on. We don't wanna scare off our sexy writer."

Sam huffed and put her sandals back on. She was bored. It felt like they had been here forever. An older woman headed toward the store with two kids in tow. "Oh, I bet that's our mystery writer. Look, she's in pajamas and has kids. Just like I said."

"Jesus, I hope that's not her. Pass me a soda."

"Where is it?"

"In the cooler in the backseat."

"You brought a cooler?" Sam turned around. "Oh my, you did. You brought a cooler. How long is this stakeout gonna last?"

After unzipping the red, soft-sided Igloo, she assessed the contents. Not much of a variety: Coke, Diet Coke, and more Coke. A bottle of water would have been nice, but evidently that wasn't on the menu. As she was grabbing a can of soda, she noticed a bag behind Jade's seat and peeked inside. It was everything from aisle one in a convenience store: multiple bags of Doritos, a sizeable bag of regular M&M's, some sandwich cookies, and beef jerky—a lonely protein in a sea of carbs.

"My God, you have enough food in here to last for days." Sam took in all the empty plastic cups, wrappers, and chip bags strewn on the floor in the back. "And you should clean your car. Cluttered car, cluttered mind they say."

"Who's they?"

"Me." Sam handed her a soda. She was super envious of Jade's metabolism. Girl ate like a pig and never gained an ounce. And she never chose healthy options. "You shouldn't be drinking that stuff. Do you know what it must be doing to your insides?"

Jade waved her off. "Blah, blapity, blah." Suddenly she straightened. "Wait—hellooo."

They both saw her at the same time, strolling out the front door with a big, brown dog following close behind.

Sam pulled the sunglasses down her nose to get a better look. The woman went over to a customer and began talking and smiling, showing off perfect, white teeth. She was tall and lean, with long dark hair and a body that screamed fitness freak. She wore a tank top, cargo shorts, and a baseball hat that was like a cherry on top of the sweetest dessert.

Sam's breath quickened. A surprising heat gathered between her legs. Who was this attractive mystery woman? She nibbled on her lip. There was something hypnotic about her. "Are you seeing what I'm seeing?"

"You mean those delicious calves?" Jade asked.

"I was looking at those delicious arms."

The woman helped the customer load plants into their car, muscles rippling with every movement. When she finished, she glanced in their direction.

"Shit. Shit. She sees us." Sam slipped down in the seat.

Jade gave a dismissive wave. "Relax, she doesn't see us."

The woman went back inside, and Sam breathed a sigh of relief. She had no intention of being caught stalking some woman, even one as lovely as the brunette. She didn't want to be on the front page of the *National Enquirer*.

"We should go. Now."

"We're not going. Did you see that chick?" Jade turned to Sam, bug-eyed.

"Yeah."

"She's hot. What if she's our writer?"

"We are not that lucky."

They waited a couple of minutes and the woman appeared again, carrying flowers for the display out front, the dog close on her heels.

"Lordy Jesus, what's it like to fuck a body like that?" Jade asked.

"You are so crude. And that's another dollar." Sam stared, fascinated by the woman's graceful movements.

"C'mon, you ever sleep with a body like that?"

"No."

"Don't you wanna know what it's like?"

"You're ridiculous." Sam admitted to herself that yes, she did wonder what it would be like to touch that body. Of course, she wouldn't tell Jade that.

The woman exuded confidence with her impeccable posture and head held high. She kept moving the plants, then stepping back to critique the setup. It took a good four times of rearranging before she nodded with satisfaction.

Sam was mesmerized, finding it hard not to follow her every move. The woman spoke to the dog, and Sam tried to catch what was said, but they were too far away. Soon they both walked back into the store, and Sam's shoulders sagged with disappointment.

"Where you going, beautiful?" Jade called softly.

Sam made a conscious effort to stay rooted in the car, because her body was compelled to follow the woman into the store and buy every plant in sight just to have the opportunity to speak with her. She took a deep breath. Time to get a hold of herself. She was the one being ridiculous.

"Hey, Columbo, how long are we going to sit here?"

"For as long as it takes."

"As long as it takes to what?"

"Figure out if this is our writer."

Five minutes later, the woman came outside with more plants. Sam's body temperature skyrocketed again, her heart palpitations increasing. This stakeout was gonna be the death of her.

"We need to speed up this sleuthing process." Jade leaned out the window. "Alexa!"

Sam's mouth dropped open and she yanked Jade back inside. "Stop it!"

The woman scanned the parking lot until her eyes rested on their car again.

Jade slapped the steering wheel. "It's her."

"You are an idiot. That's not her."

"She looked."

"She didn't hear you."

They began arguing, oblivious to the woman approaching their car.

* * *

Alex had been watching the two women in the blue car for fifteen minutes now. She couldn't make out their faces very well from her vantage point inside the store. They both had sunglasses on, that much was clear. One wore what looked to be a large, floppy hat. Alex's gaydar pinged. A whack to the butt made her jump.

"What are you looking at?" Lenna asked, resting her chin on Alex's shoulder.

"Those two women in the dark blue Mercedes have been sitting there for a while. Just found it odd."

"Maybe they're stalking you. Jilted lovers or something like that," Lenna said. "Sophia wants to know if you wanna get dinner out tonight."

"Sounds great. Your treat, right?"

"Guess so. Be careful when you go back out there. Don't need my baby sis being kidnapped by some psycho ex-lover."

"One less mouth to feed."

"Yeah, but Yogi would miss you."

Alex playfully shoved her. After Lenna walked away, Alex turned her attention back to the women. Picking up the last of the plants, she pushed open the door. While arranging pots, she thought she heard someone call her name. She spun around, but no one was in the vicinity. Odd. She headed toward the car to ask if the women needed help. They were arguing when Alex strolled up and said, "Hey."

The brunette screamed. "Aaahh! Holy shit, you scared me."

Alex smiled and checked her out. Chestnut-brown hair fell just below her chin. A white sleeveless shirt showed off strong tanned shoulders. Probably an athlete. She glanced at the blonde in the other seat, who stared straight ahead. *Now, there's a beautiful profile.* Alex sensed she'd seen this woman someplace before, but the where eluded her. "Can I help you ladies?"

The brunette stammered, "Uh, well, we were, um, just sitting here..."

Both women were attractive. Not a bad thing if they were indeed stalkers. Alex rested her arms on the door and glanced around at the mess in the car. "Wow. How long have you guys been here?"

They exchanged a look, and in unison said, "We just got here!"

Their jangled nerves were on full display. The brunette incessantly tapped her fingers on the steering wheel and the blonde jiggled both legs.

"Are you interested in any plants or landscaping, or anything?"

The brunette spoke first. "Yeah, we were interested in landscaping." She turned to the blonde for confirmation. "Right?"

"Right." The blonde nodded but kept her eyes forward, refusing to make eye contact.

They seemed oddly afraid to leave their car. "Do you want to come inside?" Alex asked. "Or I can get in the backseat if it makes you more comfortable."

The blonde snickered.

Alex leaned closer, eyeing her up again. Damn she looked familiar. Maybe they'd slept together. Blondes were her weakness.

The brunette quickly said, "No, we can go inside if you want."

"It's not what I want, it's whatever you want." Alex tried to catch the blonde's eye, but no luck so far.

"Let's go in. I'll go in." The brunette turned to the blonde. "Why don't you make, um, that phone call, and I'll pop inside and talk landscaping."

Yogi appeared and hunkered down beside the blonde's window, growling and whining. Alex smiled at her. "Yogi must like you. He only talks to people he likes."

"Yogi?" she asked.

"Yeah, Yogi Bear."

The blonde stretched a hand out of the window and rubbed his head. "Wow, you do look like a bear. Hi, Yogi Bear. You're so handsome." She opened the car door and stroked Yogi's back. "I wish I had a treat for you, but Jade ate everything."

Alex cocked her head, fascinated by the blonde as she fussed over Yogi. A small throbbing started below her belt. Even though Alex had yet to get a clear look at the woman's face, her body knew what it liked. Her sexual interest was piqued.

"Should we go inside now?" the brunette, Jade, asked.

The voice came from far away, because Alex's mind was busy removing the blonde's clothes. She needed a better angle to guess bra size. Yogi began planting wet, sloppy kisses all over the blonde's face, which she must have enjoyed, judging by the peals of laughter. Sexy *and* sweet. A deadly combination.

"Hellooo?"

Finally, it registered that the other woman was speaking. Alex nodded without looking at her.

"Let's go."

In the interest of keeping her head intact, Alex tore her eyes away from Yogi and his new girlfriend, ducked when the door swung open, and followed. She glanced back just as the blonde gave Yogi a kiss. "Lucky dog," she murmured. Alex had to jog to catch up to Jade. She managed to beat her to the door and opened it. "C'mon back to my office. I'm Alex Novato." She extended a hand. "I do all the design work here."

"I'm Jade." The woman gave Alex's hand a firm shake.

"Nice to meet you, Jade, and your partner's name?"

"Partner? Oh yeah, no, that's, um, Sama…Sa…Sarah."

Alex pursed her lips in confusion. Did she not know her own girlfriend's name? Maybe it wasn't her girlfriend. "Okay, have a seat. What were you guys interested in?" She waited for reply.

Jade gave her the once-over and then shifted in the chair. "Jade?"

"Oh, yes, she, we just bought a house, and the yard needs a lot of work. There's a pool that looks like shit, and gardens that look like shit, and a patio that basically looks like shit. We were thinking of redoing everything."

Alex bit back a smile. If the backyard truly was as bad as she said, it would be right up Alex's alley. Fixing disasters was her specialty. "It sounds like a pretty big job. The best thing to do is for me to come over and see the space."

"Oh, you'd come to the house?"

"Yep. Is that okay?" Jade was fixated on Alex's lips for some reason. Alex patiently waited for her to resume eye contact. "Is that all right? If I come to the house?"

"Yeah, that's great." Jade shifted in the seat again.

Alex would have to check that chair later. Maybe the cushion was bad. "Do you want to schedule an appointment?"

"Sure, what's good for you?" Once again, Jade's brown eyes wandered.

Alex took a quick peek down at herself to see what had Jade so enthralled. It was her bicep. This woman was checking her out but good. Alex flexed, and Jade's eyes grew big. Alex almost laughed. She tried to get Jade back on track. "Where you guys at?"

"Where's who?" Jade asked, clearly distracted.

Alex knew women found her attractive, but this was over the top. "Where do you guys live?"

"Oh, Sama…Sarah lives in West Hollywood. I mean we… her and I…live in WeHo. Together. We live together in WeHo. Recently. We got together, and moved in. I mean, we were together before, but we just moved in. Recently. Like yesterday."

Alex just kept nodding like a marionette as the woman stammered and stumbled over her words. This interaction ranked right up there with the weirdest in recent memory. Like top five. "You just moved in yesterday?"

"Did I say yesterday? No, I didn't say yesterday. I said… yesterday last month. You must have heard me wrong, or maybe I said it wrong, but that's what I meant."

Scratch that, this was number one. Alex continued nodding, because she didn't know what else to do. "Well, I'll be in the area on Wednesday, so I can stop by in the afternoon, around three. Is that good?"

What was she was getting herself into? She made a mental note to make sure someone knew her whereabouts that day.

"Yes, you're perfect. I mean, that's perfect, really perfect." Alex's head nodding must have been contagious, because now Jade was doing it.

"What's your address?"

Jade wrote down the address, along with a phone number.

Alex passed a business card across the desk. "I'm one of the owners, so I'll take good care of you. Here, take some of these catalogs. They might give you some ideas." She slid the books over and sat back. "So I'll see you Wednesday?"

Jade sat unmoving, fingering the business card, staring at Alex's chest.

Alex raised her eyebrows. "I'll see you Wednesday." First she couldn't get the woman out of the car, and now she couldn't get her out of the office.

Jade's eyes snapped back up to Alex's. "Oh, yes, Wednesday." She stood and reached across to shake Alex's hand. "We'll see you then."

After Jade left, Alex leaned back in the chair. She weighed the pros and cons of this upcoming meeting. Pro: hopefully meeting the blonde again. Con: never making it home because they were a couple of ax murderers. Easy decision. Pros outweighed the cons. Hopefully the two women were just roommates.

* * *

Jade scampered to the car and settled into the driver's seat. "You're welcome."

"What?"

"You're welcome."

Sam looked askance at her. "What am I thanking you for?"

"She's coming to the house on Wednesday to look at the yard."

Sam's heart leapt into her throat. "What? Are you kidding me?"

Jade grinned. "No, I am not kidding. And I have confirmed she is our writer. That was Alexa, aka Alex. Sam, she's perfect."

"Perfect for what?"

"Your fuck buddy."

"*Whaaat?*"

"You heard me."

"Is that what this is all about? Finding me a fuck buddy? I thought we were just having fun 'sleuthing'!" She made angry quotes around the word.

"Sam, she's fucking hot. I mean, smokin'. Green eyes, your fav-or-ite." Jade sang the last part.

"Oh, my fucking God!"

Dollar bills floated around the car. "Chick oozes sex. I swear it was seeping from her pores. Those lips, oh those lips were begging to be kissed. And I almost did. What else? She flexed, and my undies got wet. Whew."

The more Jade talked, the more animated she became. "She has these muscles, actual chest muscles—I couldn't take my eyes off them." She took a quick swig of Coke and burped up the carbonation. "You know me. Nobody makes me nervous, but this chick had me squirming. She's a perfect sexy ten. I am seriously in love already. I was kind of in a daze in her office, and she had to kick me out the door just to get rid of me." Jade took a deep breath.

Sam just stared for a few seconds, horrified. "Jesus Christ, she probably thinks we're nuts. First, we're hanging in her parking lot for, I don't know, an hour, like we have some irrational fear of landscaping, then you're sitting in her office in a catatonic state drooling over her."

Jade started the car and cackled. "This is gonna be fun." She glanced in the rearview mirror. "Where's the dog?"

"Yeah, don't run over her dog. That'll put a damper on your plans."

CHAPTER FIVE

On Wednesday, Alex headed to WeHo. Following the GPS, she turned into the driveway of the address Jade had given. At the security gate, she leaned out the window and pushed the button. The house was much larger than expected. Homes in this area were worth a few million at least, and Alex wondered what jobs the two women had to afford this piece of real estate. Her head was still outside the window when the security camera zoomed in on her face. She slowly backed away as the lens kept coming closer and closer.

Static crackled, then a faceless voice gurgled, "Hello?"

Alex shifted closer. "Hello?"

"Hello?" echoed the disembodied voice.

Alex paused. "Hello?" Was this a game of hello chicken? Who would be the first to give in?

"Who dat?"

"Ah, Alex Novato. I'm here to see Jade and Sarah?"

The gate slowly swung open.

Taking a deep breath, she pulled through the entrance and turned a critical eye to the landscaping surrounding the house.

A long, terracotta-tiled driveway looped up to the home and back, surrounding a neglected patch of greenery. In the middle of the green patch stood an antiquated fountain with water slowly trickling from the spout. She stopped driving, opened a manila folder, and jotted down a quick note: *Replace intake hose on fountain in front yard.* Depending on their budget, a whole new fountain was in order. The cherub spitting water out of its mouth felt a little 1940s. But some might consider it retro. She needed to get a feel for their style and taste. The weeds around the fountain grew hip high, and Alex wrote another note: *Industrial strength weedwhacker needed, or possibly a small hand grenade.*

After parking her black pickup truck near the front door, she studied the two-story house. The architecture was impressive, with its white stucco and red trim. English ivy surrounded a large picture window in front and snaked its way up to the second story Juliette balcony. Brick-colored clay tiles covered the roof, giving the house Spanish flair. A blue stone patio led to an oversized black front door. Alex scratched down a few more notes, then grabbed her briefcase and rang the bell.

Jade opened the door immediately, startling her. She had a strong inclination that it had been Jade operating the super zoom.

"Alex, good to see you. Come in, come in."

"Thank you. Wow, the house is beautiful."

"Thanks. Sam will be right down."

"Who's Sam?"

"My, uh, partner."

"You mean Sarah?"

Jade took a quick glance sideways. "Uh, yeah. That's what I said, Sarah. Follow me."

Alex had two thoughts. One, she was disappointed that the blonde was Jade's partner. And two, Jade was as bizarre as she remembered.

As they walked through the house, Alex took stock of the interior. The living room gave off a warm cottagey vibe. An overabundance of throw pillows made the space inviting and comfortable. They entered the dining room and Alex caught a view of the backyard through the French doors. "Holy shit." She held a hand over her mouth. "I'm sorry, excuse me."

"Oh, don't worry about offending me. Fuck is my middle name." Jade dug into a pocket, pulled out a dollar, and stuffed it in a jar on the dining room table. A jar chock full of bills.

Alex smiled and Jade blushed. She walked to the French doors. "May I?"

"Sure, and hopefully Sarah will be down soon." Jade walked over to the staircase just off the dining room. "Sarah! Alex is here!" She grunted when she received no response and joined Alex, who opened the door and followed her outside.

They both stopped and stood on the patio, staring at the wasteland that was the backyard.

"Well?" Jade asked.

Alex took stock of everything. One word came to mind. Deplorable. The outdoor kitchen appliances were rusted and rickety. Perennials were choked and stunted by the weeds that sprang from every corner of the gardens. The concrete surrounding the pool was cracked and chipped. This poor space had been neglected for years, but she lived for renovating things like this. If they were willing to spend the money, Alex could do wonders with it. A house like this deserved an incredible backyard.

"Yeah, you were right, it does look like shit. I don't think I've ever seen weeds that tall. You could lose a small child in there."

"Funny you should say that. We lost our friend Emma back here for an hour once. But that's a story for another time. So, it's fixable, right?"

"Absolutely, but it depends on how much you want to spend."

"Pfft! Money is no object."

"Well, let's crunch some numbers before you make a statement like that. I can fix the landscaping in the front yard too, if you want. Maybe get a new fountain?"

"Don't you like our chubby-cheeked 1920s statue?"

"Oh, well, if you like it, I can certainly work with it."

"I'm fucking with you." Jade reached into a pocket and came up empty. "Don't tell anybody I said that."

Alex nodded, not sure if she meant the fucking with you part, or the liking the statue part. She'd get clarification on it later. "Let's go inside and browse through some catalogs. Then I'll take some pictures and measurements."

* * *

Sam checked the living room, but her bestie was nowhere to be found, so she went into the kitchen. Suddenly, the French doors opened, prompting Sam to say, "Hey jackass, why are you yelling Sarah? Do you have some woman tucked away in here I don't know about?" just as Jade entered the kitchen with Alex.

They all froze and stared at each other. Well, mostly Alex stared at "Sarah," who stared back at Alex.

Sam had lost the ability to speak. She figured her mouth was hanging open. She should probably close it. Or say something. Anything.

Thank God Jade came to the rescue, making the formal introductions. "Alex, meet Sarah Cass...I mean Sam, Samantha Cassidy. Sam, this is Alex Novato. Alex, sorry for lying to you before. Sam likes to keep things on the down low. She's an actress."

"Yeah, I recognize you, and I totally understand about the down low part." Alex's eyes never left Sam's face as she walked across the room with an extended hand. "Nice to meet you."

Sam stayed frozen in place, not moving until Alex was directly in front of her. Alex had a couple of inches on Sam, so she had to tilt her head back to maintain eye contact. While shaking the offered hand, her gaze wavered. Alex's stare was intense. Too intense. She felt exposed. Naked. And she still hadn't spoken, because evidently, being around a hot woman rendered her mute. Her body was reacting much the same way it had in the parking lot. The crazy arrhythmia was back, along with a hot flash that went from toes to cheeks. She prayed nobody noticed the flush in her face.

"I'm actually her manager," Jade said. "Not her girlfriend. I have my own girlfriend."

Sam finally found her voice. "Yeah, and I have a boyfriend. Brian Davis!" Well, that came out louder than she would have liked. "We're dating," she added, just to sound more like a dumbass, because if he was her boyfriend, of course, they would be dating.

Jade gave Sam the stink eye.

"Okay, now that we've got that out of the way." Alex smiled at both women.

"Yeah, so, ah, do you have a boyfriend or...a girlfriend?" Jade asked.

Alex didn't miss a beat, obviously unfazed by such a personal question. "It would be a girlfriend, but no, nothing serious."

"Why?"

She shrugged and bent down to pick up the briefcase. "Not my style, I guess. I enjoy sex, not relationships."

Jade made eye contact with Sam and mouthed, "Perfect."

Sam glowered back.

Alex lifted her head and caught the interaction between the two women. Her brows creased. "Are we still interested in landscaping?"

Sam was mortified. Alex must think they were idiots with the way they were acting. "We're definitely interested in landscaping."

"All right. I can show you my portfolio. Maybe it'll give you some ideas. Or if you guys have something in mind?"

"Sam sketched some stuff," Jade said. "I'll get us some water. Let's sit in the dining room."

Sam and Alex headed into the dining room, and Jade soon joined them with three glasses.

"Alex, you sit here, and we'll sit on either side, so we can both see."

With sketchbook in hand, Sam took a seat next to Alex. She tried to quell her nerves. Jade was right, this woman was sexy as hell, and every time Sam met those green eyes, it felt like Alex removed a piece of her clothing. Hearteyes? More like Sexeyes. With shaky hands and sweaty palms, she opened the book.

"Let's see what you have here." Alex flipped through a few pages. "Wow, these are good."

Sam blushed like a schoolgirl. "Thanks." She wanted to crawl under the table. What the hell was the matter with her? Sam couldn't recall if she'd put deodorant on, because right now it didn't feel like it. She felt a trickle of sweat between her breasts. Could this be any more awkward?

Alex put a binder on the table and flipped through a couple of pages. "Here. I can see this type of retaining wall to replace the one behind the pool."

As Sam inspected the pictures, she heard an audible sniff.

Jade's nose hovered above Alex's shoulder.

The second sniff was snuffed out as both Sam and Alex stared at Jade.

"Ah," she stammered, "you smell nice. What is it?"

"Calvin."

"Yeah, well, I like it. Sam, doesn't she smell nice?" Jade gave Sam the old take-a-whiff-of-this-chick look.

Sam's eyes widened. Did she want to engage her sense of smell? It was difficult enough controlling the other senses. Jade's scowl demanded action, so she leaned in toward Alex's shoulder and took a whiff, and—oh boy—it went straight to her crotch.

"Uh, nice, yes. Fits you. It's, uh, a nice smell."

"Thanks."

Alex laid a thousand-watt smile on her, making her feel faint and giddy. Sam envisioned herself passing out with a stupid grin on her face. Was it possible? Around this woman, yes. Yes, it was. Her chest heaved with relief when Alex turned her attention back to the binder.

But the relief was fleeting, because now Jade was making goo-goo eyes at Alex. She winked at Sam and mouthed, "Go for it."

"Knock it off," Sam mouthed back, worried Alex might pick her head up at any moment and catch Jade's antics.

But Jade continued, at one point flicking her tongue in a seductive manner. A tiny, embarrassed squeak escaped Sam's throat.

Alex finally sat back in the chair. "Are you guys wanting a three-way or something?"

Sam turned beet red. "Oh my God."

Jade blurted out, "No, no. My God no."

"Just getting a weird kinda vibe here." Alex looked back and forth between the two women.

Jade defused the situation by throwing herself under the bus. "This is totally my fault. I'll admit, I find you super-hot. And sexy as shit. And believe me, if I didn't have a girlfriend, I'd do you in heartbeat. You got a body—"

"Too much," Sam murmured.

"What? Oh, all right. Sorry for acting kinda weird. Please don't freak out."

"Okay." Alex turned to Sam.

"I have a boyfriend!" Sam blabbered again, louder than the last time.

"Yeah, you said."

With Jade behind Alex's back mouthing "Stop it," Sam knew this was one of the most humiliating days of her life.

"Okay, we good?" Jade asked, glancing between Sam and Alex. "Good. Let's get it together ladies. Let's look at some pictures."

They were all staring at Alex's catalog when Jade asked, "So have you ever had a three-way?"

Sam groaned and reached for the water, wishing it was alcohol.

"Yes. I have," Alex said matter-of-factly.

Sam choked on the water.

"You okay?" Alex asked.

"Yeah." More coughing and sputtering followed, along with a few chest thumps. "Went down the wrong pipe."

Jade put an elbow on the table, chin in hand, fascinated. "So what was it like?"

Alex took a moment before answering. "Distracting in a way. It was hard to concentrate."

"Huh. Yeah, I guess so. Was it with two other women?"

"Yep. Anyway, I can say I had one, but I doubt I would do it again. One on one is much better." Alex turned to Sam. "Don't you agree?"

But Sam was barely listening, wondering if it really was possible to die from embarrassment. Finally realizing Alex was talking to her, she gazed into those eyes and was lost, drowning in a sea of green. "Huh? I'm sorry, what?"

"Don't you think one-on-one sex is better?"

Sam's eyes left Alex's face and shifted slightly left, focusing on Jade, who leaned past Alex and mouthed, "Answer!"

Her focus returned to the green eyes in front of her. "Ah... yes, much better. It's much better, to...ah, have sex with one person at a time." What shade of red was her face at this moment? Scarlet? Crimson? Candy apple?

"Well, I'm glad we agree." Alex's lips quirked up at the corners and her eyes danced with mirth.

Suddenly, Sam's seat felt warm and something caused a small pool of moisture in her panties. Probably the cushion on the chair. Damn microfleece.

"Which of these designs do you like best?"

Sam tried to cool down and concentrate. She picked a few interesting ones and Alex spent the next half an hour discussing how to bring those ideas to life. When they finished going over all the details, Alex walked outside to measure.

Jade slapped the table. "That was a disaster. What the hell were you doing?"

"Me?" Sam pointed an emphatic finger at Jade. "I was gonna get you a lobster bib you were drooling so much!"

"She must think we are complete and utter morons."

"She obviously sleeps around. And she's out of my league sexually. I mean, a three-way? Who has three-ways?"

"She does, apparently!"

"Well, that's intimidating as hell."

"Stop it. You're fine. You're Samantha Cassidy. Emmy-award-winning actress. Alex should be shaking in her boots just to meet you."

"Well, that's not what's happening, in case you haven't noticed. I'm the one who can barely look *her* in the eye."

"Why did you keep saying you have a boyfriend?"

Sam winced. "I panicked. She makes me nervous."

"Do you think she's attractive?"

"Hell, yes! She's...extremely attractive. Those eyes. You know how I love green eyes."

"Well, okay. Come hell or high water, she's gonna be your fuck buddy."

Alex came back inside and gathered up her things.

Jade's phone rang. "I have to get this. Alex, it was nice seeing you again. We look forward to hearing from you." She waved goodbye.

Sam was left to show Alex out. Time to channel her inner Callie. *Be strong. Be confident.* They walked to the front door. "Do you have our contact info?"

"Yeah, I have Jade's phone number and email."

"Let me give you mine."

Alex handed Sam her iPhone. "Type it in my contacts."

Sam's nervous fingers kept hitting all the wrong numbers and letters. After much backspacing and deleting, she handed the phone back. "You can email me the prices, or call, whichever is best for you."

"Great. Here's my card. You can call or text if you think of something we didn't cover today." Alex leaned against the doorjamb. "Probably take me a few days to put something together."

Sam took the card, and when their fingers brushed, it felt electric. Schoolgirl crush, that's what it felt like. At twenty-eight. How pathetic. "Sorry about all that. You probably think we're nuts."

"No, I don't. I was flattered, to be honest."

Sam drew a shaky breath. This woman was a cool customer. *So* out of her league.

Alex continued to stare. "You have beautiful eyes. I'm sure you hear that all the time."

Sam felt another blush coming. "Me? God, no, you...you have the beautiful eyes. Green eyes are my fav—are great. Really great."

Alex gave a warm smile. "Well, blue eyes are pretty great too. I hope your boyfriend appreciates them. It was a pleasure meeting you." She offered a hand.

Sam took it, feeling the strength in Alex's grip, the calluses from hard work—and feeling her insides turn to mush.

Alex walked away but turned back. "I am a fan of your show."

Another hot rush of pleasure shot through Sam's body. "Oh yeah? What did you think of this season?"

"The ending sucked."

"I know," Sam said. "I wish it would have turned out differently."

"So does my sister and her wife. They were depressed."

"Not you?"

Alex winked. "I guess I'm made of stronger stuff." She turned and continued walking, not looking back, but waving a hand in the air. "Goodbye, Samantha Cassidy."

Sam couldn't wipe the stupid-ass grin off her face as Alex walked down the driveway. Such a tight ass. She could have eaten Alex up with a spoon. When the truck disappeared through the gate, Sam closed the door. A cold shower topped her to-do list.

* * *

On the drive home, Alex processed the events of the past hour. *The* Samantha Cassidy. Wait until Lenna and Sophia heard about this. No wonder she'd looked so familiar. And now Alex had a chance to interact with her every day. She was as gorgeous in person as on TV, if not more so. And she blushed like a champion. A serial blusher. Which was hard to fathom, since the woman lived in the public eye. *Boyfriend my ass.* Alex could sense sexual interest a mile away, and Samantha Cassidy was interested. She'd felt the spark between them when they touched, like a small jolt of energy. Alex wanted this job. Alex wanted this woman.

When she walked into the house, she found Sophia in the kitchen wearing an apron. Being an excellent cook, Soph was the self-appointed family chef.

"Perfect timing, I have the filets in the broiler, and we'll be ready to eat in a minute."

"Smells delicious."

Shortly after Alex arrived home, Lenna came into the kitchen and gave Sophia a kiss on the cheek. "How was everyone's day?"

"Great!" Alex could barely contain her excitement as she set the table.

As they sat down to eat, Lenna asked, "So how was your meeting in WeHo?"

"Interesting to say the least." Alex reached for the vegetables.

"Oh yeah, why?"

"Because of whose house it was."

"Whose was it?" Sophia asked.

"Guess."

"Whoopi," Lenna mumbled with a mouth full of potatoes.

"No."

"Ellen. Ellen has a secret cottage," Sophia said.

"No."

"The Queen of England," Lenna said.

"No," Alex said evenly, ignoring Lenna's sarcastic tone.

"Give us a damn hint."

Alex snickered at Lenna's exasperation. Patience was not her strong suit. "Let's see. She's blond."

Lenna rolled her eyes. "You've narrowed it down to a million women in LA county."

"She just got laid a couple of months ago on TV."

Both of their mouths dropped open. "No!" they responded in unison.

"Yes."

Lenna jabbed a fork in the air. "That blonde on *Real Housewives of LA*?"

"No, you shithead. Callie, your favorite character."

"I know, I was kidding. So holy shit, you met Sam Cassidy?"

"I did."

"What was she like?" Sophia asked.

Alex recalled the rosy, pink cheeks of a blushing Sam. "She ah, she was pretty...pretty beautiful actually."

"Listen to you!" Sophie teased. "You sound smitten. Smitten like a kitten."

"What else? Was she nice? Was she funny?" Lenna asked.

"Oh, she was sorta funny, I guess. Oddly shy. Her manager was there—she's a bit of a wingnut. They were uncomfortable and acting strange. And I know you're gonna think I'm cocky, but I think they were hitting on me."

Lenna's eyebrows shot up and the fork paused on its way to her mouth. "Both of them?"

Alex nodded.

The fork arrived at its destination. Lenna slowly chewed and swallowed. She put the fork down and cleared her throat. "Both of them were hitting on you."

Alex sensed Big Sis wasn't buying it. "Seemed that way."

"So, what, pray tell, did you do, Alexa?" Lenna always reverted to Alex's full name when annoyed.

She shrugged. "I asked if they were interested in a three-way."

Lenna's expression didn't change at all. "Let me get this straight," she paused for effect. "You go over to Samantha Cassidy's house, famous actress." She nodded at Sophia, who nodded back. "Emmy-award-winning actress, possible client, dates some actor?" She snapped her fingers at Sophia.

"Brian Davis."

Lenna pointed. "Right, Brian Davis. You go to her house and ask if she's interested in a three-way?"

"Yes."

"Are you a fucking moron?"

Alex howled with laughter. "You weren't there! They were acting strange."

"What was their reaction?" Sophia asked.

"Well, Sam said, 'Oh, my God,' and Jade, the manager, said, 'No, no. God no.'"

"You say it like you just shed light on the whole thing," Lenna snapped.

Alex was still rolling. The serious expressions on Lenna and Sophia's faces were priceless.

"Wait, no wait. Jade admitted they were acting weird, and it was her fault, that she was, ah, that she found me super-hot, and she was sorry. For acting so weird."

Lenna's eyes dug into Alex. "I can't wait to hear what else happened."

"Well, Jade did ask if I'd ever had a three-way."

"Oh no, you didn't." Lenna covered her face with a hand. "Ugh."

Alex cracked up again. "What? She asked. I wasn't gonna lie."

"And what was Sam's reaction to your answer?" Sophia asked.

"She choked on her water."

Lenna's head bowed in resignation. "Needless to say, we won't be getting that job."

Alex wiped the tears of laughter from her eyes. "Trust me, I'll get the job."

And the girl.

CHAPTER SIX

Two days later, Sam and Jade sat in the office of Zach Barrett, Emma's older brother. He worked at Creative Management Group and represented both Emma and Sam. Good looks ran in the Barrett family. Zach's sun-streaked chestnut hair was slicked back from his forehead, and he shared his sister's warm brown eyes. At thirty-two, he was an up-and-comer, already ensconced in a corner office with a view.

Zach slid a contract over to Sam. "Sign this. It's the Lancôme spokesperson contract we've been working on. They want you to start shooting these spots next week. And, what else?" He shuffled through some folders on his desk.

Sam continued checking her phone for emails and texts. A certain brunette had her nervous and jittery. And anxious. And impatient.

Jade snapped her fingers in front of Sam's face. "Hey, pay attention."

"Sorry, I was checking my email. What did you want me to sign?"

Jade gave Sam a playful shove. "Oh, just a multimillion-dollar contract, that's all. Sign it. I need a new car."

"Oh great." Sam absently signed the paperwork.

Zach cleared his throat to bring Sam's focus back. "I have this script for you too. Someone backed out last minute. Now, it's not a big part, but the headliners are big. Read it ASAP because they want an answer by the end of the weekend. The director would love to have you. And it'll only be a couple months in Vancouver, so it should wrap up before the series begins shooting again."

"Great, thanks." Sam considered herself lucky to have Zach, especially right now since the only thing on her mind were green eyes and a hot body. She had no clue what she was signing, but he was trustworthy.

They had attended high school together. Zach was a senior when Sam was a freshman, and they were paired in the Big Senior/Little Freshman mentoring program. The two had bonded and kept in touch, so it was only natural she would hire her pseudo big brother to look after her career.

"Have you heard from her?" Jade asked.

Sam frowned. "No."

"Damn, I hope we didn't scare her off. And when I say we, I mean you."

Sam's mouth dropped. "Me? You asked her about three-ways for God's sake."

"Well, I wasn't the one who kept shouting, 'I have a boyfriend. I have a boyfriend!' You might as well have yelled, 'Move along, nothing to see here!'"

Sam had no retort. She had said that. Multiple times. Was it a turnoff for Alex? Maybe. But there had been that tiny jolt of electricity when their fingers touched while saying goodbye. She hoped Alex had felt it too and wasn't put off by their shenanigans.

"Well, it's only been two days."

Zach's brows crinkled in confusion. "What are we talking about?"

"Sam's potential fuck buddy. She needs to get laid. By a chick."

Zach groaned. "Okay, I don't need to hear this. I'll be right back. I want to make copies of these." He stood and left.

"Don't you got a secretary to do that shit?" Jade called after him.

"I think you made him uncomfortable."

"Why don't you text her?" Jade asked.

"No."

"Why not? Alex said you could."

"I feel stupid. I'm still embarrassed over the whole scene the other day. She probably thinks I'm a nutcase."

Jade snatched Sam's phone.

Sam's heart jumped into her throat. "Hey, what are you doing? Give it back!" She tried to grab her bestie but whiffed.

Jade scooted around the chairs and locked herself in Zach's bathroom.

Sam ran over to the door and pressed her forehead against it. "Please don't do what I think you're doing. Please, I'm begging. I'm sure she thinks very little of me already. Please don't humiliate me." It was too late. The telltale swoosh of a text being sent echoed through the door. "Ugh. I hate you." Dejected, she slid down the wall and sat on the floor.

Jade opened the door and tossed the phone into her lap.

Sam peeked at the phone screen, half afraid to read the message.

Hey Alex, if it's not too much trouble please include a spa in your quote. Thanks, Sam.

Heaving a huge sigh of relief, Sam leaned her head back against the wall. "Thank God. You scared the shit out of me."

"Hey, I'm not gonna make you look like a douche, okay? C'mon, I'm hungry. Let's go find some place to eat."

They left Zach's office, picked up Sam's copies of the contracts, and said a quick goodbye before heading to the elevators.

They both twitched when Sam's phone vibrated and then read the text at the same time.

Hey blue eyes, I was just thinking about you.

The elevator doors opened, and Jade pushed Sam in. "Ha! I knew it. Success. Do you need me to answer?" Jade reached for the phone.

"No." Sam slapped her hand away. "In fact, I need some privacy." She shot back out of the elevator. "I'll call you later. I promise." The elevator doors closed on a disappointed Jade.

Sam snuck into an empty office, shut the door, and sank to the floor. With trembling fingers, she typed, *You were?*

Absolutely. Been thinking about you for weeks.

Sam stared at the phone for a second. *You only met me two days ago.*

Wait, who's this?

Sam did a double take. Was Alex teasing? She had to be, right? Sam's name was in Alex's contacts. *It's Sam.*

Oh, Sam. I thought you were another Sam.

Sam smiled. *There's only one Sam.*

Trudat.

Sam giggled. Before she could reply, her phone dinged again.

Almost have your pricing done. But now you've added to my workload, which means I have to stay up late.

Sam mulled over a response. *Guess you'll have to pull an all-nighter.*

It's gonna be hard to stay awake. Why don't you come over and keep me up?

Sam almost dropped the phone. She took a deep, calming breath. *Be cool, Sam. Be cool.* She had a brief image of Alex's fingers flying over her phone as she texted, and from there, Sam pictured those fingers doing something else. She needed to get her thoughts out of the gutter immediately.

Drink coffee, she typed.

The reply was instant. *But coffee ain't beautiful.*

Sam blushed. *You obviously don't have the right coffee.*

Maybe you should bring me some beautiful coffee.

Sam told herself to keep playing it cool. She typed, *Maybe you should take a cold shower and call me in the morning.* She was feeling it now. Why, she was almost cocky.

Alex's reply was quick. *I like a woman who plays hard to get.*
Then you're gonna love me. Mic drop. Sam put a fist in the air.
LOL. Later, Sam.

"I got an LOL," Sam said out loud. One step closer to not
being a complete dork around this woman.

* * *

On Sunday, Sam met Jade and Emma for brunch. They'd
chosen a chic deli off Sunset Boulevard and were cozied up in
a corner booth, sipping mimosas while waiting for their orders.

"Zach said he gave you that script. You're taking it I hope?"
Emma asked Sam.

"Yeah, it's good. I told him this morning I would do it."

"When do you start filming?"

"Not for a month."

Emma took a selfie with her mimosa.

"*What* are you doing?" Jade asked.

"Sending a text to Logan."

Logan and Emma had met on the set of *Gemini* three years
ago, but his character was killed off at the end of season one.
After he'd left the show, their romance had blossomed and
grown, and they were now one of Hollywood's hottest couples.

Sam fiddled with her phone.

"No emails?" Jade asked.

Her face drooped with disappointment. "No."

When Emma was finished texting, she put her phone down.
"Who's gonna email you?"

"Sam's potential fuck buddy."

Emma straightened in her chair. "Fuck buddy? Spill it."

"Sam's gonna get it on with her landscaper, who's a perfect
sexy ten."

"Landscaper? When did this happen?"

Jade took a quick glance around and lowered her voice.
"We've been reading this fanfic, by Hearteyes, Sam's future
wife. So last week we did a little detective work—" Jade started.

"We stalked her—" Sam corrected.

"We kinda sat in her parking lot for a few minutes—"

"It was hours. There was a cooler—"

"And I went into her office to talk landscaping—" Jade continued, ignoring Sam's commentary.

"Where she drooled over her—"

"And then she came to the house—" Jade continued.

"Where we both drooled over her—"

"So, we were sitting at the dining room table—"

"And she asked if we wanted a three-way—" Sam cut in.

"To which we replied no—"

"Then Jade asked if *she'd* ever had a three-way—"

"To which she replied yes—" Jade said.

Emma was by this point completely agape with incredulity. "She had a three-way? Holy cow. With two other women?"

Sam nodded.

Emma sipped her drink. "Wow. Are you gonna have sex with her?"

Jade huffed. "Well, if she doesn't, I will."

"I'm sure Calynn would love that," Emma said.

"We have an open relationship."

"Bullshit."

"Actually, I've been thinking," Sam said. "I can do this. I think I can do this."

"Really?" her besties asked at the same time.

"Yeah, I'm ready for some fun, some casual sex. No strings attached."

"That's my girl," Jade said.

"I am so ready, baby. Cheers!" They all clicked glasses just as Sam's phone rang. She glanced down and panicked. "Oh, shit, oh shit, it's Alex!"

"Answer!" Jade demanded.

"I can't. Oh shit, oh shit." In a panic, Sam tossed the phone over her shoulder, and it bounced off the wall and hit her in the back of the head. "Ouch."

Jade retrieved it. "Oh, for the love of God." She swiped and held the phone to Sam's ear, forcing her to take the call.

"Hello?" Sam timidly took the phone and held it like a live grenade.

Emma and Jade gave encouraging signals while leaning in to listen.

"Sam, it's Alex."

She once again channeled her inner Callie. She could do this. "Hey girl, long time no talk. How are you?"

Emma winked and gave a thumbs-up, but Sam could tell Jade was waiting for the proverbial shoe to drop, because she started giving the relax sign, motioning for Sam to take deep breaths.

"I'm good, how are you?"

"Oh, you know, living the dream," Sam said nonchalantly, hoping for approval from her besties. Emma looked happy. Jade looked constipated.

"Yeah, I guess you are. Hey, I have prices for you. Thought maybe I'd stop by and go over everything."

"That sounds great. When can you make out with me…it… uh… When can you make it out, this way? To me…with prices?" The proverbial shoe dropped on her head. A size sixteen, to be exact. Sam's confidence was fading fast. She looked to Jade for some much-needed support, but all she got was Jade's horrified face and a swirling finger in the air as she mouthed, "Wrap it up, wrap it up!"

"How's tomorrow night?" Alex asked.

"Perfect. I'll be home after five. Whenever you're free, stop by."

"All right, cool. I'll see you then."

Sam ended the call and put the phone down. "I am so not ready. I am *so* not ready."

"You're fine," Jade said.

Sam covered her face with both hands. "Why am I acting this way?" She felt like a virgin. And just like that, Madonna was singing in her head.

"You're attracted to her, that's all," Jade said.

"I've been attracted to people before." But no one had ever rendered her incoherent like this woman.

"Maybe she's your lobster, you know, like *Friends*," Emma said.

Sam raised her eyebrows. "She is not lobster material. She had a three-way, for God's sake."

"Oh, right."

Jade asked, "Do you want me there tomorrow night?"

"No, it's better if I tackle this alone."

"Picture her in her underwear," Emma suggested.

"What?" both Sam and Jade asked with questioning looks.

"You know, like *The Brady Bunch*, when Jan needed to give a speech, and she was all nervous. They told her to picture everyone in the audience in their underwear. To make her more comfortable."

"What the fuck channel do you watch?" Jade asked.

"You don't watch *The Brady Bunch*?" Emma asked.

"I don't watch *The Brady Bunch*."

A confounded Sam stuttered, "So you...you want me to picture this...this perfect ten of a woman in her underwear. Do you hear how asinine that sounds?"

"Oh." Emma pursed her lips. "I forgot she was hot. That's probably not gonna work."

"You think?"

Sam's insides twisted. She had thirty hours to get her shit together before one of the most attractive women she'd ever met came knocking on her door. She hoped she could pull it off.

"Is *The Brady Bunch* even in color?" Jade asked.

CHAPTER SEVEN

Sam paced around the living room waiting for Alex. At the Lancôme shoot today, she'd been an unfocused mess, obsessing over this meeting. Why did this woman make her so nervous? The whole thing was absurd. Okay, she was attracted to Alex. No big deal. She didn't have to sleep with her if she didn't want to. Ugh. Maybe a drink would calm her frayed nerves.

Mistake number one. Sam was no drinker, aptly nicknamed Two-Beer Betty by her friends. But desperate times called for desperate measures. Going to the cabinet, she grabbed a bottle of tequila.

Maybe a quick shot. Isn't that what you did with tequila? No shot glass was handy, so Sam took a quick swig from the bottle. Was that enough to help her relax? She shrugged. Maybe one more, and down the hatch went another mouthful. A few ounces of the finest Jose Cuervo sloshing around with her lunch from this afternoon. As she wiped the bottle off, her lips curled in disgust. The aftertaste was wretched.

After liquoring up, Sam wandered around the living room doing mindless tasks, rearranging the copious pillows on the sofa, moving the vase of freshly cut flowers from one table to the next, anything to sap the nervous energy. She decided to treat this like an acting role. Her character would be a cool, together woman. Perhaps a powerful business executive, accustomed to getting what she wants. Yes! Perfect. Alex could be an industry rival, ripe for seduction. Sam could play this role. On tequila, she could certainly play this role. Right after she took a nap, because Two-Beer Betty was suddenly sleepy. She flopped onto the couch and shut her eyes.

The buzz from the gate startled Sam awake, and she stumbled over to push the button. She couldn't feel her face. Did tequila cause face numbing? The doorbell rang, and, ACTION!

Sam opened the door and mentally slapped herself on the ass for encouragement. "Hi, Alex, thanks for coming. I hope you didn't hit a lot of traffic."

Alex smiled and took Sam's outstretched hand. "Oh, you know, you're not in LA if you're not in traffic."

Sam was reluctant to release Alex's warm, sexy hand. Her alcohol-addled brain wanted to hold it for the rest of the night. Shouldn't be a problem, right?

Alex gave a slight tug to get her hand back.

Evidently, she was going to play hard to get.

Stepping back, Sam assessed the situation—or at least what Alex was wearing. Her body looked fine in tight pants and a formfitting shirt. Flip-flops showed off bright blue-painted toenails.

"Nice toes."

Alex rewarded her with the first of many award-winning smiles and wiggled her toes. "You like the color?"

"Adorable." Wait, was that in the script? "You wanna beer?"

"Only if you're having one."

Mistake number two. Never mix liquor and beer.

"Sure, I'll have one." Sam wandered into the kitchen and opened the refrigerator. "How about a lager?"

"Great, thanks. I'll just set up on the dining room table."

When Sam opened the second beer bottle, the cap shot off and skittered across the floor. She bent down to search for it but came up empty. She'd be stepping on that in bare feet later. She stood and swayed, grabbing the counter to steady herself. No worries. Her body was just loose and relaxed. The room was *not* spinning. Keep the camera rolling.

Taking a couple of deep breaths, Sam moseyed into the dining room and handed Alex one of the beers. "Here you go."

"Thanks. I have your written proposal." Alex took out a folder. "And I have your design loaded in the computer."

Her fingers flew over the keyboard, making Sam dizzy. "Whoa, you type fast."

Alex turned and smiled, and Sam felt...butterflies? At twenty-eight? This should not be happening. And now her face was hot. Evidently, blushing was her part-time job around this woman.

"Well, I'm a landscaper by day and a writer by night. So I type a lot."

Of course, Sam knew about the writing, but played dumb anyway. "You write? That's cool. What do you write?"

"Believe it or not, science fiction."

Sam playfully slapped her shoulder. "Get out! Is that why you watch the show?"

"Yep. That and the lead actress is kinda cool."

That was a flirt. Sam was sure that was a flirt. The butterflies returned with a vengeance. She took a swig from her bottle. Beer killed butterflies, right? This was the exact moment when loose slipped into tipsy. "Slow...show me what you have."

Alex took Sam through each section of the backyard, giving the breakdown on costs, showing the least expensive way of doing things and the most expensive.

"Listen. It's cute you keep showing me these less expensive options, but trust me, I can afford it." She leaned in close and whispered, "I'm on television."

Alex whispered back, "I know."

Sam giggled and made mistake number three: finished off the first beer and went for another. This one for courage.

With some bottled moxie in hand, she returned from the kitchen and sat. "I want to get it all done. Where do I sign?"

"Why don't you mull it over for a few days?"

Despite not being of sound mind, Sam waved her off. "Where do I sign?"

"Okay, but please, if you have a change of heart in the morning, call me."

Sam nodded.

Alex slid the proposal in front of her. "I've got duplicate copies, one for us, one for you. You just need to sign both. Then you keep one and I keep one."

Sam tried to focus on the paperwork in front of her, seeing triplicate even though Alex insisted there were only two. Her head pounded, and her ears were on fire. She took the pen Alex offered and stroked her arm. "Thank you."

The signature line on the contract kept moving up and down. Was this some sort of animated proposal? Sam slanted her signature up to split the difference and put the pen down. "When can you do me?" Her brow furrowed. Something wasn't quite right with that statement. *Oh Christ, fix it!* "When can you do the work?" Reaching out, she grabbed Alex's bicep. "Oh my. This is nice." That was her inside voice, right? She giggled again.

"Ah, thanks."

Sam held on as Alex closed the laptop. Muscles inadvertently flexed, and the warmth in Sam's ears spread to her chest and just kept plummeting, sinking and settling in at the top of her thighs. She groaned and put her head on Alex's shoulder, wanting to feel a lot more than bicep and triceps.

"Is next Monday a good time to start?" Alex asked.

Sam nodded, still groping, still flushing, still wanting. All the flushing and groping and wanting induced a massive headache and a bilious stomach. She was afraid to stand, because she might fall over.

CUT! Somebody yell CUT, please! This take was going down the shitter fast.

"Are you okay? You don't look so good."

"I don't feel so good. God, I'm sorry. I'm so sorry." Sam flopped her head onto the table to try and stop the spinning.

"Why?"

"I didn't eat enough today, and it was a stressful day. I was up at four a.m., and then you were coming over and I needed to relax, so I did a shot of tequila. I think two shots of tequila, and here's the thing. I don't drink. I have a beer once in a blue moon. And now I don't feel so good, and I'm sorry for messing this all up."

"Aw, Sam. You didn't mess anything up. I just hope you don't regret signing this contract tomorrow morning," Alex said lightly.

"I won't. I promise." Sam squeezed Alex's hand. Her cheek remained on the table, the coolness feeling good against her overheated face.

"Please call or text if you have any reservations."

Sam managed to lift her head without tossing her cookies but was reluctant to let go of Alex's hand. It was so soft and comforting that she wanted to press a kiss into the palm. She wanted to press a kiss on those full lips. Reaching out, she laid a finger on Alex's mouth.

"You got pretty slips," she slurred.

"Thanks. You do too."

"Oh, you're nice." Sam traced Alex's bottom lip with her index finger, fascinated by the plumpness.

"Do you want to lie down?"

"Oh. You wanna cuddle? Okay."

"No, no, I meant just you. Maybe you should lie down, since you don't feel good?"

"I think that is a very good idea. However—" Sam belched. "'Scuse me. However, I fear when I get up, I will immediately fall down, thereby capping off another humiliating moment with Alex. It's my new reality TV show: *My Humiliating Alex Moments*."

Alex laughed. "I'd watch that show."

"You...are being kind. I'm a hot mess."

"It's fine. Happens to everybody. Let's get you up and over to the sofa."

Alex helped her stand. Putting an arm around her shoulders, she steered Sam toward the living room. Sam's legs thought it an opportune time to go to sleep, or maybe they died, because she started to slowly slip to the floor.

"Whoa." Alex caught her before she hit the ground and swooped her up, like a groom carrying a bride over the threshold.

"Did we get married?"

Alex set her down gently next to the couch and tossed a few pillows on the ground. When she had cleared enough space, she shifted Sam onto the cushions.

Sam stretched out and groaned. How could she have possibly screwed this up again? Jade was gonna bitch-slap her. Her eyes drooped, and just like that, Two-Beer Betty was down for the count.

* * *

When Alex returned from the kitchen with water, Sam's eyes were closed. She set the bottle on the coffee table. A blanket was draped over the back of the couch, so she tucked it around Sam.

Deep in thought, Alex gathered her things. There was something about this one. She was nutty and sweet. Not the prototypical Hollywood diva you read about in the gossip magazines. As she walked to the door, her phone buzzed. She pulled it out and read the text from Sam.

Thank you.

Across the room, Sam's phone dropped from her hand and fell to the floor.

Alex walked over and placed it on the table. Sam's eyes were still shut, her breaths shallow and even. Alex sat down on the coffee table and studied her for a minute. She had such long, dark lashes and dark brows. And all they did was accentuate the most beautiful blue eyes Alex had ever seen, eyes that made her weak.

She adjusted the blanket under Sam's chin and moved a strand of hair away from her face, tucking it behind an adorable ear. What would it be like to wake up next to her every morning?

Rolling over to find sleepy blue eyes and tousled blond hair, sharing a morning cuddle and cup of coffee in bed.

Alex's heart stuttered, shaken by the sudden image of being with the same woman day after day. She bolted to the door, locking and pulling it shut behind her. She needed to purge that thought fast, because she did not want to be in a relationship. One-night stands? Absolutely. That's what she did. She had sex with beautiful women. Wonderful, no-strings-attached sex. If Sam wanted to explore that, well, she was certainly not going to turn her away. But cuddling and morning coffee in bed? No way.

Alex headed to the bar to find a diversion. She arrived at Monette's around nine. The West Hollywood club was a trendy hot spot for the LGBTQ community, and the owner, Monette Thompson, was a good friend of Sophia and Lenna.

"What are you doing here on a school night?" Monette asked from behind the bar. She wore a tank top that showed off her slim build and warm, amber-brown skin. Her tightly cropped afro glistened with sweat from the heat of the lights above.

"Just needed to clear my head."

"You want a beer?"

"No, just water." Alex threw the truck keys on the bar.

Monette slid the water over. "Why does your head need clearing? Let me guess, a woman?"

"Yep." Alex took a sip from her glass. "Somebody off-limits." Alex flashed back to earlier in the afternoon, and Lenna waggling a stern finger in her face and making her promise to "keep it in her pants."

"Married?"

"No."

"So why is she off-limits?"

"It's a new client. Lenna thinks I'll screw up the job if I sleep with her."

"Well, good luck with that. Let me know if you need anything stronger than water."

Alex spun around to face the dance floor, resting her elbows on the bar behind her, and surveyed the room. Every time her eyes landed on a blonde, she thought of Sam. Maybe a redhead would be better. She spotted an attractive woman with auburn hair. *Perfect*. It didn't take long for Alex's stare to be returned. After they'd held each other's gaze for a few seconds, the woman ambled over.

"Hey, do I know you?" she asked.

Alex smiled at the overused pickup line. "I don't think so. I'm Alex." She grasped the other woman's hand in hers.

"Nice to meet you, Alex. I'm Sarah."

It felt like someone threw a bucket of icy water on her. Suddenly, nothing about this seemed right. For the first time in a long time, Alex didn't want to get laid by some beautiful stranger. Probably just a temporary reaction to spending time with her favorite actress. She was saved from an awkward situation by the ringing of her phone. It was Lenna.

She leaned into the woman's ear. "I'm sorry, but I have to take this."

The woman's bottom lip jutted out with disappointment and she walked away.

Alex accepted the call. "What's up?"

"Where are you? I'm checking to make sure your clothes are still on."

Alex laughed. "Yes, still fully clothed. I'm on my way home."

* * *

When she walked through the door, all three of them were sitting on the couch with expectant looks on their faces. Yogi wanted his walk, and Lenna and Sophia wanted information.

"Well? How'd we do?"

Alex proudly tossed the signed contract at Lenna. "Signed, sealed, and delivered."

Lenna paged through it. "Wow, she's doing all this?"

"Yep."

"Damn, and you didn't even sleep with her? I'm impressed."

"You owe me ten bucks." Sophia extended a hand to collect.

Lenna waved her off, not quite ready to lose an Alexander Hamilton. "No three-ways or two-ways took place?"

"Nope."

"Ten bucks please," Sophia repeated. "I had faith in you, Alex. Your sister, on the other hand, did not."

Alex pretended to be affronted. "Ye of little faith."

Lenna's eyes narrowed. "So it was uneventful?"

"Yes." Alex paused and held up a finger. "Well, she was drunk and asked me to cuddle, but other than that, it was uneventful."

Lenna and Sophia glared for a moment, then cracked up.

"I owe you ten bucks, babe," Lenna said.

Alex rolled her eyes. "I'm beat. Gonna walk the dog and hit the hay."

"Good job, Hearteyes."

Alex put Yogi's leash on and led him outside. As she walked around the block, her thoughts wandered back to Sam. Alex had smelled the alcohol on her breath right away. Drugs and alcohol were a big part of Hollywood, and Sam wouldn't be the first actress with a drinking problem. But that adorable confession, about how nervous she was, how she never usually drank, somehow made her more attractive, if that was possible.

Oh well, for now, this woman was off-limits. But when the job was finished? Game on.

* * *

"Let's recap, shall we? There seem to be three major mistakes," Jade said.

Jade and Sam were at Emma's for girl's night. Sam sat on the couch rubbing her eyes, while Jade paced around the room like a prosecutor.

"And what was mistake number one?" Jade asked.

Sam mumbled something.

"I'm sorry, what was that?"

"The tequila."

"Yes, the tequila. Miss Barrett, how much tequila are talking about?"

"Let me go back in my notes." Emma made a show of paging through her phone. "Ah, she drank an unknown quantity right from the bottle."

"I just took a mouthful. It was barely a sip."

Jade waved a hand. "At this time, the sip is conjecture. So, let's see, a mouthful, is generally, what? One or two ounces?"

"It was actually two mouthfuls," Sam painfully admitted.

"Oh. Now we're up to two unsanitary mouthfuls, straight from the bottle. Remind me to never hire you as my bartender." Jade clasped her hands behind her back and continued to pace. "What were you hoping to accomplish?"

Emma raised a finger. "Objection. Badgering the witness."

"Shut the fuck up, Jan Brady."

"I was hoping to bolster my courage," Sam said, voice barely above a whisper.

"Okay. But then we have mistake number two, which is? Jan?"

"Ah, never mix beer and liquor," Emma said.

With arms crossed, Jade stood in front of Sam. "And then, the final nail in the coffin. The second beer."

Sam grimaced. "I barely drank the second one."

"Miss Cassidy, what is your nickname?"

"Two-Beer Betty."

"And why is that?"

"Because I can't handle my alcohol."

"Bingo. Tell her what she's won, Johnny."

Emma used her best game show host voice. "You've won the chance to *not* sleep with Alex Novato!"

"I don't think it's as bad as you're making it out to be," Sam grumbled.

"Why is that?"

Sam puffed herself up. "Because she'll be at my house Monday to work in my yard, probably in a tank top. Booyah! Defense rests!" Sam stood and held an imaginary mic up high, getting ready to drop it.

"That is not mic drop worthy," Jade warned.

Sam dropped it.

Jade put her hands on her hips. "You pick that up."

Sam gave a quick shake of her head.

"Pick it up. Right now, or I swear to God…" Jade left the idle threat hanging in the air.

Sam pouted, bent over, and picked up the imaginary mic. She collapsed onto the couch in a huff.

Jade started pacing again. "Have you heard from her yet?"

"No."

"Here's what you're gonna do. Later in the week, you text her, since you just babble and drool when you talk to her, and you confirm the appointment on Monday. Got it?"

"Yes."

"Okay, maybe we can salvage something here."

* * *

A couple of days later, Sam was relaxing on the couch reading when her phone vibrated with a text from her favorite brunette.

Hey, just checking up on you, making sure you're okay.

Sam felt two things: happy and mortified. And nervous. God, nervous? C'mon, Sam. Be cool.

She texted back. *Feeling fine, now. Sorry about the other night, luckily don't remember much.*

Don't apologize, shit happens. You're good. What happens on the couch stays on the couch.

Shit. What had happened on the couch? Had she done something embarrassing? Oh God, what had she done? Did she say something stupid? Did they make out, and she didn't remember?

Did we kiss?

LOL. Honey, even in a drunken stupor, you would remember that.

Relief flooded through her. All that talk about wanting to kiss a girl again, and to think she might have missed it because she was toasted! Would Alex be a good kisser? Of course she would be with that sexy mouth. A sudden picture of Alex putting her mouth on other things came unbidden into her brain.

She shook her head to clear the image and texted back. *What happened on the couch, pray tell?*

You don't remember?

Sam frowned. That night was still a bit fuzzy. She remembered waking up on the couch, not getting to it.

No, do I need to be mortified? Because if so, it's better here on text than in person, so just tell me now.

It wasn't bad. You just wanted to cuddle.

Sam nodded. She did like to cuddle. *Obviously, I have a cuddling problem. I'm a closet cuddler.*

And there may have been some fondling at the dining room table.

Sam bit her lip. Had she gotten handsy too? *Need I ask who did the fondling?*

Well, it wasn't me.

Sam gulped. *Okay, well that narrows it down. And what, pray tell, did I fondle?*

My bicep. And I have to admit, I was digging it.

Sam's fingers whipped across her phone. *Well, it seems I once again managed to humiliate myself.*

And...

Sam groaned. *Oh wait, there's more? Goody.*

You called me your reality show, My Humiliating Moments with Alex.

Perfect. I'll make sure you get your royalty checks.

LOL. Don't sweat it, your secrets are safe with me. See you Monday? Bright and early? Seven a.m.?

Sam brightened. *Yes, seven a.m. Bring Yogi! And I promise I'll keep my hands to myself.*

Alex sent a sad-faced emoji.

Sam stared at the tiny, yellow pouty face long after Alex signed off, her body thrumming with excitement. Ever since she'd met Alex, it was like being hooked up to a slow drip of caffeine. This was the most alive she'd felt in a long time, despite the levels of humiliation.

Monday couldn't come soon enough.

* * *

Alex tossed the phone down and rested her head against the back of the sofa. Yogi had his head in her lap, snoring. She reached down and tickled his ears. She was glad she'd given in to the impulse to text. Sam had been on her mind the past couple of days. Alex had been hoping she wasn't embarrassed by the other night, and truth be told, she'd needed a Sam fix.

Picking up her phone, she scrolled back through their conversation. She thoroughly enjoyed Sam the texter. She exuded a sexy confidence. Alex glanced down at her faithful pooch, who had rolled over, offering his belly for a rub.

"What say you, Yogi Bear? Sam asked for you by name. Sounds like she has the hots for you, buddy. Maybe one of us can get to first base."

He yipped.

Alex laughed and gave him a kiss on his lips. She reread Sam's line about being a closet cuddler. It almost made her want to drive over and initiate a cuddle.

"This one may be trouble, Bear." Alex continued rubbing his belly, chuckling at his expression of ecstasy.

CHAPTER EIGHT

Sam awoke early Monday morning, all atwitter with anticipation. At four a.m., she jumped in the shower, spent way too much time on her hair, and then stood in front of the closet for half an hour, mulling over what to wear. Which outfit matched her eyes? Which shirt showed the right amount of cleavage? Which shorts hugged her ass just right? By six a.m., she was in the kitchen sipping coffee. The photo shoot didn't start until this afternoon, which provided ample time to observe the object of her affection—or rather, object of attraction. She didn't know Alex well enough to have actual feelings. Yet.

She poured more coffee into her favorite Snoopy mug and leaned against the island. Her thoughts traveled back to college, when she'd last felt this way. Six long years without feeling the giddy excitement of being in the same zip code with someone.

Finally, the clock struck seven. Sam took her mug to the front window and peered into the dewy, early morning light. How pathetic was this? Stalking her own front yard, waiting for some woman she barely knew to arrive. Hopefully in a tank top.

Her mind drifted back to the texts she'd exchanged with Alex and the mild flirting that had made her heart race. She hoped it would continue in person.

When the buzzer sounded, Sam jumped, spilling coffee all over her perfectly ironed white V-neck. With a curse, she pushed the button to open the gate and ran back into the kitchen to blot the shirt with water. Soon the entire front was soaked. And see-through. Great. Well, her bra choice was on full display. It was white, and it was lacy, and she swore her nipples were visible. Fantastic. *Hi Alex, c'mon in, and oh by the way, have you met my areolas, Titsy and Bitsy?* Before she could ponder what to do about the peep show, the front doorbell rang. She held the towel close to her chest, hustled to the door, and pulled it open.

"Good morning," Alex said.

Sam held onto the doorknob with her left hand to steady herself. "Morning." She hoped she didn't sound as out of breath as she felt.

Alex pointed to the front of Sam's shirt. "What happened there?"

Overcome with modesty, Sam readjusted the towel. "Coffee mishap." Uncertainty nagged at her. Was a handshake in order? Or a hug? Perhaps it was too early for hugging. And dropping the towel to shake hands meant it was hello nipple time. She opted to just stand there like the dork she was. "Ah, do you wanna come in?"

"I'm gonna get my crew started. I'll knock on the French doors when I'm done, and we can go over the plan for today."

"All right. I'll meet you around back. I'll just, um, go change my shirt." Sam closed the door and hustled up the steps to change, scolding herself for looking like such a huge, coffee-stained moron.

When she made it back downstairs a few minutes later, she peeked through the kitchen window. Alex walked around the yard with the crew. She was dressed much like the first day at the store, with long khaki cargo shorts slung low on her hips, a tank top that showed off a fabulous physique, and a weathered baseball hat. A mod pair of Ray-Bans completed the look. It was sexually devastating.

Sam's nerves had her jittery. Or perhaps it was the three cups of dark roast. *Something* was causing heart palpitations. Sweat beaded up on her forehead, so she headed outside to breathe some fresh air.

Yogi came running as she stepped onto the patio, creating the perfect diversion. "Yogi Bear. Hey buddy, remember me?" Sam knelt to greet him and received a big, sloppy, wet kiss, right on the lips, and then a tongue right in the mouth.

Alex soon appeared. "See, Yogi? I told you one of us would get to first base today."

Sam laughed. "Do you try to get to first base with all your clients?"

Alex smirked. "Only the blonde ones. I mean, they are supposed to be more fun."

The heat of Alex's stare radiated through her sunglasses, making Sam lightheaded. Yogi pushed his head into her hand, and she smiled at him. "He's adorable. Is he a rescue?"

"Yeah. We rescued each other about four years ago."

"Well, he's welcome here anytime." Sam stood. "I'll let you get back to work." As she walked away, her eyes remained glued to Alex.

"Sam, watch out!"

Too late. Sam turned just in time to promptly walk into the French doors, banging her forehead. "Ow."

Alex hustled over. "Are you okay?" She cupped Sam's face with her hand. "Let me see."

"Am I bleeding?"

"No, but it might bruise. You'll live." Alex rubbed the spot and smiled that sexy smile.

Sam resisted the impulse to grab that hand and nestle her cheek into it. "I guess that's par for the course, right? Just when I thought I had my shit together, the reality show continues. I'm sure I'll be on crutches by the end of the week."

Alex laughed. "Let's hope not."

Chuckling at her own ineptness, Sam jerked a thumb toward the house. "I'm gonna go, because I'm sure I have something better to do than run into things. Like put ice on my face."

"Eyes forward, Blondie," Alex instructed.

Sam completed her not-so-graceful exit and headed inside, making a beeline to the freezer for an ice bag. She chided herself for being such a clumsy ass. How was she gonna explain this lump on her head to the Lancôme people? Wait until Jade heard about this. Probably make her day. She shrugged. Why not make Jade's day now?

Her bestie answered on the first ring. "Hello?"

"I walked into a door this morning."

"Oh good, the misadventures of Sam Cassidy continue."

"And I French kissed her dog."

"Sounds like you French kissed the wrong Novato."

"Yeah. And I'm pretty sure she saw my nipples."

"I don't even wanna know."

Sam held the ice against her lump. "I don't think I'm cut out for this."

"Relax. You're fine. What's she wearing?"

Sam had already committed what she was wearing to memory and recited it easily.

Jade sighed. "Be still my gay heart. Take a picture and send it to me."

"I am not taking a picture. Don't be ridiculous."

"C'mon, just take it. She won't even know."

Alex made her way to the French doors.

"She's coming to the door. I have to go."

"Send me a picture!"

"Shut it." Sam put the phone and ice bag down just as Alex knocked. She opened the door. "C'mon in."

Alex followed Sam into the kitchen. "How's your shirt?"

Now that the Ray-Bans were on top of the hat, Sam had full access to those green eyes, twinkling with suggestion. Blush number one hundred and one. "I probably ruined it." She nervously wiped an invisible piece of dust off the countertop. "I didn't realize it was so…um…thin."

"It *was* sheer. But I'm not complaining."

The sexy smile was back. This woman was a master. A black belt flirter. Sam wracked her brain for the lowest belt. White? Invisible? That's what she was.

"So what are you going to do first?"

Alex explained all the work on tap for the next few days and then asked if Sam had any questions. Before Sam could answer, her phone vibrated with a text and they both looked down.

Tell her I said hi and to take her tank off ;)

With a pained groan, Sam snatched the phone.

Alex wore an amused smile.

"Yep. Well, uh, I'll let you get back to work. Let me know if you need anything."

"I will. Thanks."

Sam spent the next couple of hours lurking near whichever window afforded her the best view of a certain brunette. At 10:09 a.m., the tank came off, revealing the red sports bra underneath. She pulled out her phone, needing to tell someone about this glorious view.

The tank's off. I repeat, the tank is off.

Sam's phone rang immediately.

"Fuck a duck, if you love me at all, you're sending a picture," Jade said.

"I am not taking a picture."

"Why not? Just go outside and video the action, catch her sweating and straining with a shovel or something. Wait! We'll FaceTime, and she won't know we're FaceTiming. Tell her you want to video the work, or some shit like that."

"What the hell are you talking about?"

"Just do it. You owe me."

"Why do I owe you?"

"Do I have to remind you about the time you got caught half naked at that party, and I had to convince a photographer not to publish the photo?"

Jade had her on that one. Three years ago, Sam had attended a party at a co-star's house, and everyone had started skinny-dipping around midnight. Sam had been on her fourth beer, which meant she was practically asleep. Brian, her now ex-boyfriend, had convinced her to go topless and get in the pool. Little did anyone realize the paparazzi were just beyond the fence. It was not a good night for Two-Beer Betty, who ended up on a fuchsia floatie, tits up, mouth open, snoring. The picture was hall of shame worthy. Fuchsia was not Sam's color.

"Okay, I'll try. But I think that's a manager's job anyway, to keep bad things out of the press."

"That's above and beyond the call of duty, my friend. In fact, I should get a raise. Remind me to give me a raise."

"What'd you say?" Sam asked, unable to concentrate because Alex had picked up a large landscape rock and was carrying it across the yard, her lean muscles rippling with the effort. If this were Victorian England, Sam would be whipping out a handheld fan, vigorously waving it back and forth in front of her face to cool off.

"I said I'm giving myself a raise."

"Okay," Sam said dreamily.

Outside, the action escalated. Goddamn, Alex did have a shovel, and with every thrust into the earth, Sam pictured her thrusting somewhere else.

"She looks so good right now." Sam gripped the windowsill for support. "You should see her."

"I'm trying, but you won't cooperate."

"You know how some women have abs of steel?"

"All the women of my dreams do."

Sam had gone quiet, staring longingly into the yard.

"Are you drooling?"

She did a quick swipe at her chin. "No drool. Yet. What did you want me to do?"

"I'm gonna hang up, and then I'm gonna call you back on FaceTime. You're gonna walk outside and let me see this woman. Do it!"

"All right, calm down." Sam hung up and answered when her phone buzzed. "I'm not sure about this. What if she catches us? I will fucking die from embarrassment."

"She'll never suspect. Just go."

Sam began to walk toward the patio doors. "I can't believe I'm doing this." She heard an "Ahem," and looked down at Jade. "What?"

"Ahem."

"Ahem, what?" Sam asked, exasperated. She looked around and her eyes landed on the swear jar. "I don't have one." There was no room in Sam's tight shorts for dollar bills. "Besides, you owe for that little fuck a duck comment earlier. We'll just call it a wash." She headed outside.

Alex, who was shoveling dirt around the recently installed boulder, straightened when Sam walked over. "Hey there, what's up?"

"I just wanted to, um, video the progress." Sam's hands were shaking.

"Jesus Christ, stop shaking," Jade whispered.

Sam coughed to cover up Jade's voice, taking a quick peek at Alex to see if she was on to them. So far, so good. It appeared their ruse was working. She made a play of moving the phone from side to side, narrating to make it more believable. "Here is my backyard before my fabulous makeover. This is Alex, my landscaper."

Alex's wave made the vein in her bicep pop.

The vascular display distracted Sam, and she lost her train of thought. Would that vein pop out if Alex were, say, leaning over Sam, while they were in bed? Naked?

She refocused and continued her monologue. "I'm getting new gardens, and, ah, a new outdoor kitchen, and um…" This was not her finest improv. And to top it off, Jade kept grousing about the phone moving too much. "Well, that's it I guess." Sam put the phone down. "I have to go to work. Same time tomorrow?"

Alex nodded. "Sure, same time."

Sam waved and headed back to the house.

"Bye, Sam—bye, Jade."

Sam was mortified. Jade was toast.

* * *

The next day, Sam rose again at the crack of dawn. The decision had been made the night before to only indulge in one cup of coffee. And to not wear white. At least the swelling on her head had subsided. What hadn't subsided was the steamy, X-rated dream she'd had last night about Alex taking her behind the honeysuckle. Sam had tossed and turned for hours after, finally succumbing to some self-satisfaction to relieve the tension. Thankfully, she didn't have to work today, because she was exhausted. And her hand was stiff.

At seven a.m., Sam pressed the button to open the gate. Alex was dressed the same as yesterday, only today the tank was green, and Sam was sure it would match her eyes. It was time to step up her game. Although she had no idea how. She bit down gently on her thumb, trying to think of something. This fuck buddy business was hard work. She still wasn't sure she could pull it off. "Fuck buddy" implied two people simply hooking up, but Sam needed more of a connection to have sex with someone. Maybe the better term would be "friends with benefits." Yes. Perhaps that was the answer. Become friends, establish a connection, then have sex.

Her buzzing phone startled her. Luckily the coffee sat safely on the countertop. "You're up early."

"Are you having sex yet?" Jade asked.

"No. But I have a plan."

"Do tell."

"I'm not feeling the fuck buddy thing."

"Okay."

"I'm gonna call it 'friends with benefits.'"

"Whatever you need to call it to get that chastity belt off."

"I'm gonna take it slow, get to know her—"

"Then bang her."

"Well, that's the plan. I just need to feel a connection."

"Good. Go make friends."

Sam spent the rest of the morning propping up her confidence. Around lunchtime, the crew left to get something to eat, leaving Alex and Yogi in the backyard alone. Time to implement the plan. Sam breezed through the doors with a bowl full of water for Yogi. The best way to a woman's heart was through her dog. Wait. Heart? Libido. That's what she'd meant.

Alex sat with her back against the old retaining wall drinking a bottle of water, boots and socks lying in the grass. Her tank was still on, much to Sam's disappointment. Maybe the temperature would rise through the afternoon.

"Do you want something other than water?" Sam asked.

"No, I'm good thanks."

Sam placed the bowl on the ground next to Alex. "I brought Yogi some, just in case he was thirsty."

Yogi padded over and lapped at the water.

Alex looked on with mock disgust. "God forbid he drinks from the bowl I put down."

"Well, he obviously adores me," Sam said.

"Who wouldn't?" Alex whispered.

"What?"

"Nothing." Alex took a swig from her bottle.

A joyous thrill passed through Sam, tickling her insides, and she sat down next to Alex, pulling her knees up to her chest and resting both arms on them.

Alex's hat was off, and the sunglasses now perched precariously on top of her head. "I don't know if I'd get that close. I'm kinda gross right now." Sweat glistened all over her body.

Sam wanted to run her hands over those strong arms, wanted to taste the salt on Alex's neck. "I don't care. How's it going?"

"Pretty good. How's your head?"

Sam rolled her eyes skyward and absently touched her forehead. "I'm such an idiot. You bring out the idiot in me."

"You're not an idiot."

"I am. It's like *The Three Stooges* around here. I literally walked into a door."

"I think your knees were weak from Yogi's awesome kiss."

Sam giggled. "You're funny." She tilted her head towards the sun and took a deep breath. "You know, I can be funny. I can be cool funny."

"I think you're funny."

"No, I'm dorky funny around you. Not cool funny. I say stupid things and do stupid things. I walk into doors. I babble. I get drunk."

"And you're blaming me?"

"Yes, I am." Sam playfully shoved her, and Alex toppled over. "It's all the sexual energy you give off. It's uncomfortable for us mere mortals."

Alex laughed, righting herself. "I'm sorry I make you uncomfortable. I'll try not to be so sexually appealing."

"How you gonna do that? You'd have to show up for work dressed in a burqa. And that wouldn't be enough, because those peepers would still be showing. You'd have to be in a burqa *and* your Ray-Bans. Then maybe you wouldn't turn me on." As soon as the words slipped out, Sam groaned. *Good God.* That was definitely her outside voice.

Alex's eyebrows shot up. "I'm sorry, what was that?"

"Nothing." Sam covered her face with her hands.

"Oh, it wasn't nothing."

"It was nothing!" Sam hid behind her hands.

"It was far from nothing. Am I turning you on?" She poked Sam in the ribs.

Sam tried to ward off the onslaught by grabbing Alex's hands. "No, no, I didn't say that."

Alex held onto Sam's hands. "You did. You just did. You said I'm turning you on."

Sam pulled her hands back and turned away, hiding blush number one hundred and two. "I don't think I did."

Alex stretched out on the grass and put her hands behind her head. "So I'm turning you on. That's titillating."

"Titillating? That's a big word."

"Yeah, writer, remember? The burqa comment was cool funny, by the way."

"Yeah?" Sam asked.

"Yeah. You were cool funny and titillating all in one conversation. I think you've put your past struggles behind you."

Sam settled into the grass next to Alex, all her nerve endings firing. "You know, just because you turn me on doesn't mean I'm gonna fall into bed with you."

"Whoa!" Alex's eyes widened. "Who said anything about falling into bed?"

"We should just be friends."

"Absolutely." Alex's lip quirked up in amusement and she shot a sideways glance at Sam. "How's your boyfriend?"

"Ugh. You saw through that, didn't you?" On a whim, she sat up, snatched the sunglasses from the top of Alex's head, and put them on. "How do they look?"

"You look hot."

She beamed at the compliment. "We're gonna be friends, right?"

"Yes. Besties. Do besties get to flirt with each other?"

Sam didn't hesitate. "Yes, flirting is allowed." Friends with benefits would absolutely flirt.

"What about random touching?"

"How random?"

"You know, like…" Alex took her bare foot and ran it up Sam's bare leg.

She got chills despite the ninety-two-degree heat. "Yeah, random touching's okay."

"Cuddling? I only ask because of your current condition."

Sam nodded, still rocking the sunglasses. "Definitely. I cuddle my friends all the time. Ask Jade."

Alex's brow creased with thought. "Kissing?"

"With or without tongue?"

"With."

Sam's lips pressed together. "Hmm. I don't think so."

"Sounds like it might be a gray area."

"No, not a gray area. More like a no-fly zone."

"Without tongue?"

"Like a kiss hello?" Sam asked.

"Yeah. A kiss hello."

"That's fine."

Alex tilted her head. "What happens if I go to kiss you hello, and my tongue accidentally finds its way into your mouth? Like it slipped or something."

"Like on a banana peel?"

Alex struggled to keep a straight face. "Yes, yes, on a banana peel. Like would you reject it right away, or would there be some possible lingering?"

"Hmm. I may allow some lingering."

They both giggled.

"Nice guns, by the way," Sam said.

"Thanks." Alex gave a wink and flexed.

Sam figured she might as well get all her favorite parts out on the table. "*And*, nice six-pack."

"Do you like them?" Alex pulled up her shirt.

"No, you don't have to show—oh, fuck me," Sam murmured when she got the close-up. God help her. And her wallet. "We good? We'll be friends. Promise me we'll be friends."

"I have to promise?"

"Yeah."

"Okay, I promise."

"You have to raise your hand like this," Sam put her two fingers together, "and swear."

"I prefer a pinkie swear. Because it involves random touching."

"Okay, pinkie swear."

Alex sat up and they locked pinkies. "I promise to be your friend, and only your friend, until you deem otherwise."

They held their fingers together for a couple of seconds longer than necessary.

Sam licked her lips. Random touching felt pretty damn spicy. "Good. And now, I'm gonna head inside." Sam stood and started walking away. "I'm paying you to work, not get me all hot and bothered."

"Oh, I can do both."

Sam grinned and skipped into the house, brimming with newfound confidence. Friends with benefits felt like a winner. She passed the powder room and stopped short, gazing at her reflection in the mirror. Hot damn, she did look good in these sunglasses. She finger gunned herself. "FWB," she said out loud. "Friends with benefits." She took the stairs two at a time, and tripped over the last one, landing with a thud.

CHAPTER NINE

On Wednesday morning, Alex prowled around looking for something to eat.

It didn't take long for a hungry Sophia and Lenna to wander into the kitchen.

"So, how's the job going?" Lenna asked, stifling a yawn as she poured a cup of coffee.

"Good so far."

"How was Sam?"

"Sam who?" She received a soft smack on the head. "Ow. She was good. It was…interesting."

Lenna groaned, taking a seat at the table next to Sophia. "What does that mean?"

Alex decided on cereal for breakfast. "Well, there was some kissing." She poured some into a bowl before sitting down. "Of the French kind. And some heavy petting and rubbing." Alex stopped to monitor her audience.

Sophia's look was one of mild interest.

Lenna's look said, *I'm gonna cut your tits off and put them in a blender.* "What did you do?"

Alex poured milk into the bowl. "Tsk, tsk, tsk. Always assuming the worst."

"Alexa?" Lenna's cheeks took on an angry reddish hue.

Alex peered down at Yogi. "Ask him. Yogi, what did you do to Sam? You Frenched her, didn't you."

Yogi whined and wagged his tail.

Alex pointed at her faithful pooch. "You Frenched Sam right in the mouth. It was wet, and it was sloppy, buddy. You might have to clean that up if you wanna get to second base."

Yogi barked, stood up and stretched, then plopped down again.

Alex looked at Lenna. "I think they're a thing now."

"You're a shithead."

Alex chuckled and shoveled a healthy spoonful of toasted oats into her mouth. After swallowing, she made a face at Lenna. "Your lack of faith in me is disheartening. I promised I would behave, and I did—sorta."

The tit stare returned. "Sorta?"

"Well, there was some flirting. But in my defense, I didn't start it. And have no fear," Alex put a hand up, "it's not going anywhere. She just wants to be friends."

Lenna stood and whacked Alex on the head again. "Behave. I need to get ready for work." Lenna started up the stairs. "And when do I get to meet her? She's my favorite actress. Invite her to dinner."

"Yes, we all know she's your favorite actress. And thanks for the concussions!" Alex glanced at a wickedly grinning Sophia. "Oh, Jesus Christ, what's with you?"

"You're into Sam."

"What?" Alex blew out a quick breath. "Please. We're just gonna be friends."

Remembering the pinkie swear promise made Alex smile. It was adorably silly, and she loved it.

Sophia's silence made Alex paranoid. "What?"

"Nothing."

"I see your wheels turning."

"My wheels aren't turning."

"Listen, I know you're a shrink and all, and you love to psychoanalyze people, but family members should be off-limits. So stop."

"Some of the best relationships begin as friendships."

"Relationship? Who said anything about a relationship?"

Sophia ignored her. "Your sister and I were friends first."

"I know. For two years. Your courtship is in the *Guinness Book of World Records*. You were the anti-U-Haul."

Sophia's eyes took on a dreamy quality. "Yeah, we were."

"Ain't love grand."

"It is. You should try it again sometime."

Alex swirled her spoon in the bowl, sadness creeping into her voice. "I tried it once. Didn't end too well." The heaviness of her past still weighed on her soul.

"I know, honey." Sophia squeezed her hand.

They sat in silence for a few moments until Alex changed the subject. No sense dwelling on painful memories.

"How's the planning going for Lenna's fortieth? Is Monette ready to close down the bar so we can party?"

"We're all set."

"Good."

"Hey, why don't you see if Sam will come over for dinner? Lenna would get a big kick out of it. Maybe sooner rather than later, as an early birthday present."

"I'll ask her. I mean, we are good friends now."

* * *

Sam's long hours meant no interactions with Alex on Thursday. Thankful for an early dismissal on Friday, she hustled home, hoping to catch Alex before she left. Time to institute the new plan. FWB!

Sam's heart rate accelerated as she pulled through the gate. The truck was still parked in the driveway. She hurried through the house and stepped onto the patio. Alex was at the other end of the yard alone, her crew having already left for the day.

"Hey, Sexeyes. I think you should stay for dinner tomorrow night."

Alex smiled broadly. "Wow, we just became friends. Isn't it a little soon for that?"

"Friends have dinner together. We can get to know each other. What do you say?"

Alex rested her arms on the shovel. "Only if there's cuddling."

Sam's brows knitted in thought. "No guarantee. I mean, it's only our first friend dinner."

Alex put the shovel down and wandered over to the patio. "Are you a good cook?"

"No, if I'm being honest. Better eat a snack before you come."

"Let's see. No cuddling and the food will suck. You're not making this very appealing."

"Well, there's a chance the food won't suck."

"Which would mean there's a chance of a cuddle?"

"I dunno about that," Sam said with a small smile.

"Should I bring anything?"

"Nope. Just yourself." *And your sweet, tight ass. And your sexy smile.* That was her inside voice, right?

* * *

Later that evening, as Alex stared at the computer screen, a certain blonde was front and center on her mind. When she closed her eyes, she could see Sam's smile, the dimples deeply indenting her cheeks. Without overthinking, Alex grabbed the phone and fired off a text.

What's the dress code for tomorrow night?

She stared at the screen, hoping for a quick reply. When it didn't come, she put the phone down and glared at the laptop. Restless energy made for jumpy legs, so she went downstairs to get some water.

Sophia and Lenna were curled up watching a movie. Alex hovered beside the sofa.

"What's with you?" Lenna asked.

"Nothing."

"Sit down. You didn't miss much. It just started."

"Na, I'm working on a chapter."

Sophia picked her head up from Lenna's shoulder. "Was that somebody's phone?"

Alex took off, stumbling over Yogi, who had planted himself at her feet. She righted herself and flew up the steps.

"Whoa! Be careful!" Lenna shouted.

Alex charged into the office, door slamming behind her. She smiled when she saw the answering text.

Do you have anything formal?

I have a tux. You taking me to prom?

A smiley face emoji came back. *Wouldn't mind seeing you in that.*

What are you going to wear? Alex typed.

I have a white Giorgio Armani gown for special occasions.

Well, I wouldn't mind seeing YOU in that.

Oh yeah?

Actually, I wouldn't mind seeing you get out of that.

Smooth.

I'm here all night.

Let's scrap the formal and go casual.

How casual? Alex asked.

PJs?

Laughter bubbled up from Alex's chest. Sam positively killed it on text.

* * *

The next day, Sam arrived home at three p.m. She bustled around the kitchen and kept checking the clock, anxious for dinnertime. By five p.m., things were almost ready. Poking her head outside, she called to Alex, "Hey, everything's almost done. You wanna come in?"

"Sure." Alex grabbed the shovel and rake, putting them in a neat pile by the patio. She stepped inside, carrying a backpack. "Can I shower?"

"Yeah." Sam led the way to the guest bathroom upstairs. "Just come down when you're done."

Fifteen minutes later, Alex came sauntering into the kitchen.

Sam's gaze lingered. This was the first time she'd seen Alex with her hair down. It fell in loose waves around her shoulders. Auburn highlights shimmered. She'd had the privilege of hanging around a lot of stunning women, but none could hold a candle to this one. She averted her eyes, not wanting to be caught staring.

Alex peeked into the baking dish that sat on the counter. "What is it?"

Sam was overwhelmed by the scent of vanilla shampoo and Alex's signature cologne. She almost forgot to answer the question. "Chicken?"

They both peered into the dish, studying it closely, heads only inches apart.

"What happened to it?" Alex asked.

"I happened to it."

"I've never seen chicken that color before. Maybe in a cartoon, but never in a baking dish."

"It might taste okay."

"It's purple." Alex took a fork and lifted one of the pieces. She shrieked and dropped the fork, startling Sam, who pulled away from the dish.

"What?" Sam feared the worst, a bug or a hair in her signature dish.

Alex's eyes were comically wide. "I think it moved."

Sam laughed and pushed her. "Stop it! You shouldn't be making fun of me. It's the first time I'm cooking for you."

"Au contraire, we are just friends, and friends are honest with each other. Now, if this were a date, I'd have to choke that shit down."

"Aw, you would do that for me?" Sam batted long lashes at Alex, who remained inches away.

"Yeah, if it meant getting laid." Alex leaned in closer and glanced down at Sam's mouth, then back up to her eyes.

"You are so romantic. No wonder women fall all over you."

"I try." Alex leaned in even closer.

Things were getting hot, and it wasn't from the steam of the purple chicken. It was Sam's turn to gaze down at Alex's mouth.

She shuddered and bit her lip. How would that mouth feel pressed against her fevered skin? Or nibbling on certain sensitive areas? Now was not the time for this line of questioning. She needed to reel herself in.

"What should we do?" she asked, returning her attention to the chicken.

"I think…"

The air sizzled with sexual energy and Sam's breath hitched. Those emerald eyes screamed that a kiss was imminent. And she would be powerless to stop it.

"…we should order pizza."

The spell was broken, and Sam's body wilted with disappointment. Immediately she chided herself for it. What was the matter with her? It was too soon for kissing. "No purple chicken?"

"I don't think so."

Sam sighed. She had hoped to appear competent in the kitchen. Just once. "I told you I couldn't cook."

"Well, next time I'll cook."

After the pizza was delivered, they sat around the table happily munching and chatting. "Much better than purple chicken." A string of cheese hung between Alex's mouth and the slice she'd just taken a bite from.

Sam resisted the urge to twirl a finger around it and searched for a safe topic of conversation. "Did you go to school for writing?"

"Yes, Arizona State. Go Sun Devils."

"Have you written a book?"

"I have. It's not published though. It's book one of a trilogy."

"How come it's not published? How does that work?" Sam reached for another slice, making a mental note to up the cardio tomorrow.

"The first thing you do is send out query letters and hope someone calls you back. It's hard though. You need to know someone, or at least have an agent working for you. And, unfortunately, I don't know anybody, and I don't have an agent. Minor detail, right?"

"Can I read it?"

"Sure, I'll email you a PDF."

They finished eating, and Sam gathered the dishes and put them in the sink.

Alex stood. "Here, let me do those."

"Well aren't you thoughtful."

"Didn't know that about me, did you?"

"No, I did not. See?" Sam pointed between them. "We're getting to know each other."

* * *

Doing the dishes enabled Alex to bolster her wavering willpower. When Sam bit her lip earlier, Alex had almost lost it. It had taken all her steely resolve not to kiss Sam right then and there. And if this were any other woman, they would have skipped pizza altogether and headed to the bedroom. But this was Sam. And there were promises to keep.

When the dishes were done, Alex wandered into the living room.

Sam was relaxing at one end of the couch, but the remaining space was covered in throw pillows.

Alex whistled. "That's a lot of pillows."

"Oh, sorry." Sam grabbed the pillows in bunches and tossed them on the floor.

When the coast was clear, Alex sat.

Before she had a chance to settle in, Sam kicked off her sandals, leaned back against the arm of the sofa, and put her feet on Alex's lap.

She prayed for self-control. While she waited for the prayer to be answered, she grabbed Sam's foot and began massaging it. Time for some random touching. "Are your feet ticklish?"

"No." Sam closed her eyes and moaned. "Oh, that feels good. Forgive me if I start drooling. Foot rubs are heaven."

Alex was mesmerized by the look of ecstasy on Sam's face. She'd like to see that face under different circumstances. When the lip was caught between white teeth again, she had to look away.

"I have a confession to make." Sam opened her eyes. "Promise you won't get mad?"

"Is this a pinkie swear promise?"

"No." She chuckled before taking a deep breath. "Jade and I read your fanfic."

Alex stopped rubbing for half a second, then started again. "Okay. When?"

"When you first posted it."

Alex tried to put the timeline together. "That was before we met."

"Yeah. Are you mad?"

"No, why would I be mad? And how did you know it was me?"

"It was in the comments. Friends of yours kinda called you out by name."

"Right. Now I remember."

"Anyway, we read it, and we loved it. We even commented."

"What was your comment?"

"I think Jade wrote, 'dude, that was a fucking awesome sex scene.'"

"I remember that one." Alex started on the other foot. "You liked that scene, huh?"

"Um, it was pretty good." Sam's color heightened. "After we read it, we thought it would be fun to track you down."

"And you ended up in my parking lot." Alex grinned. "Explains a lot. You two were acting super weird. *Sarah*."

Sam gently whacked her with a throw pillow. "That was Jade's idea, not mine!"

Alex tossed a small fuzzy pillow back. "Okay...Sarah."

"Stop it...Hearteyes."

Alex threw her head back and laughed. "You got me there."

"Where did that come from?"

"It was a high school nickname. I had a crush on an older girl. My friends said I stared at her with hearteyes."

"Have you ever been in love?"

Alex's body stiffened at this new line of questioning. "Sure, who hasn't?"

"When was the last time?"

Alex looked away. "A while ago."

"Oh, you're being vague. Did someone break your heart? Is that why you're such a player? What's her name? I'll take care of her," Sam teased.

Alex shifted uncomfortably. "Can we talk about something else?"

Sam's baby blues filled with sympathy. "Wow, she must have really broken your heart."

"It's no big deal. Everyone gets their heart broken at some time. You must've had yours broken."

"I did. In college I dated someone, and she cheated on me. It sucked. There hasn't been anyone serious since."

"College? That was a while ago."

"When your life is public knowledge, it's hard to be out and in love. I guess you could say I've chosen my career over my personal life."

"That's sad, Sam. You seem like someone who should be in love."

"What about you? Why shouldn't you be in love?"

"Not my thing, I guess." Not wishing to elaborate or open old wounds, Alex stopped rubbing Sam's feet. "Well, I've enjoyed our little get-to-know-you session, but I do have to head home."

"Damn. Right when we were getting to the good stuff." Sam swung her feet onto the floor.

"I know." Alex stood and put the pillows back. "Oh, I have a favor to ask."

"Anything."

"My sister and her wife would love to meet you. They wanna invite you to dinner."

"Only if they make purple chicken."

"I wouldn't count on that."

"I can't believe you didn't love my purple chicken."

"I did love it. As a garden gnome."

"But it was purple."

"I told you. There would've been strings attached for loving that purple chicken."

Sam nodded. "Oh right, the getting laid part."

Once again, the air popped with tiny sparks of attraction.

Alex was thankful it was time to leave. There was only so much self-control to go around, and things were becoming more dangerous by the minute. "So, dinner?"

"I'd love to."

"Great. Maybe next week?"

"Sure."

Alex gathered her things and they both headed to the front door. She jiggled her truck keys. Was the timing right for a kiss goodbye? Should she execute an 'on the lips, no tongue' goodbye kiss? But if she touched those lips, there would be no stopping her tongue. She decided to let Sam call the shots.

"Uh, so…I guess this is…good night," Sam said.

Alex rocked back on her heels. "Yeah. I had a great time. Thanks for the pizza. And the chat." She waited patiently for Sam to make some sort of move. The silence stretched on for a few awkward seconds. When it became clear no move was forthcoming, Alex hitched a thumb in the air. "I'm gonna hit the road." She turned to leave.

"Wait!" Sam said. "I think we're at the hug stage of our friendship, don't you? I mean, we just spent a couple of hours together. Surely that's enough time to warrant a hug."

Alex took the truck keys and dramatically tossed them over her shoulder. She pulled Sam into a hug and planted a soft kiss on her cheek, surprising them both. "Good night."

Sam's body sagged against her. In a throaty voice she whispered, "Good night."

They separated, and Alex picked up the keys. Before walking out the door, she turned to give one last knee-knocking smile.

* * *

Sam waved goodbye from the doorway. That sexy smile would be the death of her. Maybe it was her favorite thing. Better than the ass? Hmm. Too close to call. To make a decision of that magnitude, one needed a more comprehensive body of work. Sam absently touched her cheek where Alex's lips had landed. She hadn't been prepared for a kiss, and this one had caused a mountain of movement inside her chest. This wasn't just about sex anymore. Something else simmered below the surface. Something warm and wonderful bloomed near her heart. Time for a new plan.

Jade answered on the fourth ring. "Hello?"

"I had Alex over tonight." Sam's voice crackled with excitement.

"I'm intrigued," Jade whispered. "But I'm at dinner with my monster-in-law and Calynn, so make it quick."

"Okay," Sam whispered back. "We had dinner and talked for a couple of hours."

"Good."

"Here's the thing."

"There's a thing?"

"I don't want Alex to be my fuck buddy."

"Okay, but I thought you were gonna be friends with bene—"

"I want her to be my girlfriend." Sam listened for Jade's reply, but all that was audible was some sort of commotion. "What's going on?" she asked, continuing to whisper.

Jade talked in the background. "Babe, I'm sorry. Carol, let me get that. Here's my napkin…"

"What happened?"

Sam listened as Jade excused herself from the table. The noise in the background grew fainter, and finally Jade came back on the line. "I spit my water out on my future mother-in-law is all."

"Oh, that's not good."

"You think?"

"Why'd you do that?"

"I don't know, Sam. *Girlfriend?* Are you kidding? She's not lobster material. You said so yourself."

"I know what I said. But that's not how I feel."

"When did this happen?"

"Tonight. She gave me a hug, and it was an epiphany."

"Must've been some hug. Listen, as your previous attorney of record, I would advise against this decision."

"Why?"

"She told us herself, she's not into relationships. Alex has three-ways, you have one-ways. It wouldn't work."

Was Jade implying she used the vibrator too much? "Alex said she only had the one three-way and wouldn't do it again."

"Minor detail. Why do you want her to be your girlfriend?"

"I like her. I *really* like her. I knew from the first moment I laid eyes on her."

"What are you saying, love at first sight? That's movie shit and you know it."

"I can't stop thinking about her."

"It's a crush. An infatuation."

Sam's voice rose defensively. "I want Alex. I want her *bad*."

"Like sexually? 'Cause a quickie will take care of that."

Maybe she wasn't explaining it well enough. Although, how could she explain something she herself didn't understand? "No, it's more than that. I know it's what I want, okay? Are you going to be a friend and support me or not?"

"All right. Don't get your panties in a bunch. What do you wanna do?"

Sam smiled, relieved to have Jade's support. "Well...I'm going to woo her."

"What now?"

"I'm gonna woo her. You know, woo."

"I guess I missed the part where we were teleported to nineteenth-century England."

Sam huffed. "I'm going to get to know her, and she'll get to know me, and we'll see where it leads."

"Tell me one thing. Is sex in your future?"

"If things progress, yes. But I think it's important to have a foundation of friendship first. The best relationships start as friendships."

"Jesus Christ, are you watching *The Brady Bunch* with Emma?"

"No." Sam snickered.

"Okay I'm getting the death stare from my girl. I gotta go. All I have to say is, I hope Wooing Sam is less of a dork than Fuck-Buddy Sam."

"I think she will be."

CHAPTER TEN

Alex sat in her home office sifting through rejection letters. Numerous times over the past two years, she'd been besieged by self-doubt. Fretting her dream wouldn't come true. That she wasn't good enough. These letters fueled her determination and strengthened her resolve.

Footsteps in the hallway paused at the open door. Lenna did a double take and leaned into the room. "What are you doing here?"

"Uh, I live here?"

"It's Saturday night."

"What's your point?"

"Isn't this your prowl night? Your get your groove on night?"

Without speaking, and never breaking eye contact, Alex closed the door with her foot.

Their hushed voices carried through the closed door. "It's Sam. She likes Sam," Sophia said.

"Really? You mean for more than a one-night stand?"

Alex looked to the heavens. "I hear you. Jesus, you're right there."

Lenna cleared her throat. "Have a good one. We're going to dinner."

Sophia whispered, "Ask if she wants us to bring her anything to eat."

"You mean like Sam?"

They both giggled.

"You're not funny," Alex said.

"We'll be back later," Lenna said.

Alex sighed. No work would get done tonight. Sophia was right. She had Sam on the brain. Her phone was on the desk, but she didn't want to appear too eager. Jesus, when had this happened? If she wanted to text a woman, she did it.

She tossed the phone onto the chair across the room. "Yogi, this one is driving me nuts. How was that kiss, lucky dog?" He remained quiet, evidently not one to kiss and tell.

Alex closed her eyes, remembering the look on Sam's face during the foot massage. Her imagination took off. Sam naked in her arms, biting her lip as Alex's mouth roamed all over her body. The buzz of the phone interrupted her fantasy. She jumped across the room to grab it.

Sam had sent a picture of the purple chicken with a stake through it, perched in a flower bed. Like a garden gnome.

Alex's mood brightened. She sent off a quick reply. *I hope you don't leave it outside overnight. You'll have every coyote in the county in your backyard.*

I'll be right back.

Alex laughed, picturing Sam running into the backyard to bring the purple chicken inside. Probably in her pajamas. Had she ever met anyone this goofy, sweet, and beautiful? A teeny flicker of warmth seeped into her chest, unsettling her, because it didn't feel like lust. Sam might be trouble. She needed to be careful.

Here I am. You were right. He's been mauled. She sent another picture, of the purple chicken half eaten.

At least someone enjoyed it.

Where are you? At the bar cruising for Miss Right? Or should I say Miss Right Now? A wickedly winking emoji followed.

Maybe. Alex tried for flippant. When there was no reply, her heart skipped a beat. Was Sam disappointed? Or hurt? She quickly snapped a selfie with Yogi and sent it off. *Spending time with my main squeeze. Mr. Yogi Bear.*

A smiling emoji came through. *Give him a kiss for me.*

Alex breathed a sigh of relief. *You should be here doing that yourself.*

I'm hard to get, remember? Don't want him thinking I'm easy.

He's pining for you.

Just him?

Alex's fingers froze. How should she respond? Should she admit that Sam was on her mind constantly? Or that her favorite pastime was daydreaming about taking off Sam's clothes? Maybe she was overthinking it. She shrugged.

Did I ever tell you blondes are my weakness?

I don't think you mentioned it, Sam replied.

Blondes make me weak. So be nice to me. I'm fragile.

I'll be gentle with you, promise.

Alex grinned. Sam and her promises. *How's next Wednesday for dinner?*

Done! Send me the address and tell me what to bring.

I can only tell you what not to bring.

Very funny. Hey, Jade and Emma are coming over to swim tomorrow. Why don't you stop by?

Sounds titillating. What kind of bathing suit do you wear?

LOL. Bikini.

Alex didn't hesitate after getting this intel. *What time?*

One, and bring my boy.

Okay. Alex put the phone down and groaned. Sam in a bikini. Now how was she supposed to sleep tonight?

* * *

On Sunday morning, Sam met the girls at the trailhead to Brush Canyon. Weather-wise, it was a perfect day for a hike.

"I have news," Jade said. "Zach is gonna hire me as an agent."

"That's great!" Emma high-fived her.

"Yep, I'm ready to spread my wings. Don't worry, Sam, you'll still be my main squeeze. I can manage you and maybe represent a few more clients."

Sam stared down at her phone, at the picture Alex had sent last night of her with Yogi. She couldn't stop drooling over it, wanting to make it her wallpaper, her background…

"Sam!"

"Sorry. That's wonderful! Congrats." Sam hugged her.

"I have news too." Emma proudly extended her left hand.

"When did that happen?" Jade asked.

"Last night."

"A ring!" Sam hugged Emma. "I am so happy for you. You guys are great together. Tell Logan congrats too."

"So. Look at us, all with big news." Jade directed a questioning stare at Sam.

"What?"

"How's the wooing?"

"What wooing?" Emma asked.

"Sam's wooing Alex."

"She's not gonna bang her?"

"No. She's wooing it, friendship style."

"When did this happen?" Emma demanded.

"After the hug."

"There was a hug?"

"Yes, and the earth moved," Jade teased.

"And the angels sang?"

"Something like that. Sam has a plan."

Sam groaned in frustration. "Shut up. We're becoming friends and getting to know each other, because—"

"Sam wants Alex to be her girlfriend," Jade said.

Emma's forehead puckered. "But I thought this chick wasn't girlfriend material."

"Well, the hug changed everything."

"Wow. Must've been some hug," Emma said. "When was all this?"

"She came over for dinner the other night," Sam said. "I cooked."

Jade stopped short. "Jesus Christ. You didn't say you cooked!"

"You cooked?" Emma asked. "I thought you liked her?"

Sam playfully shoved her. "Stop it."

"What did you make?" Emma asked.

Sam peered up at the cloudless sky, pretending not to hear the question.

Jade groaned. "Oh no, not the chicken."

Sam's hackles rose. She always had to defend her signature dish. "Yes, I made the chicken."

"The purple chicken?" Emma asked.

"Yes. My chicken—that sometimes turns purple."

Jade's lip curled in disgust. "It always turns purple."

"You made it for me once," Emma said. "I thought I was eating Donald Duck. Wasn't he purple?"

"Okay, number one, Donald Duck is a fucking duck," Jade said. "And number two, there's a control on your TV called color tint. You should try it sometime."

"Maybe I'm thinking of Foghorn Leghorn. Wasn't he some sort of chicken?"

"Well, you're getting warmer. He was a rooster. Who fucked chickens. And I say all this in the past tense because he's no longer on TV. For like fifty years. Jesus Christ, we need to update your cable package."

"Did you eat the purple chicken?" Emma asked.

"No, we ordered pizza and chatted for a while. It was a nice, friendly get-together."

"You call it a friendly get-together, the rest of us call it dating," Jade said.

"We're not dating. Dating would involve kissing good night. We're not at that stage yet. Although she did give me a kiss right here when we said goodbye." Sam stroked her cheek.

"Have we not washed that spot yet?" Jade asked.

"Shut up."

"Does Alex know you want her to be your girlfriend?" Emma asked.

Sam's brows drew together. "No! You just can't blurt that out. I don't want to scare her off."

Emma nodded. "Gotcha. You're gonna woo her and make her love you. Cool."

"Love? It's too soon for that. And I'm not gonna *make* her do anything."

Emma started singing, "I'm gonna make you love me…yes I will…yes I will."

"Jesus Christ, first *The Brady Bunch* and now the Supremes? What's next, *Leave It to Beaver*?" Jade asked.

"Maybe you should let the Supremes sing that," Sam suggested.

Emma stopped singing and cocked her head. "Does one have sex while wooing? Or does that come after wooing?"

"Sex? We just became friends!"

"Emma, these things take time," Jade said. "Sam and Alex will have sex around the summer of 2022."

"I'm supposed to go to her house next week to have dinner and meet her sister and her wife. And, I invited her over to the house today to hang with us. I wanted you guys to get to know her."

Emma clapped. "Finally. I get to meet this woman."

"Yes!" Jade pumped a fist in the air. "I haven't seen her in so long I forget what she looks like. I need to put a face to my vibrator."

Sam glowered. "Shit, Jade. You're picturing my possible future wife while you use your vibrator?"

"I'm kidding. My God, just kidding."

Sam pursed her lips and looked away.

Out of the corner of her eye, she saw Jade mouth to Emma, "I'm not kidding."

Emma laughed and put an arm around Sam. "Well, I can't wait to meet her."

Sam pulled them to a stop. "Now, we have to set some ground rules. Under no circumstances are either one of you to undermine Wooing Sam."

"I thought *you* were Wooing Sam," Jade said.

"Wooing Sam has been pretty cool, she has her act together, and I'm proud of her. I will lose my shit if you make me look like a moronic dork in front of her. Am I clear?"

"I'll behave," Emma said.

Jade made a face. "Okay. But where's the fun in that?"

"And I did not mention being fuck buddies, so mum's the word."

Jade's face fell. "Shit, we have nothing to talk about now."

Sam slipped an arm around her. "Don't worry, we'll have plenty to talk about. You can tell Alex how you've named your vibrator after her."

Emma raised her voice an octave. "Oh, Alex, oh, Alex, OH, ALEX!"

Sam and Emma enjoyed a rare laugh at Jade's expense.

"I hate you both."

* * *

Jade, Sam, and Emma sat around the pool, eagerly awaiting Alex's arrival. When they heard the truck, Sam put everyone on notice to be on their best behavior. Yogi was the first one to charge around the side of the house and run to the pool.

"Yogi!" Sam laughed when he jumped on her chair and began licking her face.

Alex appeared soon after, wearing her signature hat, board shorts, and a skimpy, barely-there white tank top.

"Hi." Sam popped up from the chaise and adjusted the bottoms of her floral-print bikini.

Alex wrapped her in a hug, and strong hands caressed her naked back, causing goose bumps to dance along her arms. Soft lips brushed the side of Sam's neck, and she almost keeled over. She held on for dear life. When Alex released her, she nearly teetered into the pool.

"How you doing?" Alex asked.

Sam held a hand to her chest, still flustered. "I'm good. You remember Jade?"

Jade stood. "Hey, give me a hug, girl." She pulled Alex in and ran a hand under her skimpy tank top.

Sam scowled.

Jade wiggled her eyebrows in response.

Sam would deal with her later. "And this is Emma."

"Yeah, from the show! How are you?"

Emma hugged her. "So good to meet you finally."

"Alex, what would you like to drink?" Jade asked.

"Water's fine for now."

Jade linked arms with Alex and began walking toward the battered fridge. "What have you two been up to?"

"Not much. I've been working every day. Sam and I have been hanging out, getting to know each other." She smiled back at Sam.

"Welcome to Sam's plan," Jade said to no one in particular.

"Plan? What plan?" Alex stopped walking and turned around.

Sam's stomach dropped. "Nothing, there's no plan."

Alex turned back to Jade, who handed her a bottle of water.

Sam flipped both middle fingers at Jade, bending at the knees for emphasis.

Jade just winked at her.

Alex turned around just as Sam was coming up from the double-bird flip-off. So she did what anyone who was caught in an unflattering position would do. She pretended she was dancing. Because who doesn't dance to the rhythmic stylings of a pool filter? When Alex turned her attention back to Jade, she flopped down next to Emma, muttering, "I'm gonna kill her."

"I'm going in," Jade announced. "Who's coming in with me. Alex?"

The motive was clear. To get Alex undressed. Now, this particular action had Sam's stamp of approval.

Alex tugged the tank over her head, revealing a black string bikini that covered...nothing.

Sam gawked as she dove into the pool.

Emma whispered, "Close your mouth."

Sam did as she was told. Sometime soon, she needed to lay hands on that body.

"You two coming in?" Jade asked.

Alex swam up and put her arms over the side of the pool. "Come in, Sam."

There was the smile, and those eyes, unabashedly staring at Sam's ample cleavage. Sam was quite satisfied with her choice of bathing suits. "Okay."

Holding on to her top, she hopped in.

"Let's play some pool basketball," Jade said. "Me and Sam against Emma and Alex." Jade swam by Sam. "You can thank me later," she mumbled.

"Thank you? I'm gonna kill you." She was still sore from Jade's loose lips.

As Jade swam over to guard Emma, the genius of the game plan came home to roost. Sam would guard Alex, and there could be all sorts of random touching in pool basketball. Okay, she could forgive Jade.

Emma tossed the ball to Alex, who caught it and taunted Sam. "Whatcha got, Blondie?"

"Oh, big talker, huh?" Sam bum-rushed Alex and jumped, but not before Alex displayed perfect shooting form and hit nothing but net. Sam groaned. "Great. She's a ringer."

Alex smiled, pulling her into a playful headlock. "Maybe next time, beautiful."

Sam made a half-hearted attempt to throw off Alex's arm by wrapping a hand around her bicep. And since her other hand was unoccupied, why not rest it on Alex's rock-hard abs? Sam got the bicep and the abs all in one sober grope.

"Okay, you two, this isn't *Dancing with the Stars*." Jade tossed the ball at Sam, who somehow managed to catch it before it smacked her in the face.

Now that she had possession of the ball, Sam mocked Alex by extending the ball, then pulling it back. "You want this? You want this?"

"Yeah, I want it."

Sam was knocked off kilter by the innuendo in Alex's eyes, and her slight hesitation enabled Alex to slap the ball away.

Emma grabbed the ball and Jade jumped her, pushing her underwater. She sputtered to the surface crying, "Foul! That's a goddamn foul."

"Bite me, Jan." Jade threw the ball to Sam, but Alex was too quick, and she intercepted it, successfully dunking another shot.

"How about a little defense?" Jade said.

Sam flipped her the bird.

"Maybe I wasn't clear on the teams."

Sam flipped the finger on the other hand. The ole middle finger was getting quite the workout today.

Alex swam up to Sam and winked. "Nice try."

Sam wanted to yank her underwater and plant one on those luscious lips. "I guess you're good at everything."

"Well, some things I'm better at than others." Alex grabbed Sam's stomach.

"Yo, grope a dopes. Let's go," Jade said, calling their attention back to the game.

After fifteen minutes, Jade and Sam surrendered and headed for the lounge chairs while Alex and Emma continued shooting at the hoop.

Jade plopped down next to Sam. "Goddamn she's hot. I'm gonna have to wear a panty liner around her. Are you looking at that bod? Do you see it?"

"Oh, I see it. I see it *real* good." Truth be told, Sam's eyes hadn't left Alex all afternoon. She reached for her newly acquired Ray-Bans.

"Your willpower is admirable."

"I'm hungry," Emma called from the pool.

Sam was eager to flex her cooking skills. Or lack thereof. "I can make us something to eat."

"No!" said all three at the same time.

"You guys suck."

They ordered pizza and enjoyed a couple more hours of fun in the sun before Alex stood to leave.

"Ladies, it's been a pleasure hanging with you today, but I have to work tomorrow, and the client is a real pain in the ass."

"Yeah, but I hear she's a great cook," Sam said.

"I dunno about that." Alex grinned. "Yogi, are you coming with me, or are you gonna slobber over Sam all night?"

Sam laughed. "He likes your pain in the ass client."

Emma stood and hugged Alex. "Good job, partner."

Jade was next, and she kissed her smack on the lips. "See you soon."

Alex took a quick peek at Sam. "Yeah, see you soon."

"I'll walk you out." Sam looked none-too-kindly at Jade.

They walked in silence through the house, with Yogi dutifully following.

"Thanks for inviting me. Your friends are a blast."

"They're assholes, but I love them."

"Funny assholes."

"Yeah, definitely funny." Sam felt jittery standing in the doorway. They were on the cusp of another goodbye, and she was hoping for a lip-to-lip kiss. No tongue, of course. Not yet.

Alex pulled her in for a hug. "Night."

Sam melted into Alex's arms for a long hug. She nestled her chin into the base of Alex's neck, where they remained still, both content in the moment.

Finally, Alex pulled away and cupped Sam's cheek.

Sam's breath hitched in anticipation. This was it. This was finally it. But when Alex just kissed her softly on the cheek again, she wanted to drop to the ground like a three-year-old and kick her legs in disappointment.

After saying goodbye, Sam practically skipped to the backyard.

"Well, did you lock lips?" Emma asked.

"No. She hit the cheek again." Sam sat and directed a steely gaze at her bestie. "And don't think I didn't notice that kiss on the lips."

Jade's eyes widened. "What? It was an accident."

"Accident my ass. I haven't even kissed her on the lips yet." Sam crossed her arms, perturbed.

"Guess you have some catching up to do."

She stewed for a few moments, but then curiosity got the better of her. "How was it?"

"You don't wanna know. Let's just leave it at that."

Sam silently agreed. Best not to learn this torturous information. Better to discover it on her own.

"Those lips were soft. That's all I'm gonna say. Especially that bottom one, but I've already said too much. I almost slipped her the tongue—"

"Jade, enough!" Sam pouted.

"You guys are cute together," Emma said. "Alex is a ten. Well, maybe a twelve, if that's possible."

Sam perked up. "Thanks, E."

Resting her head back on the lounge chair, she let herself daydream about her perfect twelve.

CHAPTER ELEVEN

Sam pulled into the driveway at Alex's house, and shifted the car into park. The special tiles for the spa had been backordered, so Alex and her crew had been elsewhere for almost ten days. The longest ten days of Sam's life. She shot off a text to Zach. *If you have news on the book, let me know. I'm with Alex now.*

Last week, she'd sent the manuscript to Zach, and he, in turn, had sent it to the literary department at his agency. She rarely used her clout to receive preferential treatment, or to force people to go above and beyond, but if Alex needed an agent, then by God, Sam would get her one.

The object of her attraction sat barefoot on the front porch step with Yogi by her side. Even dressed casually in jeans, Alex was stunning.

Grabbing the bottle of wine she'd bought this morning, Sam got out of the car.

Yogi bounded up to greet her. "Hello my handsome man." When she finished scratching Yogi's back, she pouted at Alex. "What? No hug?"

"I'm not sure of the protocol. Is public hugging allowed?"

"Yes. Get up here." Nestling into Alex's warm embrace, Sam wondered if she would ever get over the thrill of being wrapped in these strong arms.

With much reluctance, she pulled away, and they both sat on the stairs. "Why are we on the porch?" Sam asked.

"Sophia wants this to be a surprise for Lenna. We'll wait for her to come downstairs, and then we'll go in."

"Cool."

"I'm hoping she doesn't act like a big dork around you."

"It would be nice to have another dork to talk to."

"Sometimes she lacks a filter."

"She can't be that bad." Sam rested her elbows on the step above. "Did you miss me?"

Alex mimicked her pose. "Oh, definitely. I don't know how I survived without you."

Sam playfully nudged a shoulder into her. "It's okay. I'm here now." She snatched Alex's baseball hat and put it on.

"You gonna take my hat too?"

"Maybe. How's it look?"

Alex leaned away and drank her in, arching a brow. "You almost look athletic."

"Good. I'm ready for a basketball rematch."

"I wouldn't say that. Am I getting my hat back?"

"No."

"Damn it."

Sam glanced down at Alex's toes. "You do have some cute toes."

"You do too." Alex covered Sam's toes with her own and tickled them.

Sam slid off her sandals and soon they were engaged in a hot and heavy toe wrestling match that had them both giggling.

After putting their toes in timeout, Sam took a breath and exhaled. "God, I'm gonna miss you."

Alex gave a start. "Why? Are you going somewhere?"

"I have to leave Sunday for a movie shoot."

"This Sunday?"

"Yeah." She'd been secretly wishing the schedule would be delayed, which was why she hadn't mentioned it until now.

Disappointment clouded Alex's eyes. "For how long?"

"I'm not sure." Melancholy seeped into Sam's voice. "Six to eight weeks."

"Well that sucks."

"And I have to explain something about how I work. When I'm shooting a movie, I try to keep my distractions to a minimum and stay in character as much as possible."

"Like method acting?"

"Yeah. I don't talk to my friends, or my mom, or anybody."

"How about texting?"

"No texting."

"No talking or texting for two months? Wow."

Sam grimaced and shook her head. "Believe me, I'm not looking forward to it." How would she survive that long without Alex? Suddenly her heart felt tight. Eight weeks was a lifetime. So much could happen. What if Alex found somebody else? Or grew bored waiting? A knot of worry lodged in her belly.

Alex sighed. "I guess I'll have to survive."

Sam tried to keep it light, because thinking about no Alex for two months was unbearable. "I'm sure you'll live. You'll probably find another distraction while I'm gone." Sam put the hat back on Alex's head, tucking in a stray strand of hair.

"I'm not easily distracted."

Sophia opened the door. "You guys ready? Hi, Sam, I'm Sophia."

Sam stood and gave Sophia a quick hug. "It's nice to meet you." She handed her the wine.

"You too. I've heard a lot about you. Thank you for the wine, that's very sweet."

They made their way to the dining room, where Lenna had already taken her seat.

"Why aren't we eating in the kitchen?" Lenna's mouth dropped open when she saw Sam. "Oh shit. You're...oh shit...I can't believe it."

Everyone laughed.

"Stop stammering like a toddler," Alex said. "I told you she's a dork, Sam."

"Well, I'm happy to meet a fellow dork." Sam walked around the table, and Lenna stood to shake her hand. "Oh no, I'm a hugger." Sam gave her a big hug before taking the seat next to her.

Alex sat across from them.

"I'm a… I'm a…," Lenna stuttered. "Ugh. Sorry. I'm an idiot."

"Aw, Sam, she sounds like you," Alex teased.

"She's right, I act like a dork around this one." Sam pointed in Alex's direction.

Lenna inched her chair closer. "Why would you act like a dork around her? She's not worth it."

Alex smirked. "Go ahead, Sam. Tell her why."

"I told her she gave off a lot of sexual energy, and it made me nervous."

Lenna scowled at Alex. "I told you to behave."

"I'm innocent in all of this."

Alex's toes slipped across the floor and grabbed Sam's, making her jump. The long tablecloth acted as a cover.

"You hear that, Lenna? She's innocent."

"If she bothers you, tell me, and I'll pull her off your job."

"Oh, I'll put up with it. Occasionally she takes her shirt off. And I'm not ashamed to say, I look. I mean, I'm human."

Lenna rested a hand on Sam's arm. "You can look. Look all you want. Alex, from now on, sports bras only over there!"

"Thank you, Lenna." Sam reached across the table and stole Alex's hat again.

"Wow, I'm impressed," Sophia said. "That's her favorite hat. Nobody touches it."

"Sam likes to take things that don't belong to her."

Meandering toes traveled up Sam's leg.

"Only your things," she said sweetly, trying not to flinch.

"Alex, let her have your hat." Lenna smiled at Sam, clearly smitten. Like a kitten.

"She already took my sunglasses."

Lenna glowered at her. "This is Samantha fucking Cassidy, you'll give her whatever she wants."

Alex's lip curled into a playful sneer. "You give her your hat."

Now the toes were above Sam's knee, traveling up her thigh, toward an area that was probably a no-fly zone. Sam discreetly reached under the tablecloth and pinched the wandering phalanges, stopping them in their tracks.

"She just said she likes to take *your* things." Lenna stared adoringly at Sam.

"Shit, I won't have anything left. I'll be walking around naked."

Sam glanced at Lenna. "Naked? I wouldn't mind that."

"Alex, take your clothes off!" Lenna yelled.

Sam and Sophia guffawed.

"Sam you're my hero," Sophia gushed. "Someone who can actually hold their own with the Novato sisters. Now, are we ready to eat? Lenna, help me get the food on the table."

* * *

Once in the kitchen, Sophia pulled Lenna's arm. "Are you seeing what I'm seeing?"

"Sam Cassidy?"

"No!" Sophia softly slapped her arm. "Are you seeing what's going on between them?"

"You mean the fact they dig each other majorly? I see it. I'm wondering if my baby sis has kept her promise."

"She has, because there's a bunch of sexual tension between them. If they were sleeping together it would be a different vibe." Sophia stole another peek at the happy non-couple. "They're so cute together. Alex hasn't acted this way around someone in a long time."

"I know."

"Do they realize how they look at each other?"

"Probably not. I don't know Sam, but Alex can be dense. Hey, maybe we'll have a famous sister-in-law in the family."

They both snickered.

"Can you imagine? Thanksgiving with Sam Cassidy," Lenna said. "We have to encourage this."

"Oh, so you're okay with it now?"

"Absolutely."

Lenna and Sophia returned to the dining room, arms loaded with plates of food.

"Wow, everything smells delicious. Thanks again for inviting me over," Sam said.

"It's us who should be thanking you for coming. It's nice to finally meet you," Sophia said.

They all dug in.

"Sam, Sophia is a shrink," Alex said as she spooned some vegetables onto her plate. "So watch what you say to her. Unless you want to be psychoanalyzed. Then, you put a nickel in the jar, like Lucy from *Peanuts*."

"I love *Peanuts*."

"Well, there you go. Meet Lucy, and my dorky, dykey sister is Peppermint Patty."

"Who are you?" Lenna demanded.

Alex puffed up her chest. "I'm Snoopy, of course. Cool and aloof."

"Oh pa-lease. Who am I?" Sam asked.

"You? Hm." Alex glanced at the ceiling, her index finger tapping her chin. "Linus."

Sam crinkled her nose. "Linus? Why Linus? He sucks his thumb."

"He does. However, more importantly, he cuddles that blanket. He's a cuddler. Sam's a cuddler," Alex told Lenna and Sophia.

Sam nodded. "She's right. I'm a cuddler."

"Although I wouldn't know. Right now, it's hearsay." Alex cocked an eyebrow at Sam.

Lenna and Sophia looked at each other. Then looked away.

After dinner, Sophia announced the dessert options. "We have two choices, apple pie with ice cream or Alex's homemade brownies."

"I'll take a brownie, please." Sam's phone buzzed and she took a quick peek down. "I'm sorry. I never do this, but it's important. Please excuse me." She hurried into the other room with Yogi trailing after her.

As Sam left the room, Alex's eyes followed her. When she turned back, she had a stupid grin on her face and a dreamy look in her eyes.

Lenna and Sophia gawked at her.

Alex frowned. "What is it with you two? You've been chicken hawking us all night."

"What's going on here?" Lenna asked, pointing to where Sam had been sitting and then at Alex.

"Nothing." Alex's lips twitched up slightly. "What?"

"How far along is this thing between you two?" Sophia asked.

"This thing? It's not a thing."

They both continued to stare.

"Nothing's going on. You made me promise."

"All I ask is that you just don't break my favorite actress's heart," Lenna said.

"I'm not gonna break her heart. Geez, give me a little credit."

Sam came back into the room smiling.

"Good news, I hope?" Alex asked.

"Very good." Sam sat down at the table.

Lenna threw an arm around her. "So it's my fortieth birthday this weekend."

"Well, congratulations!"

"We're having a big party. Consider yourself invited."

"Well, that sounds fun. Alex never mentioned it." Sam shot an accusing glance in her direction.

"Ah, it's at a gay bar in WeHo. Kinda like a no-go for you," Alex explained.

"Why? It would be fun."

"It's definitely gonna be fun," Lenna said.

"Sam," Alex said gently, "there's going to be over a hundred people at the party. All taking selfies with you. Your agent would not appreciate you being headline news. If you thought Twitter blew up from your show's last episode, this might be worse. Everyone would be posting all over their Facebook pages."

Sam looked pensive for a moment, and then her eyes flashed with excitement. "What if I brought a bunch of other cast members and crew?"

"You could do that?" Lenna asked.

"Why not?"

Alex frowned. "Sam, this is a bad idea."

"Don't worry. It'll be fine. And so much fun."

"Yes!" Lenna shared a happy high five with Sam.

Sophia placed the desserts on the table, and Sam grabbed a brownie, taking a healthy bite. "Wow, this is good. You're obviously better in the kitchen than I am."

"Yeah, Sam can't cook," Alex told Lenna and Sophia. "But it's okay, you can't be good at everything."

"Well, I'm not very good at pool basketball either," Sam pointed out.

"You have my hat now. It's bound to make you more athletic."

"I'm not good at drinking."

"Well, who wants to be good at drinking?"

"You've never seen me behind the wheel. My driving can be horrifying."

"I'll drive."

Lenna and Sophia looked at each other. And looked away.

A few minutes later, they all finished eating and sat back, hands on their bellies, feeling overly stuffed and satisfied.

Sam cleared her throat. "The phone call earlier was from my agent, Zach. Alex, I have something to tell you."

Sam's tone had everyone's attention.

"I sent your book to him, and he shared it with the head of their literary department." Sam paused. "They loved it. They wanna represent you."

Alex's mouth dropped open. "What?"

"No way," Sophia and Lenna said simultaneously.

Sam continued. "Not only that, but Zach has a friend at a publishing house in Chicago. He wants to send the full manuscript to him. Guy owes him a favor. So, at the very least, they'll read it."

"Oh my God!" Sophia threw her arms around Alex. "This is wonderful!"

Alex remained frozen in place, her eyes wide with shock.

Sam raised a hand. "Now, there's no promise they'll publish it, but at the very least, someone will read it. And if they don't want it, Zach will keep shopping it until he finds someone who will."

"Holy shit!" Lenna hollered, jumping to her feet to put Alex in a choke hold. "I told you. I told you! Write the fanfic, get a following, get your book published. Though I never expected your following to be Samantha fucking Cassidy!"

"Who would expect that?" Sophia laughed and slapped at Lenna's arm. "Honey don't kill her before the book gets published."

"Oh, right." Lenna released Alex and duffed her in the head for good measure.

Once freed from the headlock, Alex jumped to her feet and pulled Sam from her chair. "Are you serious? I have an agent?"

"Yes, if you want him."

Wrapping Sam in her arms, she twirled her around. When Alex set her down, moisture pooled in her eyes. "I just can't believe it. I can't believe you did this for me."

Sam wiped at her own watery eyes. "I'm just glad I could help. The book is great. I loved it."

Alex pumped her fist in the air. "I've got an agent, bitches!"

Everyone hooted and hugged.

With a hand over her heart, Alex said, "I can't even express in words how happy you've made me. This is totally unexpected. And, quite possibly, the nicest thing anybody has ever done for me. Thank you."

Sam grasped her hand and squeezed. "You're so welcome."

"How am I gonna repay you?"

"Oh, I'm sure I can think of something." Sam's eyes sparkled with mischief.

Lenna and Sophia looked at each other. And looked away.

After a celebratory toast and more conversation, Sam finally stood. "I guess I should get going. Sophia, wonderful to meet you. Dinner was delicious. I would reciprocate, but only if Alex cooks. And Lenna, great to meet you too. I'm gonna work on that birthday thing." Sam hugged them both.

"I'll walk you out," Alex offered.

Lenna and Sophia stayed behind to give them privacy.

"I like her," Sophia said. "She's so down-to-earth. And a breath of fresh air."

"She's adorable. I hope Alex doesn't screw this up."

"Have some faith in your sister. She hasn't been with anybody since she met Sam. She's been home every weekend for the last few weeks."

"True." Lenna peeked out the window to monitor the action.

"Maybe this is finally it. Maybe she finally met someone she can be with, long term."

"Well, I hope you're right. Been a long four years for her. But it's gonna be longer if she doesn't step up her game out there. You should see this. C'mon, kiss her, you ass. My God, when did she become so inept? I swear sometimes I think we're not related. Is this the same woman who beats them off with a stick? It's embarrassing."

"Will you stop gawking like some Peeping Tom?" Sophia scolded. But then curiosity got the better of her. "What are they doing now?"

"It's like some awkward teen dance. They're just staring stupidly at each other. Alex has her hands jammed in her pockets like some douchebag. Jesus Christ, it's almost unwatchable. Oh wait, here we go, hands out of the jeans, and…a hug. A goddamn hug…and…Sam is in the car. Yogi got a kiss though. Only Novato getting somewhere." Lenna lowered the curtain and grinned wildly. "Since Sam can't cook, I guess we'll have Thanksgiving here."

* * *

On the drive home, Sam called Jade.

"Sami, what's up? How's my girl?"

"I'm good."

"Not you, damn it, my perfect sexy ten. I haven't seen her in so long."

"It was less than two weeks ago."

"Feels longer."

"I'm not comfortable with you lusting after her so much."

"Well, I suggest you step up the wooing." Jade switched to her sweet voice. "So, don't hold out on me, how is she?"

"She's fab. I just left dinner with her family."

"Oh, the gay family dinner. How'd it go?"

"It was fun. Her sister cracks me up. Her wife is sweet, and a pretty good cook, I might add."

"So, you were able to actually eat what was cooked. That's good. Baby steps. You'll get there. Learn from others."

"We played footsy under the table."

"I'm sorry?"

"Footsy. We played footsy."

"Footsy?"

Sam laughed. "Yeah, seriously. Footsy. And it was hot."

"Footsy. Huh. I didn't know the word was still part of the English language. You go, Betty White. You'll be pregnant in no time."

"I'm serious, it was kinda hot."

"Well, when you're relegated to hugs and pecks on the cheek, I guess footsy is downright pornographic."

"Very funny. Did I tell you she wrote a book?"

"No!"

"Well, she did. I gave Zach a copy, and he loved it. I told Alex he's interested in representing her."

"Holy shit, that's awesome! So, what did Alex say? Is she gonna sleep with you out of gratitude? Will she sleep with me out of gratitude?"

"Stop it. She was happy, and that made me happy."

"Sounds like love, Sami. The footsy thing seals the deal."

"No, I'm not saying that. I'm just saying, it made me happy to make her happy. She got teary…I got teary."

"Uh-huh. Keep talking."

"It's not love. It's way too soon for love. That's a big word."

"It's only four letters."

"All right, let's change the subject, shall we? Her sister, Lenna, invited me to her fortieth birthday party this Saturday. And I wanna go."

"Oh, fun, where's it at? Their house? 'Cause I am so crashing that party."

Sam hesitated before answering. Jade was gonna have a cow. "No, it's at a gay bar in WeHo."

"What now?"

"You heard me."

"You can't go to a gay bar."

"But I have a plan."

"Oh goodie, another plan. Can't wait to hear this one."

"Well, I need your help."

"You always do."

"I need you to get a bunch of people from our show to go with me, as a cover. Cast, crew, whoever."

"Sam, that's three days from now."

"You can do it. Use your awesome powers of persuasion."

"Sounds like another raise to me."

"Isn't there a limit on how many raises one can get in a year?"

Jade ignored her. "So we're all going to a gay bar Saturday night. We're gonna surround you and act like a protective shield, like a social condom."

"Yes. And Lenna is a huge fan of the show. It would be a cool PR move, since we pissed off the whole LGBTQ community. C'mon. It'll be fun. Lots of food, drinks, a DJ…"

"Drinking and dancing and dykes, oh my. Listen, Betty. You know how you get when there's dancing and drinking. If you thought your last alcoholic escapade with Alex was embarrassing, this could be worse."

"Are you saying I'm a bad dancer?"

"No, dancing is probably the one thing you're good at. It's just, uh, you tend to get a little touchy-feely when you dance. A little too, how should I put this...sexual. You're very sexual on the dance floor when you've been drinking. And I don't know how that happens, since you are a bit, how should I say, awkward when sober. And, God help all of us if you're tipsy and dancing with my perfect sexy ten. Sexual Armageddon. In front of a hundred women taking pictures and posting on social media."

"I think it sounds kinda fun."

Jade groaned.

"Okay, I'm kidding. I'll behave. It's not like I don't have self-control. I've managed to keep my hands off her for this long."

"What does PS10 say?"

"Who?"

"My perfect sexy ten. What are Alex's thoughts on you going to the party?"

"She's *my* perfect twelve, and she wasn't too fond of the idea either."

"Great minds think alike."

"It'll be fine. What's the worst that could happen?"

CHAPTER TWELVE

Sam sprang from bed the morning of the party feeling majorly stoked. Tonight she would get to see Alex, who'd been at another job site for three long days Which meant no hugs or kisses on the cheek for *three long days*.

A cup of joe was in order, so she headed down to the kitchen. While getting a mug from the cabinet, a handwritten note taped to the fridge caught her eye. Jade must have put it there last night before she left. Sam pulled it off and began to read:

RULES OF NONENGAGEMENT

No wooing. Clearly Sam should have used another word when she'd told Jade about her plans because now the word found its way into all their conversations. Jade had told her to stop wooing the coffee yesterday. And let's not forget the classic, "What are you wooing?" And, of course, "Woo said you can't do that?"

No drinking, Two-Beer Betty. Okay, Sam owned that one.

No dancing. That was ridiculous. Of course there would be dancing, hopefully with a certain brunette.

No touching a certain brunette. Damn it!

Sam crumpled the note, tossed it in the trash, and headed to the patio with her coffee. The sun shone brightly, and the sky was a cloudless blue. A perfect morning for relaxing and daydreaming about the upcoming evening. What should she wear? Something alluring and simple. Something that would light a fire in those deep-green eyes. Her black skinny jeans, of course. And something with a plunging neckline. What would Alex be wearing? Something drool-worthy for sure. Maybe tonight they would share a kiss on the lips. Would Alex dare to make the first move? Was Alex waiting for her to do it because of the pinkie-swear promise? Perhaps she should be the one to initiate. Yes. Tonight Sam would try and initiate a kiss on the lips.

* * *

The whole crew waited in the living room for Sam to join them. Jade and her girlfriend, Calynn, lounged on the couch. They'd met a year ago, almost running each other over while rollerblading at Santa Monica Pier. After dropping a few f-bombs and accusations about who ran over whom, they'd had lunch at Del Frisco's Grille, and the rest was history. Calynn, with her sharp wit and tough personality, could more than hold her own around Jade.

Emma and Logan, Zach and Jessica, and Jackson, the head writer of *Gemini*, and his girlfriend, Riley, rounded out the group.

When Sam finally came downstairs, she was grinning from ear to ear. "I wanna thank everyone for coming with me tonight."

"We're gonna have a good turnout, Sami," Jade said. "Another car is picking up eleven more people. They're meeting us at the club, so we can all go in together."

Sam rubbed her hands together. "This is gonna be so much fun."

"Fun for you," Jade grumbled. "I'll probably be gray before the night's over."

A honk signaled the arrival of the limo. Jade held the front door open as they filed outside and into the stretch Cadillac Escalade.

"Okay, Sami, up front." Jade pointed to the passenger door.

"Why am I sitting up front?"

"Because we have things to discuss. We need to talk about you behind your back. Now go."

Jade shoved Sam into the car and joined the crew in the backseat. She closed the privacy glass and settled in. "Okay, as we all know, we are headed to a birthday party at a gay bar." She paused to let this sink in. "As we all may not know, Sam has the hots for a perfect, sexy ten lesbian who will be attending said party and who shall henceforth be known as PS10. Tonight our mission is simple." Jade glanced around with fingertips raised and pressed together. "We keep Sam in our sights at all times. We *must* limit her interactions with PS10. And under no circumstances is Sam to have more than two beers. We have all witnessed Two-Beer Betty on the dance floor. Am I right?"

Everyone nodded.

Riley raised a hand. "Should I be taking notes?"

"Notes?" Jade narrowed her eyes. "You can't remember this?"

"Well, sometimes it's nice to refer back to something. I can do it on my phone."

"Fine. Take notes." She turned back to the others. "Now, when Sam has more than one beer, she's a sexual animal on the dance floor. With all the people at this party, that means cell phones ready to capture our paycheck in some compromising position with a hot woman. All it takes is one posting on Facebook to go viral, and it could be career threatening. And when I say our paycheck, I mean my paycheck. You with me?"

"Yes, Colonel!" Emma shouted.

"Who's Colonel?"

"Colonel Jade. 'Cause you're in charge. And we need a name for this mission. All missions have code names."

Jade rubbed at the dull ache settling in her temples. "Okay, let's brainstorm some names so Emma can keep the mission straight. The one mission we're on."

"Ah, Betty something," Jessica said.

"Betty Jean King," Emma said.

"You mean Billy Jean King?" Jade asked.

"Oh, right." Emma's shoulders drooped and she paused a moment before yelling, "CassiNova!"

All eyes locked on Emma.

"CassiNova—Sam *Cassidy* and Alex *Novato*. Their last names together make CassiNova. It's their ship name. Get it?"

Jade pursed her lips. "E, I can't believe I'm gonna say this, but that is brilliant. A ship name. I think you just had a neuron fire off in that brain of yours. Hopefully it didn't hurt." Jade put a hand up. "However, CassiNova implies we're trying to get them together. Our mission tonight is to keep them apart. But I like your enthusiasm, and we're gonna revisit CassiNova later."

"CassiNova's good, honey." Logan put his arm around Emma and kissed her cheek.

"Let's get back to our mission name," Jessica suggested.

"How about Just Betty," Jackson said.

"Just Betty!" Emma and Riley yelled.

In the interest of moving things along, Jade nodded. "There you have it—Operation Just Betty. Okay, E? Do you need to write it down or anything?"

Emma elevated her middle finger.

The colonel continued. "All right, first things first. We need to be prepared for disaster, for the absolute worst thing that could happen. So what *is* the worst thing that could happen? Anyone?"

Riley raised a hand. "Sam gets royally trashed and has actual sex on the dance floor with PS10."

"Whoa, okay, that is definitely a worst-case scenario and borders on pornography. But let's back up. Let's say Sam has a second beer and she's getting close to PS10 on the dance floor. What are we going to do? Anyone?"

Everyone just stared at her, mouths agape, and Jade knew she'd be getting limited help from this crew. "We infiltrate. We buffer. We get between them. We don't allow grinding. We don't allow long, passionate looks. We don't allow touching of any fashion because, quite frankly, if they start touching, it's all over. I mean, they've been drooling over each other for weeks and haven't even kissed yet."

"You're kidding. What the hell are they doing?" Calynn asked.

"Wooing. Wooing is what they're doing. Evidently you don't touch during the wooing phase of relationships, according to Sam's book of woo. Now, if Sam and PS10 are on the dance floor, this means we're all on the dance floor. If we need to tag team to keep them apart, that's what we'll do. Someone grab Sam, and someone grab Alex. Keep them apart!"

Jade turned to Calynn. "And, honey, I'm just saying this now—I'm gonna have to sacrifice myself for the good of this mission. I will intervene and keep Alex occupied as much as possible. You may not like what you see, but you'll have to take one for the team."

"That's okay." She pointed at Jade. "But you're going down on me later."

"Deal."

A collective groan rolled through the car.

"Oh God," Jackson said.

Zach grimaced. "TMI, TMI!"

"What happens when a slow song comes on?" Jessica asked.

"Excellent question. That would be Code Red. A serious Code Red. Grab them, and dance with them. Don't let them near each other if a slow song starts to play."

Riley raised a hand. "So, PS10, is she reasonable? If so, then she should understand the situation, and maybe we can get her to stay away from Sam."

"I don't know. They're pretty hot for each other. Right, E?" Jade extended a hand toward Emma.

Emma was busy rooting around in her purse. "What?"

"The chemistry. The chemistry between them."

"Oh, their chemistry. Yes. It's like oil and water."

Jade frowned. "God, I had such high hopes after the CassiNova moment."

"Uh, oil and water kinda repel each other, honey," Logan said. "You know, the water lays on top of the oil, so they don't mix well. Like on a salad."

"I failed chemistry in school," Emma admitted.

"Salad? Who puts oil and water on salad?" someone asked.

"I failed chemistry too, E. Don't feel bad." Jessica patted Emma's hand. "Let's get off the periodic table. How about peanut butter and jelly?"

"Since when is balsamic vinaigrette on the periodic table?"

"I love peanut butter and jelly."

"People!" Jade took a deep breath. "Let's get back on point here. Now, where were we?"

"Ha! I have notes," Riley said. "Let's take a look-see, shall we?"

"Good. Read me back the last thing we said before E's brain fart."

"Okay." Riley studied her phone. "Well, I'm not sure what this is... Um, here we go, the clambake before sample and Lexus. Hmm... Clambake? Did we mention clams at any point? And is someone driving a Lexus?" She glanced around at the confused faces in the car. "I may have fat-fingered a few letters."

"The chemistry between Sam and Alex," Calynn said.

"Yes." Jade snapped her fingers. "Thank you, babe. Riley suggested asking PS10 to stay away from Betty, which may work, but what if she's drinking also? I'm not as familiar with her as I would like to be, so I don't know what happens when she drinks."

Calynn scowled. "What do you mean you're not as familiar with her as you'd like to be?"

"The team, honey, remember the team."

The privacy glass opened, and Sam stuck her head through. "Hey, guys, how's it going?"

Jade's heart pounded. "Oh my God, what is in your hand?"

"A beer."

"Where did you get it?"

"The driver brought some for us. Who wants one?"

"What the hell? How many have you had?"

"I'm about to start my second one."

A collective gasp went through the back of the limo.

"Give me the beer. Give it here."

Sam handed Jade the unopened bottle. "What? I was just gonna sip it."

"I'll sip you right in the head. Now, give me the rest of them."

Sam stuck her tongue out and handed Jade the cooler. "Killjoy."

Jade pushed the button and raised the glass.

"We're one beer into it, and we're not even there yet. What now, Colonel?" Emma asked.

The privacy glass came back down with a smiling Sam on the other side of it...wearing a chauffeur's hat. "Hey, guys. What's up?"

"Oh my God, is she tipsy already?" someone in the back whispered.

"Sam, did you eat anything recently?" Jessica asked.

"No, I forgot."

Jade pushed the button to shut the window.

Sam followed it up with her head, saying, "Booyah," right before it closed.

Jade's insides turned cold. Her worst nightmare was about to become reality. A drunken Sam cavorting around a gay bar. "Who has something to eat, for God's sake?" she yelled.

"I have Tic Tacs."

"I have a Life Saver. It's got fuzz on it, though."

Jade waved a hand at Emma. "Give me your purse."

"Why mine?"

"You're the only straight woman within reach, so give me your damn purse." Jade seized the bag and emptied the contents all over the floor of the limo.

"Hey," Emma said.

"I'm gonna pass this around. Put anything edible in this purse."

The bag passed from person to person, filling up with breath mints and hard candy.

When it landed in front of Emma, she sifted through the former contents of her Louis Vuitton bag. "Here, I have a Jolly Rancher. Oh, wait, I think I might have already had this in my mouth." She frowned at the half-wrapped candy and pulled a hair off it.

"Put it in." When the purse returned to Jade, she pushed the button for the window. "Sam, honey, I need you to eat everything in this purse, okay?"

Sam peered inside. "Booyah! A Jolly Rancher." She popped it into her mouth.

Emma winced and made a face.

Jade closed the glass. "I can't work like this. How am I supposed to work like this?"

Calynn put an arm around her. "It's okay, babe. I'll do you later."

The next time the partition came down, Sam had two large spearmint Life Savers stuck to her closed eyes. "Hello?"

Jade poked her head up front and addressed the driver. "We're gonna need some coffee in here, stat." She closed the glass.

"It'll be okay, Jade. It was only one beer," Zach said.

"Is that from *one* beer?" Calynn asked.

"She's a lightweight," Emma said.

The glass came down again, revealing a smiling Sam.

"Sam, long time no see," Calynn said.

Sam chuckled. "Jade, I'm fine. I'm busting your ass."

An audible sigh of relief went through the car.

"I didn't actually have any beer. I'm fine. You should have seen your face. We're almost there. Bye." Sam giggled and shut the window.

The limo pulled to a stop when they reached the club.

"All right, hands in," Jade said.

Everyone put their hands together in the middle of the car.

"Listen up. This is a covert operation. Let's keep Betty in the dark. First Just Betty shift will go to Logan and E. Next shift will be Zach and Jessica. I'll roam around and keep my eye on PS10. Ready? Let's do 'Just Betty' on three. One, two—"

"Just Betty!" Emma and Riley shouted.

Jade blew out an exasperated sigh. "On *three*."

"You were saying 'three,'" Emma said.

"On three usually means *after* I say three."

"Well, you should say after three, not on three," Riley said.

Jade took a deep breath. "Ready? 'Just Betty' after three. One, two, three."

"Just Betty!"

"Just Betty!" came Emma and Riley's delayed response.

"Jesus Christ."

CHAPTER THIRTEEN

Alex leaned against the bar. The soft waves of her hair cascaded down her back. She wore a pair of low-slung black jeans and an almost see-through white tank that stopped an inch above her belt. She had applied dark-brown eyeliner and red-shaded lipstick, hoping to impress a certain blonde.

Two women were on either side of her, both vying for her attention, but her eyes were locked on the entrance to the club. The party had been in full swing for two hours. The birthday shots Alex had done earlier with Lenna had loosened her up. Maybe too much. She wouldn't call herself drunk, but this fourth beer could push her past tipsy.

Her libido was wide-awake, last night's dream playing in an endless loop. Sam naked in her arms, writhing in ecstasy. Sam's hot mouth driving her over the edge. The whole week had been chock-full of similar thoughts. Sam in her bikini, Sam out of her bikini. Sam, Sam, Sam, everywhere. If Alex slept, she dreamed about her. Awake? She fantasized.

Lenna walked over to get a beer. "When's Sam gonna be here?"

"She texted that they'd be here in five."

"Cool. How much have you had to drink?"

"Why?"

"Your eyes are glassy. Maybe you should slow down."

* * *

Jade led the *Gemini* gang into the bar. The buzz of the crowd was palpable. After a moment of calm, flashes went off, and everyone crowded around the celebrity arrivals. A groundswell of bodies carried Sam and Jade away. They endured much backslapping, handshaking, hugging, and high fiving.

When they made it through the initial wave, Jade cupped a hand to Sam's ear. "This is more than a hundred people."

Sam nodded while scanning the room. She froze. At the bar, looking sexy and beautiful, stood the object of her affection. Latching onto Jade's arm, she pointed. "Fuck me." Sam pulled a dollar from her back pocket.

Jade followed Sam's finger, and her mouth dropped open. "Let's declare this free-fuck night. Because...holy fuck, Sam." She pushed Sam's dollar away.

"Fuck me."

"Holy fuck."

Sam couldn't tear her eyes away. "She looks like she belongs on a magazine cover."

Jade whimpered. "My PS10 just became a PS20."

"How is it possible anybody could look that fine?"

Jade gurgled.

Sam put a hand over her chest. "It makes my heart hurt just to look at her."

Finally, their eyes met. Alex grinned. But before Sam could make her way over to the bar, Lenna and Sophia appeared and pulled her into a group hug.

"Sam!" they both said.

Lenna dragged Sam to the shot table, and they both downed a pair to toast the birthday girl.

* * *

Jade was cruising the bar in search of Sam when Riley found her.

"Uh, Colonel, we have a situation."

"Oh God, what?" Jade's heart plummeted into her stomach.

"Betty did two shots over at the shot table."

"What the hell? Where are Logan and E? They had first shift."

"They're dancing."

Jade walked onto the dance floor and put an arm around Emma. "Where's Betty?"

"Betty was with you, so I thought we would take the next shift. You know, tag team."

"Betty just did two shots."

Emma's eyes widened. "That can't be good."

"You think?"

"We'll go find her."

* * *

Sam zigzagged through the crowd, still trying to get to Alex. She passed the appetizer table and ate a few crackers. That should help absorb those shots. After shaking at least fifty hands, she finally stood in front of Alex.

"Hey." Sam extended her arms, expecting a hug.

Alex stepped into the embrace and put her lips close to Sam's ear. "Hi, *Sarah*."

Sam pulled back and stared into heavy-lidded emerald eyes. She smirked. "Are you drunk?"

"No, I am not drunk." Alex swayed before whispering into her ear, "I may be a little drunk." She stared at Sam's low-cut shirt.

"Okay, eyes up here."

Alex's eyes climbed higher but didn't make it past Sam's lips.

"Higher." Sam smiled when Alex made eye contact. "There you are."

"Here I am. That's a nice shirt."

Warmth flooded Sam's cheeks. "You look stunning."

"Thank you." As they both rested their arms on the bar, Alex gestured toward the barkeep. "Monette, come meet Sam."

Monette shook Sam's hand. "I'm glad you could make it. I'm a big fan."

"Aw, thank you."

Monette's smile stretched from ear to ear. "What would you like to drink?"

"Well, I'm supposed to be behaving myself."

Alex chuckled. "It's a party. Let your proverbial hair down, girl."

Alex spoke a little slower when she was "a little drunk," which Sam found incredibly sexy. "I shouldn't. I'm under orders. I've already drunk too much, and Jade would kill me."

"Why?"

"Well, she doesn't want me dancing and drinking."

"Why?"

"She says I get sexual on the dance floor when I drink."

With a shit-eating grin, Alex's hand snaked behind the bar and grabbed another beer, which she stuck in front of Sam. "I wanna dance with Sexual Sam."

Laughing, Sam put a hand on Alex's arm. "You're gonna get me in trouble."

"You have nothing to worry about."

"Until the papers come out tomorrow morning."

Alex's eyes were riveted on Sam's lips again. She bent down close to Sam's ear. "Samantha Cassidy, you haunt my dreams."

For the second time in an hour, Sam put a hand over her heart as a tingling warmth spread through her chest. It was probably the sexiest, most romantic thing anyone had ever said to her. She took a swig of beer. Screw it. Tonight she *would* let her hair down and enjoy herself.

* * *

"We thought we had her at the appetizer table, but she disappeared again. She's slippery," Emma told Jade.

Riley joined them. "Betty is at the bar with PS10. I repeat, Betty is at ground zero."

They all watched Sam as she tipped the bottle back.

"Well, we're fucked," Jade said.

Emma tried to stay positive. "Not really. We'll keep our eye on them. We'll insulate them on the dance floor, right?"

From across the room, Emma saw Alex's head dip close to Sam, who smiled like the cat that ate the canary. Their hips pressed together, and the sexual heat rising off them was almost visible.

"They make a good-looking couple," Riley said.

"They can be a good-looking couple tomorrow, but not tonight," Jade said. "Now, listen to me, everybody—"

"The package is on the move!" Emma yelled.

All heads turned as Alex and Sam moved through the crowd.

The package made it to the dance floor unimpeded just in time to dance to Katy Perry's "I Kissed a Girl."

Jade paled. "Oh shit, not that song. And we're moving. We're moving, people!"

They all rushed the dance floor. Operation Just Betty…just went nuclear. Jade's blood pressure skyrocketed as PS10 and Betty engaged in a hot and heavy *Dirty Dancing* routine. Alex had pulled Sam close, and they were grinding on each other's legs. Sam's hand was behind Alex's neck, fingers caressing her nape. When Alex twirled Sam away, Jade made her move and jumped in front of Alex.

Alex wheeled around, confusion on her face. Sam was now dancing with Emma, who gave Alex an apologetic look.

Jade gently turned Alex's face away from Sam. "Eyes here, girlfriend, eyes here."

Alex spun Jade so they were dancing front to back. Her hands wandered over the front side of Jade's hips, making Jade twitch in surprise. She peeked back, and Alex grinned.

With Alex's hands touching her everywhere, Jade almost lost it right there on the dance floor. Was it possible to have an orgasm while dancing? She grabbed Emma. "I'm out, you're in."

"What?" a confused Emma asked.

In that split second of hesitation, Betty and PS10 found their way back together, pawing and leering at each other.

Jade snapped her fingers at Riley and pointed to the targets. Riley moved in to snatch Sam, while Jade pushed Emma at Alex. Emma stumbled into Alex, who reached out a steadying hand.

Surprise flashed across Alex's face when Emma jumped into her arms and wrapped her legs around Alex's waist. Jade watched in horror and wondered what the hell kind of dance move that was supposed to be. Emma slowly slid down and positioned herself in front of Alex, who began running her hands along Emma's sides, brushing along her breasts.

Emma jerked away and came over to Jade. "I'm done, boss. To quote one of my favorite movies, *Pitch Perfect*, 'that girl could turn me.'"

Jade caught Sam edging her way over to PS10, so she pushed Zach in front of Alex, blocking Sam's path. Things finally cooled down. Alex pouted, her petulant demeanor suggesting that she wasn't enjoying dancing with him, which was a good thing because Jade was running out of bodies to throw at her. Girl cut through them like a sexual machete.

Calynn appeared beside Jade. "We have a Code Red coming. I talked to the DJ."

"Code Red, Code Red!"

The music slowed. Someone made a grab for Sam, but she was lightning quick. She slipped away and fell right into Alex's arms.

"Holy fuck, get in there!" Jade screamed.

Emma, being the shortest one in the group, squatted and squeezed between them, popping up in the middle like a jack-in-the-box. She wrapped her arms around them both, so the three of them slow danced together.

Jade's shoulders sagged in relief. The trio looked like morons, but it wasn't sexual. She had aged five years in the last couple of hours. A serious bump in pay was in order after this adventure.

* * *

When the song ended, the DJ announced, "Everyone, please make your way toward the back of the room so we can sing to our birthday girl."

The threesome separated, and Alex held Sam's hand as they walked off the dance floor. One of Sam's work friends cut between them, breaking their hands apart and holding them in her own. Alex thought she remembered the woman introducing herself as Riley.

Sophia and Lenna stood next to a magnificent three-layer chocolate birthday cake ablaze with forty flickering candles as the guests sang "Happy Birthday." Alex dragged Riley and Sam through the crowd so she could be near her sister when she blew out the candles.

The crowd chanted, "Speech, speech, speech!"

Lenna raised a hand to quiet them. "Wow, we have a lot of people here tonight. I feel honored." Whoops and calls came from the throng of attendees. "I wanna thank you all for being here to celebrate this birthday with me. It feels good to be twenty-nine again."

They all laughed.

Riley still stood between Alex and Sam. Every few seconds, they made eye contact behind her back, checking each other out with lascivious looks.

"Thanks to my wife. I love you so much. It's been twelve years, and I wouldn't want to be anywhere else or with anyone else. Baby Sis, I love you too."

Alex winked. "Right back at you, dork."

"And how about our special guests tonight?" Lenna pointed to the *Gemini* crew.

The crowd went wild, clapping and stomping.

Lenna reached for Sam's hand and pulled her close. "Samantha Cassidy, ladies and gentlemen. And all the cast and crew who made it here, thank you! Let's eat some cake."

When Riley stepped forward to get a piece of cake, Alex took full advantage of the situation and slid in next to Sam. Leaning down, she breathed in the fresh vanilla scent of Sam's hair.

Her hungry lips hovered near Sam's ear. "You wanna piece?"

Sam gulped. "Of what?"

Alex smirked. "Cake."

"I love cake."

"Me too."

* * *

Jade glanced at Jessica as she sidled up next to her.

"Colonel, we have some goo-goo eyes happening at the cake station."

"If it escalates, do something."

"I'm on it." Jessica moseyed over to the dessert table and grabbed a plate, moving closer to Betty and PS10.

Sam and Alex giggled and fed each other cake. When Sam got icing on her chin, Alex brushed it with a thumb and slowly licked it off while Sam stared.

Jessica looked up and met Jade's icy glare. She quickly stepped in front of Sam with a napkin and wiped. "Here, let me help you with that, Sam."

Soon the crowd moved toward the long sofas along the walls. Jade shoveled a generous forkful of cake into her mouth and relaxed a bit.

Emma appeared next to her moments later. "Welp, there's a photo op."

Jade whipped around and caught Sam and Alex canoodling on one of the couches. "Jesus Christ."

Her plate landed in the trash can, and she walked over and sat on their laps. Wiggling down, she managed to wedge herself between them.

Calynn came over and squeezed in between Jade and Alex. Emma joined the party, Riley followed, and soon Alex was five people removed from Sam.

* * *

Frustrated by the whole scene, Alex stood and wandered over to the bar to help Monette clean up. "Hey. This was great. Thank you for letting us use the place."

"My pleasure. It was a blast."

Alex blew out a deep breath.

"Everything all right?"

"Yeah. It's fine." Alex moved behind the bar to help put away the clean glasses.

"Is that Miss Off-Limits?" Monette gestured toward Sam.

Adoring fans competed for Sam's attention. Lenna sat next to her, grinning like a kid on Christmas morning who'd found a Red Rider BB gun under the tree.

"How'd you guess?"

"I have incredible powers of deduction. And the two of you have barely taken your eyes off each other the whole night." She wore a lopsided grin. "She's gorgeous."

"Yep. She's also a pretty special person."

"So. Sam Cassidy is gay?"

"Yeah, but no one is supposed to know."

"Her secret's safe with me."

"She leaves tomorrow for a movie shoot." Sam hadn't even left yet, and Alex was already lonely. What was happening? Why was there an ache in her chest at the thought of no Sam for God knew how long?

"Oh, now I get why you're moping."

"I'm not moping. Am I moping?"

Monette chuckled. "You'll survive. What do they say? Absence makes the heart grow fonder?"

Alex started. Heart? This was supposed to be about sex. When had heart come into play?

* * *

As the crowd thinned, Sam's buzz left the building. Sophia stood at the bar, and Sam joined her.

"Hey, Monette, could I trouble you for some water?" Sam asked.

"Absolutely." Monette placed a glass on the bar and poured.

"Thank you." Sam turned to Sophia. "This was a great party. Thanks for inviting us."

"Oh, no, thank you for coming and bringing some of the other cast members. It was so cool. Lenna loved it. You made this birthday memorable for her."

"I'm glad."

Across the room, Alex was holding court, surrounded by a bevy of women.

Sam sighed. "She certainly attracts a crowd."

"She does, but it's not who she is."

"What do you mean?"

"I know Alex appears to be a player, but she's not."

Alex began arguing with one of the women.

"She's been with a lot of women," Sam said.

"Well, yeah, the last few years. But it was her way of dealing with things."

"Dealing with a broken heart?"

Alex turned her back on the woman and rushed out the back door of the bar.

"Something like that."

"Is she here?" Sam asked.

"Who?"

"The woman who broke her heart. Does she see her anymore?"

"Madison?"

"Is that her name?"

"Was. Madison died four years ago."

Sam's heart constricted. "Oh shit, is that what happened?"

"You didn't know?"

"No, she didn't tell me." Sam groaned and covered her face with both hands, feeling horrible for teasing Alex about a broken heart. "Why didn't she say anything?"

Sophia patted her arm. "Don't worry. Alex just doesn't talk about it."

"I feel awful. I need to talk to her. Will you excuse me?"

"Sure."

"Hey, Sam!" Sophia called as she walked away.

Sam turned.

Sophia smiled. "She really likes you."

"Thank you. I really like her too."

* * *

Alex found a quiet place on the deck and slid to the ground with her back against the wall. She needed to cool her jets after the argument with Cynthia, who had given Alex an earful for never calling.

Then there was Sam. Those were different types of jets that needed cooling. All the dancing, touching, holding. Alex quaked with sexual frustration. And something more. Something she was afraid to name. She rubbed her eyes and took a deep breath. Sam would be gone for a while. Maybe it would be a welcome break.

As if on cue, Sam wandered outside and slid down next to her. "Hey. What are you doing out here by yourself?"

Alex turned, her mouth curving into a soft smile. "Relaxing. Had to get away from all the noise."

"It was a great party. Your sister's a piece of work. I do believe she's quite smitten with me." Sam playfully nudged Alex's shoulder.

"I do believe you're right."

"Can I ask you something?"

"Shoot."

"It's personal. If you don't wanna answer, you don't have to."

"Okay."

"Why didn't you tell me about Madison? You let me tease you about getting your heart broken."

Alex frowned. "How did you—?"

"Sophia."

Alex raised her eyebrows. "Ah. Well, I didn't want to make you feel bad. The conversation at the time was light."

"Make me feel bad? My God, you're the one who lost someone, not me."

"It's also not something I talk about."

They sat in silence for a few minutes. Alex stared straight ahead, her heart aching with memories. Maybe sharing would lessen the pain. "She died four years ago from cancer."

"Alex, I'm so sorry. You don't have to talk about it if you don't want to."

"No, it's okay. Madison had glioblastoma. It's an aggressive form of brain cancer." Alex spoke slowly in a monotone voice. "She was gone in less than a year. We kept hoping some miracle would happen, but it never did." Alex stopped for a moment to take a deep breath. She battled the tears that threatened to fall. "The last few weeks, I rented a house by the beach. Madi loved the beach. She grew up on Cape Cod."

Those last days had been the most painful of Alex's life, watching the light slowly slip from Madison's eyes. When death had finally come, it had brought with it a small measure of relief. Relief that Madi's suffering was over. It had also brought a measure of guilt because near the end, Alex had prayed for it to be over. Selfishly wanting her own suffering to stop.

Sam edged closer, their bodies touching now, shoulder to shoulder, hip to hip, and she slipped a hand into Alex's. "Where did you guys meet?"

"We met in college, sophomore year. After graduation, we moved back East to be closer to her family. We got married, thought we were going to be together forever. A year later, they found the tumors."

"I'm so sorry." Sam's eyes filled with tears, and she laid her head on Alex's shoulder. She kissed their clasped hands.

With a shuddering sigh, Alex rested her head on Sam's.

They stayed in that position until Jade found them.

"Oh, sorry for the interruption. You guys okay?"

They both nodded.

"Our car's here. Party's ending."

"I'll be there in a sec," Sam said.

Jade headed back inside, and Sam and Alex stood.

Sam jammed her hands into the back pockets of her jeans. "I hate that I'm leaving tomorrow."

"It's only for a couple of months." Alex tried to sound cavalier.

"I guess we should say goodbye then."

They melted into each other's arms.

"Thanks for listening," Alex whispered.

Sam pulled back and cupped Alex's face, rubbing her thumb along her cheek. "Thanks for telling me." A horn honked. "I'll see you soon."

"Bye."

Sam disappeared, and Alex was left alone to wrestle with her inner demons.

* * *

Alex's ringing phone startled her. Lifting her head and cracking open one eye, she pawed around the floor, searching for it. It was hiding under the nightstand. She pulled her wild hair back. A FaceTime call.

"Sam?"

"Hey, are you still in bed?"

"What time is it?" Alex asked, her throat dry.

"Nine a.m. Nice hair."

Alex tried to smooth it down to no avail.

"Why are you still in bed?"

"We just made it home three hours ago." Alex peered at Sam's surroundings. "Where are you?"

"I'm in the first-class lounge at the airport. My flight was delayed."

Alex stretched with the phone still in her hand.

"Oh shit, you're naked!" Sam said.

"Oops." Alex grinned and brought the phone down to eye level. "Sorry. I'm not used to FaceTiming my calls."

"Well, you should pull the blanket up."

Alex did so. "Sam, um, I'm not alone."

"Oh. Oh my God, I'm so sorry. Why didn't you say something sooner? I'll catch you later."

Alex stretched again, rolling over onto her side and extending an arm over her bed companion. "Yogi says hi."

"That was not funny."

Alex laughed.

"You are not nice!"

"Well, why did you expect the worst of me? Was that nice?"

"You are so dead next time I see you."

"You should have seen your face."

"I'm not talking to you right now." Sam pursed her lips and glared.

"Fine, we can sit here and stare at each other." Alex waited for Sam to start talking again, but when time stretched on, she wavered. The thought of Sam being even remotely upset made her insides queasy. "I'm sorry, Sam."

But Sam refused to budge.

"Would it help if I gave you another peek?" Alex slowly pulled the blanket down.

Sam waited until the blanket was almost at her waist. "Okay, I forgive you."

"Am I stopping?"

"Yes, you can stop. Stop there, please. Jesus, I have to sleep tonight."

Alex snickered and pulled the blanket back up. "I thought you needed to minimize your distractions, yet here you are, watching me strip on FaceTime."

"Well, I'm not on location yet. Distractions are still welcome. So, we were not headline news this morning, which is good. The crew was sweating it out at my house last night. I don't think any of them slept."

Alex ran a hand through her hair to try and tame it. "Yeah, what was going on at the club? I felt like we were part of a *Saturday Night Live* skit."

"They were trying to be protective. They didn't want any bad press for me or the show. And nothing's come out yet."

"That's good. How are things in the first-class lounge?"

"Nice, lots of food and beverages. Nobody else is even in here."

"Cool. I've never been in one."

"Maybe if you play your cards right, you'll see one someday."

"I guess I better behave myself."

"Crap, they're calling my flight. Give Yogi a kiss for me."

Alex gave him a kiss on the head.

"Put him on."

Alex put the phone in front of Yogi.

"Yogi, give Alex a kiss for me, buddy."

Yogi licked Alex's chin.

Sam giggled. "I can't believe he did that."

"He listens pretty well. And thanks for the kiss. Do you need another peek to get you through your flight?" She slowly pulled the blanket down.

Sam hesitated a few seconds. "No, I'm good."

"We could do this the whole time you're away, you know." Alex wiggled her eyebrows.

"I would, no doubt, get fired from my job if I watched that every day. Now, I'm leaving, so pull the blanket up."

Alex hiked it up a centimeter. "Better?"

"Farther, please."

The blanket crawled north a couple of inches.

"Jesus Christ, I think you're trying to kill me."

CHAPTER FOURTEEN

Sam was going off her rocker. It had been four weeks since she'd last talked to Alex. Four long weeks of not seeing or touching. Four weeks of thinking about Madison, and how painful it must have been for Alex to lose her wife. Could she compete with the ghost of a past love?

She imagined an angel and a devil sitting on opposite shoulders. Good, strong, confident Sam on one shoulder: No need to call. Don't appear needy. She's thinking about you like you're thinking about her. You're attractive and fun. Who wouldn't want you?

And bad, weak Sam on the other: Call her. What if she forgot about you? What if she found you lacking in comparison to Madison? She may find someone else while you're gone if you don't talk to her. You haven't even kissed her. She probably thinks you just want to be friends!

She hated bad, weak Sam.

She stared at her favorite picture of Alex and Yogi. Alex's contact photo. The number stared back at her. All she had to do was push the call button.

* * *

"Did you hear from the publisher yet?" Sophia asked while loading the dishwasher.

Alex scowled and handed her a dirty plate. "No."

When she wasn't obsessing over Sam, she obsessed over the book. When was Sam coming back? When would the publisher be in touch? How was Sam doing? Why wasn't the publisher calling? Day after day, hour after hour, minute after minute.

"I think you'll hear soon. We're gonna have a famous author in the family, I just know it."

"Well, I don't know about famous. I'll settle for published."

"I just want a famous actress in the family," Lenna said from the living room. "We're having Thanksgiving here, by the way. Make sure you tell Sam." She carried an empty glass into the kitchen and duffed Alex in the head. "Make it happen. Don't screw this up."

"You're a pain in my ass."

As Lenna wandered back into the living room, a phone rang. Alex's phone. It sat on the coffee table next to the sofa.

"Holy shit, it's her! It's Sam!"

Alex tripped over a chair leg as she came stumbling from the kitchen.

Lenna threw the phone at her.

Falling forward, Alex lunged for it, but accidentally knocked it back toward Lenna, who grabbed and whiffed. The phone slid under the couch, skittering back against the wall. They both sank to their knees and peered into the darkness.

"Jesus Christ, get it!" Lenna yelled.

"Can't you reach it? You idiot, why did you throw it?"

"Why didn't you catch it?"

Sophia rushed over and saved the day. She waved the sisters aside and simply moved the couch away from the wall, picked up the ringing phone, and handed it to Alex.

Alex slid onto the floor in front of the couch and answered the FaceTime call with a calm that belied the chaos of the last few seconds. "Hello?"

* * *

When Alex finally appeared on the screen, Sam's heart stuttered in her chest. Could she have possibly forgotten how beautiful Alex was? She wanted to get on the first plane to LA right now.

"What took you so long? Were you on the toilet or something?" Sam asked with a smile.

"No, I was in the kitchen. How's Vancouver?"

"It's good. How's Pasadena?"

"Good."

Lenna and Sophia appeared on the couch behind Alex.

"Hi, Sam."

"Hey, Sam."

"Hi guys, how's it going?"

Lenna leaned forward. "It's going, it's going. When you getting back into town? 'Cause quite frankly," she pointed at Alex, "this one is driving us nuts."

Alex shoved her. "Shut up." She stood and moved away from them.

Sam laughed. Embarrassed Alex was adorable. "Wait, put Lenna back on. I wanna know what you're doing to drive them nuts."

Lenna didn't need any further prompting. She looped an arm around Alex's neck, putting her into a choke hold. "She's been moping around for the last four weeks. It's pretty pathetic."

Alex tried to pry herself loose. "You're gonna die, 'cause I'm gonna kill you."

"Oh please, you can't take me. You never could."

Straining bodies obstructed Sam's view. "I can't see."

Sophia snatched the phone. "Hi, Sam. We'll let them get this out of their system. Sometimes they act like little boys. If you ignore them, they eventually stop."

"Well I wanna watch, because this is the highlight of my boring day."

"Tell her she's coming to Thanksgiving!" Lenna cackled.

"Shut the hell up. What is wrong with you?"

Sam frowned. "What did she say about Thanksgiving?"

"Don't mind them," Sophia said. "This is a classic case of sibling rivalry. The oldest tries to maintain a level of dominance over the youngest. The same thing happens in the animal world. In this instance, Lenna has always been Alpha, so she feels the need to exert control over the pack."

Sam appreciated the psychological implications of sibling rivalry but was much more interested in fight club. "What are they doing now?"

Sophia pointed the phone at the floor. Lenna had Alex pinned face down and was twisting her arm behind her back.

"Jesus Christ, you're gonna break my arm," Alex whined.

"Honey, don't break her arm."

"Yeah, Lenna. Please don't break her arm," Sam said.

Lenna released Alex and pointed a finger in her face. "You're lucky she likes you."

Alex winced and rolled over onto her back. "I think you're gaining weight."

Lenna plopped back down on Alex's stomach, knocking the wind out of her.

"Okay, enough," Sophia said. "Somebody's gonna get hurt."

Alex saved face at the end by flipping Lenna off and rolling on top of her. "Ha!"

"May I remind you that you're forty and you're thirty, and we have a guest here, so please kiss and make up."

They both got to their feet and glowered at each other.

"That was fun. What are we gonna do now?" Sam asked.

"We're gonna let you two talk," Sophia said. "Say goodbye, Lenna."

Lenna grinned. "Bye, Sam. Don't be such a stranger."

Alex seized the phone and headed upstairs, where she collapsed into bed.

"Way to come back at the end. How's your arm?" Sam asked.

"It hurts."

"Do you need me to kiss it and make it better?"

Alex sulked. "No, I'm fine."

It was refreshing to see Alex humbled. And Sam wasn't going to let her off the hook about it either. "Does this happen regularly? You getting your ass kicked by your big sister?"

"Lenna's a black belt, for God's sake."

"A black belt? You mean, like karate?" Sam karate chopped with her hand.

"Yes, she's the Karate Kid." Alex raised both hands, imitating the pose made famous by the movie. "And she's bigger than me."

"Well, don't worry. I don't think any less of you because your big sister beat the crap out of you."

Alex continued to pout. Her lips set in a straight line.

"So, you're not talking to me now?" Sam asked. "Are we gonna have another staring contest? Because you know I'll win."

A flicker of amusement crossed Alex's face. After a couple of seconds, she chuckled. "I'm sorry for acting like a baby."

"It's okay. You're still adorable."

"Adorable? Who wants to go to bed with adorable? Kittens are adorable, puppies, baby goats…"

"Baby goats *are* pretty adorable," Sam agreed. "I love, love, love them. Have you ever seen videos of them? Jumping around? They crack me up. I feel like I need one when I watch them. Me personally? I love to go to bed with adorable. Just an FYI."

A spark finally returned to those green eyes. "You mean you sleep with baby goats?"

Sam laughed. She wanted to crawl through the phone and settle into Alex's embrace. She wanted to tell Alex how gorgeous she was, even while getting face-planted by her sister. She wanted to kiss Alex's arm to make it feel better, and she wanted to kiss other things as well. But most of all, she just wanted her.

"I'd sleep with a baby goat. I bet they're very cuddly."

"Lucky them. I still haven't gotten a cuddle."

"We'll fix that next time I see you."

"Okay." Alex scooched up against the backboard. "So, how's the movie coming along?"

"It's going great, although one of the other actors is hitting on me. It always makes me uncomfortable when that happens."

"Well, I can send Lenna to take care of him, since she seems to be your knight in shining armor."

"Okay, missy, do I detect some jealousy? Do we need another blanket episode? Would that cheer you up?"

"Whose blanket?"

"Well, you're the one who sleeps naked."

"Don't you?"

"No, I like to sleep in my jammies."

"And I like to take jammies off."

Sam giggled. Her Alex was back. "Well there you go. I wear them, you take them off. It's perfect, like peanut butter and jelly."

"Or purple chicken and dumplings."

"Yes! Like that." Sam would've been content to just stare at her for hours. "So, when I'm done in a few weeks and fly back, I may need a ride home from the airport."

Alex visibly brightened. "Are you asking me to come get you?"

"If you want."

"Oh, I want. When?"

"Not sure yet. I'll text you the info when I know."

"Okay."

"Well, it's getting late. I guess I should say goodbye. Gotta be on set at five a.m."

"It's kinda boring around here without you."

"I miss you too."

Alex grinned broadly. "Your backyard job is finished, by the way. Might wanna find something else you need done. Just sayin'."

"I'm sure I can find something for you to do."

They stared at each other, neither wanting to get off the phone.

"Good night, baby goat," Sam said.

"Good night, lover...of baby goats."

When Sam hung up, she knew she'd be smiling for at least another hour, happy that she'd called. Maybe weak Sam wasn't so bad after all.

CHAPTER FIFTEEN

Sam hustled through the airport wearing sunglasses and Alex's ASU baseball hat. A backpack hung on one shoulder, and a carry-on dragged behind her. It was Saturday evening, and the airport overflowed with travelers coming and going. As she approached baggage claim, her heart pounded with anticipation. She'd been away for eight long weeks.

At the top of the down escalator, she froze. There she was. A vision standing at the bottom. Sam put the glasses on top of her head to get a better look.

Alex's wavy hair hung softly around her shoulders, and the way those gray slacks fit should be illegal. She stood with hands clasped behind her back and a sign around her neck that read "Sarah Cassidy."

Sam's shoulders shook with laughter, all her doubts instantly dispelled. Sam was crazy about Alex. Certifiably, unconditionally crazy about her. Had known it from the first moment she'd laid eyes on Alex in that parking lot. This woman was the one for her, and if she needed to wait for Alex to catch up in the feelings department, then Sam would wait. For however long it took.

She remained rooted in place, getting jostled by the other passengers fighting to get to their bags. She knew the exact moment Alex saw her. Mirrored sunglasses hid her eyes, but a slow smile gave it away. A wide grin split Sam's face. This was a romance movie come to life, with Princess Charming waiting to claim her. Sam rode the escalator down and walked over to Alex.

"Hi, I'm Sarah."

Alex's head bowed slightly. "Miss Cassidy, your taxi awaits."

Sam wanted to hug the shit out of her, but they were in a public place so it wouldn't be kosher. "Those sunglasses new?"

Eyebrows rose above the frames. "Yes, you like?"

"I do."

"I thought they'd look good on you. When you take them from me later."

Sam swapped their sunglasses. "Why wait 'til later?"

Alex laughed. "How are you? You look tired."

"I'm exhausted. Flying always makes me sleepy."

"Well, let's get you home and tucked into bed." Alex took Sam's bag, and they went to the baggage carousel to wait for the rest of her luggage.

A short time later, with all her bags in tow, they walked through the automated double doors and into the short-term parking lot.

"Anything from the publisher?" Sam asked.

Alex grimaced. "Nothing yet. Zach said it's still with their reviewers."

"Stay positive. It's a great book."

Alex put the suitcases in the back of the truck and opened the passenger-side door, making sure Sam was safely tucked in before closing it. When she slid into the driver's side, she glanced at Sam. "Go to sleep. I'll get you home safe."

"Okay." Sam yawned. "Hey."

"Yeah?"

"I kinda missed you."

"I kinda missed you too."

Sam snuggled into the seat, practically purring with happiness. She slid a hand into Alex's and shut her eyes with a soft sigh. All the angst and worry of the past two months melted away, and she drifted off to sleep.

* * *

Sam was still asleep when Alex pulled into the driveway. Her face was serene and childlike. Alex resisted the urge to softly explore cheekbones and lips with her fingertips.

"Hey, sleepyhead, you're home."

Sam's lashes fluttered open. With a soft moan, she stretched her arms, lips curling in a lazy, sleepy smile. "Thanks for getting me home safe and sound." She opened the door and climbed down from the truck.

"I'll get your suitcases, babe." Alex winced. Was it too soon for endearments?

"Did you just call me babe?"

"Yeah, it kinda slipped out. I'm hoping you'll forget it by morning."

"I'm sleepy, not drunk."

"Well, maybe I'll slip you some tequila. I seem to remember that giving you amnesia."

"Oh, I'm gonna remember this." Sam showed Alex her phone. "Welcome to my new favorite thing: voice memos." She hit the mic button. "Alex called me babe at nine p.m."

Alex laughed. "You just discovered that?"

"Yeah, I never knew how useful it could be until the last few weeks on set."

Sam unlocked the front door and Alex brought the luggage in. The next thing she knew, Sam was in her arms. "This is the hug I owed you at the airport." Sam rested her lips against the pulse in Alex's neck.

Alex's hands wandered down Sam's back, coming to rest at the top of her jeans. If Sam wasn't so out of it, something more might be happening, but instead Alex simply held her. When

Sam's head bobbed, Alex pulled back from the hug to cup her face. "You're exhausted. You should go to bed."

"No! I'm fine. Just let me lay on the couch for a minute." Sam moved some pillows aside and crawled onto the couch, patting the space behind her. "Where's my baby goat? I owe cuddles. Get over here."

Alex didn't need to be asked twice. "You do owe cuddles, and lots of them."

Shoes were kicked to the curb and she climbed aboard, burrowing behind Sam. Not sure what to do with her hands, she rested one on Sam's hip and tucked the other under her own head.

Sam clutched Alex's arm and pulled it tight against her belly. Scooting backward, she snuggled into Alex with a deep, contented sigh. "Mmhmm. This is nice."

Soon she was breathing evenly.

Alex nuzzled her neck, feeling happy and satisfied.

She woke an hour later with one arm pinned beneath Sam. Tiny needles radiated along the trapped limb and she tried to shift without disturbing Sam.

"Don't go," Sam whispered softly.

Alex froze as she let the words sink in. Various women had uttered the same words over the past four years. And every time, she would slip from their arms and get dressed in a rush to escape the intimacy.

This time, a quick exit was the furthest thing from her mind. She wanted to be here. "I'm not going anywhere," she whispered into Sam's ear. Sliding an arm under Sam's neck, she pulled her closer. How had she gotten here? A few months ago, there was a gaping hole in her heart, and she'd thought it would never be mended. Now she was snuggling a woman who made her believe that maybe, just maybe, she could find love again.

* * *

When Sam opened her eyes the following morning, her brows scrunched together in confusion. As things came into focus, she found herself lying on top of Alex, ear pressed to her chest. She listened to the slow, steady thump of Alex's heartbeat. A warm hand pressed against her bare back. The events of the previous evening came rushing back and a smile touched her lips. Was it possible to stay here forever? She inhaled the scent of Alex, subtle yet intoxicating, fresh and clean, with a hint of lavender.

Something had shifted between them last night. This was more than your standard cuddle, and it left her unsure of where to go next. She wanted that first kiss badly, but not with stale morning breath. The heartbeat in her ear quickened as Alex awoke. Sam stretched to relieve the crick in her back and sat up.

"Where you going?" Alex asked sleepily.

"I feel like I've been sleeping for twenty-four hours. It's time to get up."

It was Alex's turn to stretch. "Good cuddle session."

Sam laughed. "Yeah, marathon cuddle session."

"Well, you owed me. I was beginning to think I wasn't cuddle worthy."

"Oh, you're a little cuddle worthy."

Alex looped strong arms around Sam and pulled her back down. "Just a little? Tough crowd."

"Well, we can't have your head getting any bigger than it already is, can we?"

"My head's not that big."

"It is. I have your hat."

Sam had every intention of leaving the couch but found it difficult to pull away from the warmth and comfort of Alex. She whimpered when Alex's hand slipped under her shirt and slowly rubbed her lower back. But a shower was in order, and toothpaste. She found the strength and peeled herself off Alex.

"I'm going upstairs to freshen up. I'll be right back."

Alex lay prone on the couch, hands behind her head, tousled hair framing her gorgeous face. "I'm not going anywhere."

Sam stared, fighting the urge to take a flying leap right back on top of Alex. Her rumbling stomach provided a needed distraction. "You're gonna make me breakfast, right?" She headed for the stairs. "'Cause you will not believe the color of my eggs."

Alex laughed. "Yes, I'll make breakfast."

"Yeah! I'll be right back." Sam grabbed her suitcases and hustled upstairs.

* * *

Alex was poking around the fridge when her phone buzzed with a text from Lenna.

Where you at? You're supposed to be here to meet that couple about their new patio. They're gonna be here in half an hour.

"Oh shit." Alex had totally forgotten. "Shit, shit, shit."

I'm coming, she texted. *Be there in a few.* She cursed herself for forgetting the appointment.

Sam came bouncing down the steps. "I don't smell anything." When she entered the kitchen, her playful expression changed. "What's going on? What happened?"

Alex briefly closed her eyes. "I'm so sorry. Nothing happened. I have this appointment I totally forgot about, and I have to go." She sighed. "I feel awful because I said I would make you breakfast. And I wanted to show you around the yard, but I gotta go." She began gathering her things in the living room.

"It's okay. I mean, I'm devastated about the no breakfast thing, but I'll get over it. And you'll owe me."

Alex put her shoes on and stood. "I *will* make it up to you. I promise."

Sam followed her to the door. "You look like you're doing the walk of shame, with your messy hair and wrinkled shirt."

Alex grinned and they shared a hug. Pulling back, she gave Sam a quick peck on the lips. "I wish it were the walk of shame." She winked. "I'll catch you later."

"Don't forget. You owe me." Sam pointed at her. "I'm good at collecting my debts."

"How about I make you dinner tonight?"

"Deal. Bring my dog."

"I will." Alex turned and ran to the truck.

* * *

Later that afternoon, as Alex bustled around the kitchen, Lenna came in and leaned against the counter, arms crossed, watching her. "What are you doing?"

Alex continued to pile things into bags, not looking at her sister. "I'm making Sam dinner at her place, and I don't know what she has. I wanna make sure I have everything."

"Should we expect you home tonight?"

"I don't know. Why?" Alex focused on the spices in the cabinet, going over the recipe in her head. She shrugged and put a bunch of them in the bag. This was special, and not having something like basil or rosemary could be a deal breaker.

"Just asking."

Alex stared at the large frying pan in the cupboard, Sophia's go-to pan. She put it in the bag too. "Well, don't wait up."

"Okay. Do you need a pep talk?"

Alex finally made eye contact. "A pep talk? What the fuck? Am I sixteen?"

"It's been a while since you've done this."

Alex huffed and continued her mission. "Hasn't been that long." She took her favorite chopping knife and put it in the bag.

"Almost ten years, since before you met Madison."

Alex paused. "Has it been that long?"

"Yeah, you nervous?"

Alex hesitated, doubtful now. "No. Should I be?"

"I don't know, Romeo, should you be?"

"I don't think so… No. I'm not." Alex chewed on her bottom lip. "And don't call me Romeo. It has bad connotations." She brushed past Lenna to get to the fridge.

"Why does it have bad connotations?"

"It implies I've been with a lot of women." She bent over to get to the produce drawer.

"You have been with a lot of women."

"Well, not anymore." She pulled out a bag of red peppers and hunted for onions.

"Did you get her something, like flowers?"

Alex stood. "Shit. Should I get flowers?"

"You're making her dinner, you haven't seen her in two months. You should get flowers. Jesus Christ. I'm embarrassed to call you my sister."

Sophia walked into the kitchen. "Who's getting flowers?"

"I told this one to get Sam flowers, and she looked at me like she never had a date before."

Alex tried to defend herself, raising a hand in the air. "I don't know if this is a date."

Lenna snorted. "C'mon, moron. Don't tell me you're still 'just friends.' Friends don't spend the night wrapped around each other on the couch. I don't care how much someone loves to cuddle."

"Agreed. I'm with your sister on this, for once. Except the moron part. Get flowers. Be romantic."

"It's been a while since I've had to be romantic."

"It'll come back to you. Start with flowers," Sophia said. "Do you need me to make the dinner?"

Lenna nodded her approval. "Great idea, babe. I can't have this one ruining Thanksgiving."

Sophia began opening and closing cabinet doors. "Where is everything?"

Lenna smirked. "Alex is taking our kitchen with her. Evidently, Sam's kitchen is a barren wasteland, devoid of pots and pans and spices and utensils."

"Shut up!" Alex punched Lenna. "I want this to be perfect."

"Did you shower?" Lenna asked with a straight face.

"Did I...what?" Alex curled her lip. "No. No I didn't. I'm gonna go cook dinner for a beautiful woman, and I thought it would be cool if I smelled like a trash can. What the fuck kind of question is that?"

Lenna didn't bat an eye, her poker face remaining in place. "Just checking. Sometimes when you get nervous, you forget stuff."

"I said I'm not nervous." Alex took one last glimpse into the bags. "All right, I have to go. I'll get some flowers on the way. Wish me luck."

"Good luck." Sophia hugged her.

"Hey." Lenna slapped Alex twice on the cheek for encouragement, like *The Godfather*. "Romance the shit out of her."

"Jesus, you're rough." Alex rubbed the side of her face. "A hug works, too, you know."

"Suck it up. You better have something more to report tomorrow than hugs and kisses on the cheek."

"Well, all I'm hoping for is a kiss on the lips, to be honest. This is Sam, after all."

"You guys will be screwing like rabbits in no time," Lenna assured her.

Alex shook her head. "That's so crude."

Lenna pointed. "Think Thanksgiving."

"What is this obsession with Thanksgiving?"

Sophia gave her another hug. "Ignore her. Have fun. Tell Sam we said hi."

* * *

Sam threw open the front door when Alex knocked. "Hey, you, and hey, my Yogi Bear. I missed you, buddy." Sam bent over to give hugs and rubs to her favorite dog, then stood and embraced Alex. "Here, give me some of those." She peeked into the bags. "Wow, what all you got in here?"

"I wasn't sure what you had, so I raided our kitchen. And here, these are for you." With a sheepish grin, she handed a bouquet of lilac and gardenia to Sam.

"Flowers?" A surprised Sam inhaled the floral scents. "That is so sweet, thank you. So romantic. I'm impressed."

They both walked into the kitchen and began emptying bags.

Sam laughed at the frying pan. "I do have pots and pans."

Alex grinned. "I wasn't sure. Best to be prepared. And," she whipped the knife out. "Just in case."

"Most kitchens do come with knives, mine being one of them."

Alex pouted. "But it's my super, special, secret knife."

"Oh, well, if it's super, special, and secret, I get it. I would've had a problem if it was just super and special. The secret part sealed the deal."

Alex winked. "I'm glad we agree."

"What are you making?" Sam found a vase and put the flowers in water.

"I plan to show you the proper way to make chicken."

"Oh, it's gonna be a cooking lesson, is it?" She rested her elbows on the countertop, putting her chin in her hand.

"You will be my sous chef."

"Are you sure you don't want to learn my secret recipe for purple chicken?"

Alex ambled over to the sink to wash her hands. "It's called secret for a reason. Nobody should know it. How good are you with a knife?"

"Not bad. I've yet to lose a finger." Sam presented both hands, showing all digits intact.

Alex turned on the burner and poured olive oil in the frying pan. "You cut and sauté the vegetables. After they're done, I'll throw the chicken breasts into the same pan."

"Sounds like a plan." Sam sliced and diced and then put the veggies into the pan.

"I'm going to coat the chicken. Do you need help stirring those veggies?"

"I can stir, ma'am."

"I don't have to frisk you for any purple food dye, do I?"

"No, not unless you wanna frisk me," Sam sassed while stirring the sizzling vegetables.

Alex put her lips next to Sam's ear and whispered, "Don't tempt me."

Sam shivered, and tingles shot all the way to her toes.

When Alex finished mixing the marinade, she nestled against Sam's back, putting arms on either side of her and resting her hands on the stove. She leaned her chin on Sam's shoulder, looking down at the frying pan. "You ready for me?"

Sam hid a smile and shifted back, grinding her butt softly into Alex. Two could play at this game. "I've *been* ready for you." She turned her face toward Alex and their cheeks brushed.

Alex's eyes closed, and she turned her smiling face into Sam's hair, inhaling deeply. "Smells good."

Alex's husky voice sent sexual shock waves through Sam's body. She bit her bottom lip as her eyes glassed over before completely shutting. God help her if—no, when—they got to first base.

Alex groaned, and Sam's eyes snapped open. "What?"

Alex wore a pained expression. "Nothing." She moved away to get the chicken.

Something she'd done had struck a sexual cord. Sam needed to figure out what and take a memo. "Is my work here done?" Steam rose from the perfectly browned veggies.

"Yep. We'll put the chicken in and let it cook for a bit."

"Do you want some wine?" Sam asked.

"Sure."

Sam poured them both a glass while Alex took the veggies out of the pan and put the chicken in.

"Now what'll we do?" Sam asked suggestively, itching to get to first base.

"We wait."

"For how long?"

"'Til the time is right."

Sam's gaze raked over Alex, thinking ahead to later in the evening and her first true Alex kiss. The thought of Alex's lips brushing hers made Sam's legs weak. She nibbled on her bottom lip again.

"You gotta stop doing that."

"What?"

"That lip thing." Alex pointed at Sam's mouth.

Sam giggled and grasped Alex's finger. "What? This?" Sam bit her lip and batted her eyes seductively.

Alex's breathing hitched. "Yes."

"Why?"

Alex still stared at Sam's lips. "Why what?"

"Why do I have to stop doing it?"

"Because it turns me the fuck on."

Sam was proud of herself for not blushing. "Okay, good to know." She reached for her phone and pulled up the voice memo app. "Bite lip to turn Alex on."

"You gonna refer back to that later?"

"Absolutely."

While the chicken cooked, they walked around the backyard hand in hand, Alex proudly showing off the new landscaping. Although they shared multiple hugs, their first kiss remained elusive.

When they got back inside, Alex grabbed Sam from behind. "You ready?"

"For what?" Sam turned, breathless with anticipation, wondering if this could be the big moment.

"Dinner."

"Oh."

Alex grinned wickedly. "Wanna get some plates, lover of baby goats?" She removed the chicken from the pan.

Sam set the table and Alex brought the food over.

They sat down and began to eat.

"Wow, this is delicious. You're a good cook. Guess you'll make someone a great wife someday, huh?" Sam asked, but then remembered Alex's past, and her face fell. "Oh shit, I'm sorry. I shouldn't have said that. I'm so sorry."

"Hey, it's okay. Please don't feel bad."

"It was insensitive. Ugh." Sam covered her face with both hands.

Alex gently pulled her hands away. "Please, it's okay. You are one of the nicest people I've ever met. You could never be insensitive. I know you were teasing."

"I'm so stupid."

"Hey, you know what? I did make a great wife and will again someday. I hope." Alex squeezed her hand and smiled.

Sam's mood lightened. "How are Sophia and Lenna?"

"They're good. They miss you. Make sure you don't have any plans for Thanksgiving. Evidently you're coming to our house."

Sam was confused. "For Thanksgiving?"

"Don't ask me. Lenna's obsessed with you and Thanksgiving for some reason."

"Maybe she's thankful for me."

"I'm sure that's it."

Sam couldn't imagine being happier than she was right now. When they finished eating, she stood and cleared away the plates.

"I can do the dishes," Alex said.

"No, you cooked. I clean. Go sit down and relax."

Alex rose from the table and headed into the living room. A moment later, she called out, "*Addictions*? Is this a new script?"

"Yeah. It's a great story. Zach's trying to get me a reading for the lead."

"What's it about?"

"A woman in a rural town whose family is battling the opioid crisis."

"Sounds powerful."

"It's got Oscar written all over it. I'd love to get it."

Sam finished loading the dishwasher and glanced over at Alex, who was sitting on the floor with her back against the couch. *What a gorgeous profile.* Suddenly, Sam's palms were sweaty. Nerves started to get the better of her. She would never hear the end of it from Jade if they spent the entire evening together and didn't kiss. It had to be tonight. And why should she be nervous? It's not like she'd never kissed anybody before. She'd kissed plenty of people.

Sam bit her thumbnail. But this was different, somehow. A lot was riding on this kiss. She took a deep breath and walked into the living room, coming to a stop next to Alex, who smiled that sexy smile. Sam's heart fluttered, and suddenly her palms weren't the only things moist. She began tossing pillows on the floor.

"That's a lot of pillows."

"Yeah, I kinda have a thing for throw pillows."

After clearing a space, Sam sat on the sofa and leaned one arm against the end, trying to look smooth, but then she thought better of it and shifted so her back rested against the arm instead. This was a tactical decision. It afforded her a nice view of Alex's profile. More importantly, it was easier to get prone in this position. It was time to step up the wooing. Sam pulled her knees into her chest and blurted out, "So, is it time?"

CHAPTER SIXTEEN

Alex flinched at Sam's outburst, but her mouth twitched with mirth. "Time for what?"

Sam gently pushed Alex's head with her foot. "To kiss. I don't consider that peck you gave me this morning a kiss."

Alex turned, looking wounded. "You didn't like it?"

"It was anticlimactic."

"Well, if you remember, I was pressed for time."

"I'm not considering it our first kiss," Sam warned.

"Nor should you."

"I'm hoping you can do better."

Alex nodded. "I'm pretty sure I can."

Sam nervously nibbled on her thumbnail. "What's gonna happen afterward?"

"I'm pretty sure I'll get all hot and bothered and wanna rip your clothes off."

Sam smiled. "Well, that's a given."

"What do you want to happen?"

Sam tickled Alex's ear with her toes. "Does this gross you out? I like to toe my friends' ears. It's my thing."

Alex cocked an eyebrow. "Well, you've got quite a fetish, and to answer your question, no, it doesn't gross me out. I've got sensitive ears, so you're kinda turning me on."

"Interesting. Your ears are an erogenous zone. I'll remember that for later."

"How much later? I'm getting older by the minute here."

Sam laughed. "I guess you think we should be further along?"

"I know we should be further along. I'm wondering how long it'll be before we have sex."

"Jade mentioned the summer of 2022."

"Sounds about right."

Sam gathered her courage. "Do you think we should kiss now?"

"Yes. We should've a long time ago. I should've gotten in the backseat of your car that first day and kissed you then."

"Oh, c'mon! You barely looked at me. And I wouldn't have let you."

"You would've let me. I would have hit the recline button on your seat and dropped you right into my lap. And you were the only thing I was looking at."

That day remained etched on Sam's brain. She recalled with exquisite detail her physical reaction to seeing Alex for the first time. "You're probably right, but we would've missed all this. The buildup, the anticipation. C'mon. Tell me this hasn't been the most fun thing ever. You and me, the flirting, the random touching, the cuddling. Admit it." Sam shifted so she could wrap her arms around Alex's neck and bite her earlobe. She whispered, "Admit it."

Alex shivered. "You did not just bite my earlobe."

"I did. And I'll do it again. And I'll keep doing it until you admit how much fun this has been." She bit the earlobe again before running her tongue along the outside of Alex's ear.

Alex closed her eyes and whimpered. "Okay, I surrender. I admit this has been an absolute blast."

Sam stopped the assault and sat back, quite pleased with herself.

"Obviously, admitting my ears were sensitive was a tactical error on my part. However, paybacks are a bitch, blondie."

Sam spoke into her phone. "Alex's ears are an erogenous zone."

"Did you just take another voice memo?"

"I did. I love this thing." She played back the most recent memos, chortling at the "babe" comment. "Who knew voice memos could be so much fun?"

Alex grabbed the phone and pressed the record button. "Have sex with Alex before she's eighty."

Sam laughed, then became serious. "What if it's not good?"

"You don't think the kiss will be good?"

"I don't know. How do we know?" Everything depended on this kiss. Well, that may be overly dramatic, but she'd been looking forward to this moment for months, praying the reality would be as good as the fantasy.

"I guess we just do it and find out."

"Should we?"

Alex stood, grabbed Sam's feet, and slid her slowly down the couch until she lay flat on her back, then crawled onto the couch until they were lying next to each other.

"What are you doing?"

"I'm gonna plant one on you, right here, right now, so prepare yourself."

"I'm nervous. Aren't you nervous?"

"No. Close your eyes."

"Maybe I should picture you in your underwear." Sam giggled.

"Well, you don't have to picture me. Just say the word and the shorts are off."

"No, silly. Emma told me a while ago that I should picture you in your underwear, to make me less nervous."

"I would hope picturing me in my underwear would make you feel something other than less nervous."

"Believe me, it does."

"And by the way, I don't have any on. Might wanna take a memo."

"Oh." Sam caught her lip between her teeth. The visual of Alex sans undies was almost too much for her already impatient libido.

Alex began closing the distance between them.

"You realize this will be our first official kiss," Sam whispered, staring at Alex's lips, which were now millimeters from her own.

"If you keep talking, it might be our last."

"It's just—"

Alex put a finger against Sam's lips.

Sam took a deep breath and slowly exhaled, then closed her eyes and waited.

She didn't have to wait long, as Alex's lips soon replaced her finger. Both women sighed into the kiss. Those luscious lips *were* as good as advertised, and the way they gently moved over Sam's mouth was almost criminal. A spark ignited in her lower belly.

Alex turned her head for a better angle and deepened the kiss. After a few moments, she pulled back.

Sam's eyes blinked open, wondering why they had stopped. A quick glance into green eyes told her all she needed to know, and she moved in to continue what they'd started. The kisses were slow and languid, but the fire inside Sam raged.

Alex moved a hand behind Sam's head and pressed her closer. When Alex opened her mouth, Sam took advantage and slipped her tongue in.

They both moaned.

Alex was a drug, and Sam couldn't get enough. She finally understood the true meaning of the word swoon.

They continued kissing for what seemed like forever. Fingers were tangled in each other's hair. Tongues chased and played. Sighs and moans mingled together. The air around them sizzled and they both trembled.

Finally, Alex pulled back and rested her forehead against Sam's.

Sam caressed her cheek. She wanted much more but was still unsure of what Alex was feeling. She ran a thumb over Alex's bottom lip, mesmerized by the softness. Alex opened her eyes and Sam saw such want it left her breathless.

Alex found her voice first. "So was our first kiss all you hoped it would be?" She nuzzled Sam's neck, waiting for a response. When none was forthcoming, she pulled away.

Sam nodded as tears pooled in her eyes.

Alex softly touched Sam's face. "Are you okay?"

Sam placed a hand over Alex's and kept nodding. She couldn't verbalize the feelings in her heart. How could she tell Alex how crazy she was about her? How head over heels? The price was too steep if Alex didn't feel the same.

"Was the kiss bad?"

Sam shook her head.

"Was the kiss good?"

Sam's head bobbed. She was afraid to speak, not wanting to cry, not now. If she cried, then her nose would run, and then she'd be sniffling, and there goes more kissing until she washed her face.

Alex flipped over and pulled Sam to her chest. She slid both hands underneath Sam's shirt, fingertips drawing lazy circles over her back. "Hey, you okay?"

"Yeah. Sorry for getting emotional."

"It's all good. Although I must admit I've never kissed a girl and made her cry before."

Sam rolled to the side, putting her head in her hand.

Alex wiped away a trace of moisture under Sam's eye. "The kiss was pretty incredible."

"Fucking incredible." Sam moved in closer, lips brushing softly against Alex's. "Would it be okay if I said I wanna take things slow?"

"Of course. We don't have to do anything you don't want to. Not until you're ready."

"Promise?"

Alex playfully moaned. "Another promise?"

The corner of Sam's lip quirked up. "Promise?"

Alex removed her hand from under Sam's shirt and raised a pinkie.

Sam laughed, loving that pinkie swears were their thing now. "I guess this means our friendship is pretty much fucked. I mean, friends do not kiss like this."

Alex leaned forward, trying to recapture Sam's lips. "Mmhmm."

Sam continued. "You know what else this means? We're dating."

"Yes, dating." Alex ran her tongue along Sam's lower lip.

"Oh, shit." Sam momentarily lost her train of thought, distracted by the tongue. "I'm serious, Alex. We've moved on to the next stage. Right?"

Alex found a sensitive spot behind her ear.

"Ohhhh, God." Sam groaned. "No more...sleeping around."

Alex stopped. "I haven't been with anyone since I met you. I swear."

Sam's gaze lingered on plump, kiss-bruised lips. "I believe you."

Alex kissed her so deeply she almost passed out.

Both of them were almost past the breaking point, on the verge of drowning in this sea of lust and ripping off clothes. But Sam knew it was too soon to get naked, so she rolled away from Alex and purposefully, playfully fell on the floor next to the couch.

Alex peered down. "Whatcha doing?"

"Whew! Gotta cool off a bit. It's a little warm on the couch. I'm sweating in all the wrong places."

"Yeah, well, you might wanna come back. Don't want you catching a chill."

Sam giggled. "No, we don't want that." She crawled back onto the couch, crushing her mouth to Alex's.

Alex moved Sam onto her back, never breaking their kiss. A hand started to wander, going down Sam's side and finding its way under her shirt, lightly brushing back and forth across her stomach. Fingers inched higher.

Sam broke the kiss again. "That hand of yours seems to be on a walkabout."

"It has a mind of its own." Alex kissed Sam's jaw while her thumb lightly caressed around the top of Sam's shorts. She hummed into Sam's mouth. "Maybe we need to revisit our friendship rules... Well, we're not friends anymore." She made her way back to Sam's ears, flicking her tongue at the lobe. "Dating rules."

"Uh." For a moment, no sounds made it through to Sam's brain, her sense of hearing gone as soon as Alex's tongue plunged inside her ear.

"Sam?"

"Uh…huh? What? Oh, dating rules, okay."

Alex's lips were back on Sam's and all talk of rules was momentarily forgotten.

The next time they came up for air, Sam had no idea what day it was. "What?"

Alex chuckled. "Rules?"

"Oh, yeah, okay." Sam's heart threatened to beat right out of her chest. She couldn't remember ever being this turned on.

"Flirting still okay? I mean, I feel it's a given. Until 2022. Then it becomes moot." Alex's tongue lazily circled around Sam's ear.

"Yeah…flirt…good."

"Kissing with tongue? I think we have recently established that the no-fly zone has been lifted?" She buried her tongue in Sam's mouth.

Sam's eyes rolled to the back of her head.

"Sam?" Alex pulled back. "Agreed?"

"Yeah, yeah, agree…with you."

"Okay. Now that's kissing on the mouth, the original rule. What about kissing other places. Like here, for instance."

Alex's lips found their way to Sam's neck—her erogenous zone. "Oh God. *Oh God.*"

"You okay?" Alex gazed at Sam with mock concern. "Did I hit a nerve?"

Sam groaned. "You hit something."

"Mmhmm, okay. So kissing here is allowed?" Her lips traveled down Sam's neck, stopping to suck on her pulse point.

"Uh, oh shit, I'm…so… Fine, I'll allow, yeah, right there." Would it be embarrassing to have an orgasm right now?

Alex's lips traveled lower, and her teeth raked across Sam's collarbone. "Here okay?"

"Oh boy," Sam whimpered. "I think so. But maybe we should table kissing other places. And come back to it."

"Fair enough. Should we cover random touching next?"

"I…guess?" Sam was afraid of where this was going to lead, not sure if she had the self-control to get through it.

Alex's hand found its way back under Sam's shirt. "Is this okay?" She softly trailed her fingers over Sam's stomach.

"Oh, it's…" Sam couldn't finish. *Heavenly* came to mind. *Don't ever stop* was a close second.

"Okay? It's okay?" Alex caught Sam's lip between her teeth.

As soon as Sam got her lip back, she nodded. "Uh-huh. It's okay."

Alex's hand crept higher, brushing the bottom of Sam's breast. "How about here?"

"Ah, I'm thinking that might be a no-fly zone."

"Not a gray area?"

"No, I think, for now…oh…" Alex's fingers circled around her breast, coming tantalizingly close to a nipple. "For now, we'll call it off-limits. For now."

Alex's fingers traveled to the top of Sam's shorts. They paused, then continued their journey. "How about here?"

Sam gasped. "Jesus, ah, probably not."

"Okay, got it. Now, just to be clear. Just to recap." Alex's hand covered Sam's breast, giving it a tiny squeeze. "This area is off-limits, for now."

Sam almost fainted.

Alex placed her hand over the zipper on Sam's shorts and pressed down. "And here, also a no-go, for now."

And Sam did faint, or at least it felt like she did, because she didn't remember the ensuing few seconds after the question. "What?"

Alex snickered.

"What?" Sam had no clue which end was up right now.

"I told you paybacks were a bitch," Alex whispered into her ear.

"Oh God! I hate you. No, I don't, not really." It was the sweetest kind of torture.

They moved onto their sides to face each other.

"That was not nice," Sam said.

"Oh, you loved it."

"Okay, I did." Sam finally had access to the front of Alex's shirt, so she slipped a hand underneath and caressed her stomach. "You are a rare combination of very fucking funny and very fucking sexy."

"Do you owe two bucks now?"

Sam's eyebrows shot up. "How'd you know about that?"

"Because the jar says 'A Buck a Fuck.'"

"Well, the jar's for Jade. I don't put anything in if she's not around to hear it. Ssshh. It'll be our little secret."

"My lips are sealed."

Sam continued to stroke Alex's abs. "These are nice, by the way."

Alex's eyes screwed shut. "I encourage walkabouts. Just an FYI."

Sam giggled in her ear. "We have established rules regarding those things."

"Rules are meant to be broken."

"But we pinkie swore."

"Pinkie swears turn me on."

"Everything seems to turn you on."

"Everything about *you*." Alex glanced at the clock. "Wow, do you know what time it is?"

"Holy shit! That's one helluva first kiss."

"Record breaking."

"Best first kiss *ever*."

They spent the next couple of hours making out like teenagers and talking about their lives, never leaving each other's arms. Sam spoke of her dad, and how she used to perform for her family, and how she'd gotten into acting because of her father's death.

"It must have been devastating being so young and losing your dad."

"He was everything to me. I'm going to win that Oscar someday, and I'm going to dedicate it to him."

Alex shared childhood stories with Sam, too, making her laugh at all the times Lenna threw her down, trying to toughen her up.

"It sounds like she was awful to you back then," Sam said.

"Back then? Have you already forgotten the incident from a few weeks ago?"

"How could I?" Sam nipped her shoulder. "Poor baby. She almost broke your arm." She snuggled down onto Alex's chest. "Yogi's bored, he's been asleep for a while."

Alex checked the clock again. "I hate to say this, I really do, but I have to get going. I have an early day tomorrow."

Sam sat up. "No! Why don't you sleep over?"

"Where, pray tell, would I sleep? And don't say with you, because there is not enough self-control in the world if you want to take this slow."

Sam couldn't hide her disappointment. "When will we get together again?"

"Ugh. My new job is in the total opposite direction of you, unfortunately. Might not be 'til the weekend."

"I guess we'll survive." Sam sighed. "I'm getting up now." She reluctantly pushed herself to her feet.

Alex dragged herself off the couch and pulled Sam in for a hug. "Thank you for an epic night of making out."

After re-packing everything in the kitchen, they walked hand in hand to the front door. "I'll put this stuff in the truck and come back and give you a proper goodbye kiss, okay?"

"Okay." Sam bent down. "Bye, Yogi Bear. See you next weekend." She smooched his nose.

After placing the bags in the truck and putting Yogi in the backseat, Alex walked back to the porch and pulled their hips together, resting her forehead against Sam's. "Thank you again for a truly unforgettable night. You should probably get the couch steam cleaned."

"Eh, we'll just be back on it next weekend."

"Trudat." Alex smiled and rubbed her nose against Sam's before giving her a long, slow, seductive kiss.

Sam groaned and wrapped her arms around Alex's neck, pushing their bodies together. When they broke apart, Sam nestled her nose into Alex's throat. "You know how long I've been waiting for a true goodbye kiss? I mean, kisses on the cheek are nice and all, but this is so much better."

"I agree. Okay, I'm leaving now." Alex cupped Sam's face and gave her one last, quick kiss. "Goodnight, my sexy lover of baby goats." She turned to go, and Sam wrapped her arms around her from behind, walking with her. They both laughed, and Sam jumped onto her back. "Oh, boy." Alex caught her legs. "We doing this? Am I piggybacking you to my truck?"

"Yes."

"Okay, haven't done this in a while. How's the ride so far?"

"Great. You're so strong."

When they got to her truck, Alex let go of Sam's legs. "Okay, I'm leaving now."

"You said that ten minutes ago."

Alex took her index finger and lightly touched Sam's nose. "You're very distracting."

"Shouldn't you walk me back to the door?"

"We just walked here. Now you want me to walk you back to your door?"

"It could be dangerous. You wouldn't want anything to happen to me, would you?"

"God no, not before I get laid." Alex turned around, offering her back again, and Sam hopped aboard. "Oh boy, whoa, okay, take a memo, would you, babe? Alex needs to do more squats at the gym if this is gonna be your main mode of transportation."

Sam's heart felt so full it was ready to burst. She almost blabbered something that included a word starting with L and ending in o-v-e.

Back at the front door, Alex let her down. "Whew. Okay, good workout. Feels like *Groundhog Day*. Goodbye, you."

"Goodbye." Sam kissed her one last time, then kissed her again, then playfully shoved her. "Go, before I break the rules."

Alex began walking away, not looking back, waving her hand in the air. "Goodbye Samantha Cassidy."

Sam watched the taillights on Alex's truck, the happiness inside her soul overflowing. When the truck disappeared, she sprinted into the house, eager to talk to someone and share this excitement. The clock said eleven, but she figured Jade would still be awake and called anyway.

"Sam? It's late, are you okay?"

"Yes, I'm fine. Were you asleep?"

"Not yet, but I'm in bed. What's up? You're usually not up this late."

"Well, Alex just left."

"Oh yeah? And?"

"And we made out for hours."

"You made out for hours?"

"Yeah, and it was fantastic."

Jade called to Calynn. "Honey? Sam finally popped her cherry."

"Congratulations, Sam," Calynn shouted.

"We just kissed. I don't think you call that popping your cherry. We only made it to first base," Sam said.

"Hey, honey? Correction, no cherry popping. Sam made it to first base."

"Was she safe?" Sam heard Calynn ask.

"Of course, she was safe. You were safe, right? Did you make it to second?"

Sam pondered the question. "Ah, what exactly is second again?"

"Boob touching." Jade called to Calynn, "Yo, babe, second is boob touching, right?"

"Yeah, boobs," Calynn confirmed.

"Like a full grab, right?" Jade asked.

"Yeah, a full grab."

"Okay, Sam, a full boob grab is second base."

"She did kinda grab it."

"Kinda grabbed it. Hold on." Sam heard Jade move the phone away from her mouth. "Honey, what about kinda grabbed it? Is that getting to second?"

"What do you mean by kinda grabbed it?"

"Sam, we're unclear on the kinda grabbed it part. Did Alex touch the nip?"

Sam sighed and put a hand over her face. Conversations with Jade always started out so innocent, and before long, they were talking boob grabs and nips. She had no choice but to see it through at this point. "She may have inadvertently touched the nip, while in the process of grabbing the boob."

Jade pulled the phone away again. "Hey, there was inadvertent nip touching, hon."

"It sounds like she didn't really make it to second."

"You hear that, Sam? You're stuck at first. Oh, hold on, my girl is still talking. What, babe?"

"Sounds like she may have rounded first, and tried for second, but didn't quite get there."

Jade put the phone back to her mouth. "Sam you got caught in a rundown. Sorry, you didn't make it to second."

Sam gnashed her teeth. "She grabbed my crotch a bit."

"Whoa! Hold on. Hey, Cay, we got a crotch grab. Let me rephrase. Sam's crotch got grabbed *a bit*. Like the boob kinda got grabbed. Nothing's definitive in this relationship."

"Was the crotch clothed?" Calynn asked.

"Sami, was it a straight shot to the crotch, or was there cotton interference?"

"I had my shorts on." Sam's expression turned sullen, knowing she'd been gunned down at second.

"Honey, it was topside, fully clothed. She's shaking her head, Sam. I think you're still stuck with a single. So, kissing for hours."

"She's a great kisser."

"Well, you don't have to tell me. Girl's gotta a killer set of lips, especially the bottom one—"

"What?" There was no mistaking the annoyance in Calynn's voice.

"Nothing, honey. Come to bed. So, Sami, why no cherry popping?"

"We're taking it slow."

"What chapter are we on in the wooing book?"

"Is she still wooing?" Calynn's voice was closer now.

"She is, Cay. The woo-ster is still wooing."

"Stop it," Sam said. "I just didn't want to jump right into sex on our first night together."

"It's not your first night," Jade pointed out. "You've known her for months."

"Well, we're officially dating now. This was our first date, and I'm not having sex on the first date."

"What about the second date?"

"I don't think so."

"What are you waiting for?"

"I think I want to make sure Alex feels what I'm feeling."

"And what are you feeling?" When Sam didn't answer right away, Jade repeated the question. "Sam? What are you feeling?"

"I think I'm in love."

"Is that kinda in love, like kinda grabbed this and kinda grabbed that? 'Cause at some point, somebody's gotta go all-in here."

"No, I'm pretty sure I'm there. But I wanna hear it from her first, before we have sex."

"So you're gonna wait for Alex to say it, and she's probably waiting for you to say it. Meanwhile, nobody's getting laid."

Calynn mumbled something Sam didn't catch.

"What did she say?"

"She said it's getting late."

"Oh, sorry. I can let you go."

"Oh, boy, oh," Jade groaned.

"What are you guys doing?"

Jade's voice was gravelly. "Calynn's a better base runner than you, Sam. She just made it to second."

"What? While I'm on the phone with you? Really?"

"Oh…God. Evidently talking baseball turns ma girl on."

"Well, you could at least wait until I hang up." Sam received no response. "Hello?"

"Oooh. She's stretching it into a triple."

"What is third base anyway?" Sam asked. "Jade? What's getting to third, exactly?"

Crickets.

"What's going on over there?"

"Sorry, it's an inside the parker. Gotta go."

CHAPTER SEVENTEEN

Alex sat down in the grass and kicked off her boots, exhausted. She hadn't gotten home from WeHo until late the night before, and sleep had been elusive with Sam on the brain. With a deep sigh, she stretched out in the grass. Thumbing through the contacts on her phone, she stopped at Sam's picture.

After a few rings, Sam answered the FaceTime call with a wide smile on her face. "Hey, BG!"

"Hey, babe. What's BG?"

"Baby goat."

"Is that gonna be my nickname?"

"For now. Until I think of something else."

Alex laughed. "Okay. How are you?"

"I'm tired."

Alex chuckled. "Me too."

"You should've stayed over. I'm sure we could have managed to behave ourselves."

"Maybe next time."

"I talked to Jade last night."

"Oh boy."

"Did we get to second base?"

"Last night?"

"Yeah. She said we didn't."

Alex raised her brows. "Oh my, you did give her the blow-by-blow."

"Crap, sorry. I'm so used to telling her everything that goes on in my life."

"She's your best friend. I have no problem with you guys talking. Now, tell me about this second base thing."

"Well, she says we didn't make it to second base. But I thought we kinda did."

"Um…no. Technically speaking, we didn't."

"But I seem to remember a little bit of—"

"Nope."

"Damn it."

Alex pretended to get serious. "If it's important, I'm sure I can remedy that this weekend."

"No, it's not *that* important. Wait! It is important. It's just… ugh, you know what I mean."

Alex laughed. "I know what you mean."

Sam's eyes creased with worry. "Are you bummed you're stuck with someone who wants to take things slow?"

"I could never be bummed about being stuck with you," Alex said, sensing how important this was to Sam.

"Are you sure?"

Alex wished she wasn't working two hours away, because sometimes words weren't enough. She wanted to kiss away the frown lines between Sam's eyes. "I'm positive. And I'll prove it to you next time we're together."

Sam visibly brightened. "You know, if you play your cards right, second base might not be far off."

"Oh, now we're talking. Is that a promise? 'Cause I'll pinkie swear the shit out of that one."

Sam's eyes sparkled. "Yes."

"Okay. I have to get back to work."

"I miss you."

"I miss you too. And, Sam?"

"Yeah?"

"I'm an excellent base runner."

* * *

Alex strolled through the front door after work to find Lenna waiting, arms crossed and toes tapping.

"Well, well, well. What time did *you* get home last night?"

"Late." Alex threw the truck keys in the basket on the table by the door.

"Yeah, and?"

Alex smirked. "My God, I just walked in the door. Give me a minute."

"Okay, dinner's ready."

At the kitchen table, Alex purposefully ignored the questioning gazes.

"How did the new job go today?" Sophia asked.

Lenna, too impatient for such pleasantries, bellowed, "C'mon! Give it up. How did the flowers go over?"

"They went over well," Alex said. "She called it very romantic."

"I knew it! I knew it. Yes!" Lenna pumped her fist.

They both continued staring, waiting for more details.

"Can you pass the salad, please?" Alex asked.

Lenna passed the salad.

"May I please have the dressing?"

Sophia passed the salad dressing.

Alex made a mental bet with herself about how long it would take Lenna to freak out. She figured eight seconds. The Pillsbury buttermilk biscuit hit her square in the chest at five. She should have taken the under.

"C'mon, Alex! Did you kiss or not?" Lenna asked.

Alex popped a crouton into her mouth and chewed. When the smoke visibly poured from Lenna's ears, she answered. "We did…for over five hours."

Lenna's mood swung from annoyance to glee. All was forgiven as she scampered over to pull Alex into a headlock.

"Now that's what I'm talking about. That's my baby sis. Well done."

Alex was caught mid-swallow and choked, sputtering, "Uncle!"

"Sorry." Lenna gave her an apologetic duff in the head. "Now we're getting somewhere."

They spent the rest of the evening in the living room watching TV.

Around ten, Lenna stretched and stood. "I'm going to bed. We have an early delivery tomorrow at the store." She bent down and kissed Sophia. "You coming up soon?"

Sophia squeezed her hand. "I have some patient files to go over first."

Alex studied the two of them, and the way they still looked at each other with so much love and lust, then looked away, lost in her own thoughts. Would she experience that kind of lasting passion again?

When Lenna left the two of them on the couch, Alex turned to Sophia. "You guys are lucky."

"How so?"

"To still be so in love after all these years."

Sophia gave her a playful punch on the shoulder. "Well, it looks like you might have something special going with Sam."

Alex sighed and laid her head in Sophia's lap. "I like her."

"That's pretty obvious from the way you look at her. Hearteyes." Sophia ran a hand through Alex's hair and began rubbing her head.

Alex looked up at her. "Really?"

Sophia grinned. "Yeah, Lenna and I laugh about it. We figured you had no idea."

"Huh, no. I guess I didn't." She turned back toward the TV. "When I'm with her, it feels so good. For the first time in a while, I don't feel alone. But..."

"But?"

"When I'm not with her, I feel guilty."

"Guilty over what?"

"I feel like I'm cheating on Madi. Betraying her in some way. Like if I fall for someone else, I'll forget her."

Sophia continued the soothing head rub. "You're not going to forget her. She's part of who you are. She'll always be in your heart somewhere, but now there's room for someone else."

"You think?" Alex asked.

"Yep. Falling for someone else doesn't mean you have to erase your feelings for Madison. It just means you're ready to move on, and you may have found someone who's helping you do that. Madi would want that. You told me she said as much before she died."

"She did," Alex agreed, thinking back to that painful time.

It was warm for October on the Cape, but Madison still shivered in the fleece blankets cocooning her.

"You okay, babe?" Alex asked, arms tightening around her wife.

Madi nodded and snuggled back into Alex. "Promise me something."

"Anything." Alex's lips lovingly caressed Madison's temple.

"Promise me you'll fall in love again."

"Madi, stop."

"Promise me, Alex," she whispered.

"Madison, you're not going anywhere."

"Alex—"

"Ssshh. Let's not talk about it."

"I need to know you'll give someone else a chance. I don't want you to be alone because of some misplaced loyalty to me. Please, Alex. Promise me." Madi turned tired, teary eyes to Alex.

Alex's heart broke at the anguish on her face. "Okay, baby. I promise. I promise." She kissed her softly and turned away, lips trembling.

Alex wiped her eyes, and for the first time, they held no tears at the memory. "I guess you're right."

Sophia smiled. "My job here is done."

CHAPTER EIGHTEEN

On Friday night, Sam dawdled upstairs in her office, a messy ponytail spouting like a fountain from the top of her head. Bare toes tapped to the beat of the music playing on the stereo. She gave a start when the phone rang, and a wide grin split her face.

"Hello?"

"Hey, beautiful, what's going on?"

"Not much. I can't wait for tomorrow!" The fantasies were getting old; she was ready for the reality of Alex in her arms again. "What are you doing?"

"Not much. Hanging on your front porch like a hobo."

"What time tomorr...wait, what?" Sam's voice rose with excitement. "You're on my front porch now?"

"Yep. Yogi and I are here. I rang the doorbell, but you must not have heard it."

"Oh my God! I'll be right down! I can't believe you're here! I'm running—I'll be right there—" Sam bolted down the hallway, iPhone in hand, skittering around the corner to go down the steps. A quick tug at the ponytail released her curls, which bounced on her shoulders as she navigated the stairs.

"Be careful," Alex said.

"I will, I...ow! Ouch, ouch, ouch, ouch." Sam clutched at her ankle, wincing.

"What happened?"

"Crap, I turned my ankle. Hold on, I'm walking it off, I'm walking it off, ouch, ouch." Sam hobbled toward the front door, anticipation coursing through her veins. "I'm coming, I'm coming."

"Oh, don't say that," Alex said in a husky voice.

Sam giggled. "Almost there." She threw open the door, and Yogi bolted inside. Sam's heart stopped, then began beating wildly in her chest. Alex stood with one hand above her head, grabbing the top of the doorjamb. Backpack straps accentuated the muscles in her shoulders.

Fuck me. Had she gotten sexier in the ninety-two hours, twelve minutes, and thirty-three seconds they'd been apart? Sam gave Alex the once-over. Twice. She gave her the twice over. A red-hot flush of sexual heat coursed through her body, spreading in every direction until it reached even the tips of her extremities. It was going to be a long night. A true test of self-control.

Sam hooked two fingers through Alex's belt loops. "Fuck me," she murmured with her outside voice. She yanked Alex into the house and slammed the door shut.

"Okay, sure." Alex pushed Sam against the closed door, hands playfully wandering all over Sam's stomach, her mouth nipping and kissing Sam's neck.

Sam laughed and gasped for air. "I didn't mean literally."

Alex pulled back with sad puppy dog eyes.

Sam gave her a kiss hello. "Hi, sexy." She ran her hands over Alex's arms, loving the feel of soft skin and hard muscle.

"Hi, yourself."

Sam pressed herself against the length of Alex. "I can't believe you're here. Are you staying the night?"

"I planned to," Alex mumbled into her neck.

"Yeah!"

"How's the ankle? Need me to kiss it and make it better?"

The idea of Alex's lips anywhere on her body titillated, to say the least. "I think so. It's sore."

Alex led a limping Sam over to the couch. "I thought you put your idiot stage behind you?"

"I did too. But it's kinda cute, right?"

Alex smiled. "It is very cute. Here, let me see."

Sam sank onto the sofa.

Alex slid the backpack from her shoulders and kneeled to inspect the ankle. "It's starting to swell. We should put some ice on it." She kissed it, and then her lips started to wander. "Did you hurt your knee too?" Alex kissed and nibbled her way to Sam's knee.

Sam sighed, closing her eyes. "I don't remember hurting my knee, but maybe you should kiss it just in case."

Alex's mouth moved along one thigh while a hand caressed the other, slipping under Sam's shorts.

Sam laughed. "Okay, I didn't hurt that."

Alex pulled away, eyes twinkling. "Anything else hurt?"

Sam pointed to her lips and pouted. "I might have banged them a little bit."

"Oh no. Let me take care of it." Alex pushed Sam onto her back and crawled on top, softly kissing Sam's lips. "Better?"

"Yes." Sam wrapped her arms and legs around Alex, squeezing her close.

Alex groaned. "Your legs are strong. You should be piggybacking me."

Yogi came over and pushed his nose into Sam's hair.

"Oh, Yogi baby, your momma distracted me, and I forgot to say hi. I'm sorry, buddy." Sam kissed him on his nose. "I bought you a bed. And some toys."

"What?"

"I bought him a bed—well, two beds, one for downstairs and one for upstairs. And a bunch of toys."

"You got my dog a bed?"

"I got *my* dog a bed," Sam corrected.

"You're the sweetest person ever." Alex ran a finger along Sam's eyebrows. "God, I love your eyes." She gently kissed Sam's eyelids, one after the other.

Sam blew out a soft breath and kept her eyes closed.

Alex rolled onto her side. "So I was talking with Jade the other day to see if they'd heard anything from the publisher."

"And?"

"Nothing yet. But your name came up."

Sam's eyes blinked open. "Oh boy." She turned so they lay facing each other. "What juicy tidbits of my life did she share?"

Alex nuzzled her neck, and Sam squeezed her eyes shut in pleasure.

"Oh, nothing much, just that initially you wanted me as your fuck buddy."

"Rut-row."

Alex laughed. "Rut-row is right."

"I'm surprised she kept the lid on it this long."

"When did things change?"

Sam rolled Alex onto her back, and her hand wandered under Alex's shirt. "What? When did I decide I wanted more than a sexual toy?"

Alex whimpered quietly as Sam's hand stroked across her belly. She managed a breathy "Yes."

Sam stared, mesmerized by the change in eye color caused by her wandering hand. "I guess when we hugged for the first time."

Alex chuckled. "Who knew my hugs could be so life altering?"

"You're quite the hugger. But in all fairness, when this all started, I said I wanted a girlfriend. Those clowns turned it into finding me a fuck buddy."

Alex's brows rose. "A girlfriend? You wanted a girlfriend, huh?"

"Yeah." Sam paused. "So?"

"So...what?"

"Do I have a girlfriend?" Sam asked.

"You're asking me?"

"I have my hand under your shirt, so yeah, I'm asking."

"Well, we haven't even made it to second base yet."

And before the ink dried on those words, Sam's hand covered Alex's breast.

Alex's eyes slammed shut and she groaned.

"How about now." Sam's lips mouthed along Alex's jawline, her hand creating delicious circular patterns around Alex's breasts, teasing and stroking through her bra.

Alex licked her lips, and more quiet moans slipped from her mouth.

"Oh, who's helpless now? What was it you said about payback?" Sam's tongue traveled from Alex's neck to her earlobe. "I believe I have made it safely into second," Sam gloated with a wicked smile.

When Alex opened her eyes, Sam's smile slowly disappeared. Those green orbs were almost black, and they looked hungry. *Crap.*

Alex flipped their positions, Sam now on her back and Alex back in control. Sam bit her lip as Alex closed the distance between them.

Alex stopped millimeters from Sam's mouth. "You can't call us girlfriends until both of us get there."

In a millisecond, Alex's hand slipped under Sam's shirt, and her bra was pushed aside just as quick.

Sam gasped. "Oh shit."

Alex's hand began a slow, torturous exploration of Sam's breasts. Soft lips found Sam's neck, and it caused a chain reaction all the way down to her hips, which started to grind against Alex.

She could barely breathe as animal-like noises came from deep in her throat. Good Sam was in one ear telling her to slow it down, and Bad Sam was in the other telling her to keep poking the bear.

"Okay, okay, my God." Sam tapped out on Alex's back.

Alex pulled her hand away and Sam groaned in frustration over the lost contact, but she needed to slow things down.

Alex kissed her softly and rolled onto her side. "You okay?"

"Yeah." Sam reached under her shirt and resituated her bra. "That was a little unexpected, and not altogether unwelcomed."

"It's called getting to second in a big way."

"A stand-up double."

"You got that right...girlfriend."

Sam drew in a quick breath at the word. Her eyes puddled. After all these years yearning for a special someone to come into her life… "You said girlfriend."

"Well, we did just make it to second base," Alex teased. She pulled Sam into a sitting position. "Guess we should cool off a bit, right? I mean, we still have to sleep in the same bed later."

"Good idea." Sam needed a distraction right now, or the proverbial cherry *would* be getting popped. Or more like obliterated. "Did you eat?"

"No, I didn't get a chance."

"I have some leftovers and salad stuff. Want me to make you a salad?"

"Sure. Did you eat?"

"Yeah, earlier." Sam stood. "C'mon, sexy. To the kitchen, away from the couch. This thing is like a sexual black hole." As they walked, Sam jumped on Alex's back. "My ankle still hurts."

"I'll carry you anywhere, beautiful. To the kitchen we go."

* * *

They spent the rest of the evening sitting together on the love seat instead of the couch, which they figured might be safer. Alex made sure Sam iced her ankle, and at bedtime she helped Sam to the bedroom, then went downstairs to let Yogi outside. When he was done, they wandered back upstairs to the bedroom, where they found Sam in bed already, the covers thrown back invitingly.

Alex gaped. "You really do wear pajamas."

"I told you I did."

"My God, that's adorable. They match."

"Well, yeah, of course they do."

Alex took a moment to drink Sam in before reluctantly dragging her eyes away. "I'll just head into the bathroom and get ready." Yogi sprawled into his new orthopedic dog bed. "Yogi loves his bed."

"Yay! I'm glad."

Alex returned from the bathroom wearing a flimsy tank and boxers and crawled into bed.

Sam's eyes widened. "What are you wearing? You're not leaving much to the imagination."

"I get hot at night. The burqa is a no, by the way." Alex rolled across the bed to lie next to Sam. She lay on her side, head in hand, fingers itching to explore. "Hm, we have shorts, so cute and soft." Alex ran her hand along Sam's leg.

"Behave yourself." Sam grabbed Alex's hand just before it slipped into the no-fly zone.

"And we have a matching shirt." Alex's hand managed to slip beneath the PJ top, fingertips marching north.

"Behave yourself," Sam scolded again as she caught the hand.

"What did I say about pajamas?"

"You like to take them off?"

"Exactly."

"How about tonight we try to behave and wake up with our clothes on."

Alex became distracted by Sam's cleavage, teasing above her top button. It needed some attention from her lips, so she pressed them to the exposed flesh. "Mmm, these PJs of yours are super sexy."

Sam giggled. "Hey, you. Give me a kiss good night." Sam pulled Alex's lips to hers. "Good night."

"Good night, beautiful."

* * *

Alex awoke first the following morning, with Sam spooning her from behind. She yawned, but refrained from stretching, not wanting to disturb her girlfriend. Now there was a word she hadn't thought she'd ever use again.

"Do you ever wear underwear?" Sam mumbled into Alex's hair.

Alex smiled and turned her head back toward Sam. "Underwear is overrated."

"Good morning." Sam kissed Alex and then settled down on her chest.

Alex slipped both hands under Sam's shirt, stroking her back. "Good morning to you. How's the ankle?"

"Feels pretty good. Because you took such excellent care of me." Sam placed another kiss on Alex's lips, this time lingering.

Alex sighed when Sam stopped the kiss. "You are a fabulous kisser."

Sam snuggled closer. "That's high praise coming from you."

"Yes, it is. Have I told you I love morning sex?" Alex asked as her wandering hands brushed the sides of Sam's breasts.

"Are mornings your favorite time of day?"

"Well, anytime is great, let's be honest. But mornings are the best in my book." Alex's hands found their way to the top of Sam's shorts, and her fingertips slid under the waistband.

"If I had my phone, I'd take a memo."

"I can remind you."

"So is this every morning?" Her breath quickened as Alex's hands glided across her ass.

"In a perfect world, yes. I have a high sex drive."

"No, really?" Sam mocked.

Alex rolled Sam onto her back. "While we're on the subject, when the time's right, are you going to give me some sort of signal? A code word or something? A secret handshake?"

"A code word, you're funny. How about I just say *now*?"

"What?"

"Now."

"Okay!" Alex playfully dove under Sam's shirt, kissing her belly.

Sam laughed and pulled Alex's head up. "No, I didn't say it. I didn't say it."

Alex laid her head on Sam's stomach. "You said *now*. I heard it."

"Okay, just saying *now* could get me into all sorts of trouble. How about I say *now now*. It's not often you say *now now*, so that's what I'll say."

"What?" Alex asked.

"Now now."

"Okay!"

And back under the shirt she went, which started another giggle fest from Sam. She once again pulled Alex's head up. "We're supposed to be taking things slow!"

"I'm horny."

"No shit, Captain Obvious."

Alex rested a cheek on Sam's chest as they relaxed into each other.

"What's gonna happen when we finally do it?" Sam asked, running fingers through Alex's hair. "Is it gonna be like a dam bursting? Will we ever leave the house?"

"Not for the first week. We'll have a lot of catching up to do. I mean, we'll have to christen every room. And that'll be the first night."

Sam laughed. "I don't know if I have that kind of stamina."

"Buckle up, baby. You're with me now."

* * *

It took another hour to drag themselves from bed, both proud of the fact their clothes had remained on. Alex was tasked with making breakfast, while Sam relaxed at the kitchen counter in her PJs, impressed by the way Alex cracked eggs with one hand. While in a tank top. Or maybe she was just impressed with the way Alex's biceps rippled. She adjusted her newly dampened shorts.

"Have you heard anything more on that script?" Alex asked.

"It's between me and two other actresses. I don't know who, though."

"I hope you get it."

"Me too. This could be huge. I think it's a career-changer. And I know I can play that part. I can play the hell out of that part. And then, who knows? Maybe a nomination will be in my future."

CHAPTER NINETEEN

When Lenna came home from work Monday night, Alex and Sophia were already seated at the table. She duffed Alex in the head. "Romeo. How's our Juliet?"

Alex rubbed the back of her head. "First off, stop with the Romeo. I thought we covered that."

Lenna washed her hands and took a seat. "Well, *you* say it has bad connotations, but to me, it's one of the greatest love stories of all time. And as an English major, you should appreciate that." Her eyes landed on the table. "Oh, spaghetti and meat sauce, my fav! Thanks, babe." She leaned over and kissed Sophia.

"It is a great love story but super fucking tragic," Alex said. "So, you see, offensive on two fronts. The first being they both die, and the second being the current interpretation of Romeo as a womanizer type."

"Jesus Christ, I fell asleep after you said super fucking tragic."

Alex rolled her eyes. Lenna was never one to appreciate the fine arts.

Sophia slipped a carrot to Yogi. "Anything on the book?"

"Not yet. I'm starting to lose hope."

"Don't. I'm telling you. I have a feeling it's gonna happen."

"Anything new between you and Sam?" Lenna asked.

"Nope, still sexually frustrated."

"How big is her family?"

"Uh, I think just her mom and stepdad. Why?"

"Just making sure we can sit everybody at Thanksgiving."

"For God's sake, what is the Thanksgiving thing? Enlighten me."

"Jesus, somebody needs to get laid," Lenna teased.

Sophia laughed. "This all goes back to the first time you brought Sam here, and both your sister and I loved her the moment we met her. Then you said she couldn't cook, and Lenna made a joke we would have Thanksgiving at our house. Obviously hoping you two would hit it off and become a couple."

Alex smiled broadly. "Okay, now I get it. And I'm pretty sure we'll be able to fit everyone around the dining room table."

* * *

Sam waited impatiently at the door as Alex's truck drove through the gate, eager to show off the new maroon athletic shorts she'd bought today. They may be a size too small, but she liked the way they hugged her ass.

She held the door open, ogling Alex as she walked in. After the door closed, Alex dropped the backpack and they fell instantly into each other's arms, pressing their lips together.

When they broke apart, Sam caressed Alex's cheek. "You look tired."

"I am so wiped. Eighteen-hour days this week. Ugh. It's been grueling. Physically and mentally. Nice shorts, by the way."

"You like?" Sam stepped away and twirled.

"Yeah, I like." Alex stared with naked lust in her eyes. "I'd have to be dead to not appreciate those shorts."

Sam grinned and jumped back into her arms, hands entwining in Alex's hair. "I can't believe you came over on a Thursday. It feels like Christmas."

Alex held Sam tight against her body and pushed their hips together. "Well, I do have to go into the office tomorrow to finish up some paperwork. But that shouldn't take long. Then we have three days together."

"Here, let's get you off your feet. It's couch time. We need some couch time!" Sam led the way to the sofa. She had cleared off the throw pillows earlier in anticipation of a hot and heavy make-out session.

Alex sagged onto the cushions with a heavy sigh, dragging Sam down on top of her. Eager hands moved under Sam's shirt, while her tongue and lips worked the neck area. "Oh, no bra. You little temptress."

Sam bent her head away to give Alex more access. "It's almost bedtime. You're lucky I'm not already in my PJs."

"I would call that unlucky." Alex nipped at Sam's collarbone. "God, I missed you."

Alex's hands slipped lower and she squeezed Sam's ass. "Mmm. Now that's nice." She moved her hands and managed to slip them underneath Sam's underwear. "Mmm, very nice."

Sam's breath caught in her throat and a soft moan escaped from her lips. "Easy, killer. Don't start something you're too tired to finish."

"Oh, I'll find the energy to finish, don't you worry," Alex murmured into her neck.

Sam's tongue found its way to Alex's ear. She flicked the lobe and gently sucked it into her mouth. Nights this week had been filled with sex dreams, more so than usual, and she was seriously reconsidering the 'I love you' rule. Her hand slid to the top of Alex's jeans, and two fingers flicked the button open. Those same fingers slipped under the waistband and traced a path back and forth between Alex's hip bones.

Alex tried to guide Sam's hand lower.

Sam smiled. "Uh-uh."

"Please."

The corner of Sam's lips curled into a smile. "You can barely keep your eyes open and you're still this frisky?"

"I'm always this frisky. And hopeful."

"Hopeful?" Sam's fingers continued to dance below Alex's waistband.

"That your fingers might slip lower."

Sam rubbed her nose in Alex's hair. "Slip? Like on a banana peel?"

Alex chuckled. "God, you were so hot that day, wearing my sunglasses. I should've known then I was in trouble." She stifled a yawn.

"You're exhausted. I should put you to bed."

"Do I still have to behave myself? Because those PJs of yours are very sexy."

"Maybe I should wear a full-length flannel nightgown, all boxy and big. Then you wouldn't find me so appealing."

"Doubt it."

Sam laid her head on Alex's chest. "I'll make Yogi sleep between us. Then you wouldn't be able to touch me."

"If you like human torture, that's your solution. But I think there's something in the Geneva Convention outlawing that sort of behavior."

Sam chuckled. "I don't think the Geneva Convention covers that." She kissed Alex. Her body screamed for more as the kiss deepened and Alex's arms tightened around her. But when she pulled back, the fatigue surrounding Alex's eyes made her pause. "You're too sleepy. When I let you get in my pants, I want your full attention."

"Don't worry, you'll have it."

Sam nervously nibbled on her bottom lip. "I haven't been with a woman in a long time. I'm kinda worried I won't measure up."

"There's no way you couldn't measure up, so don't even say something like that."

The sincerity in those green eyes put Sam's fears to rest. "Okay. Let's get you to bed and tuck you in."

* * *

Alex came out of the bathroom and joined Sam under the covers. She inched across the king size bed, and upon reaching her destination, gave Sam a solid kiss good night. Sighing with contentment, she relaxed onto her side, leaving an arm resting across Sam's belly.

"What? I don't have to fight you off?" Sam asked with mock seriousness. "Are you over me already?"

"I'm being respectful."

"No! A little fighting off is good. It's the highlight of my day."

Alex yawned and rested her head on Sam's shoulder. "I'm saving my energy. I'm gonna try and bang you tomorrow."

Sam's laughter filled the room. "You're funny."

"Turn around and we'll spoon, then you can fight me off."

"Yeah! I love spooning." She turned over, anticipating some grade-A groping.

Alex snuggled up behind her. "Now, where to begin?" She slid a hand under Sam's shirt and placed it over her breast. "Hm. Good place to start." Her fingers teased and caressed. "Ah, here's the part where you fight me off."

Sam whimpered quietly as her nipple grew taut beneath Alex's touch, and the heat began building in her core.

"Seriously. Where's the fight?"

Sam's hips pulsed with want.

"Oh, Lord Jesus." Alex yanked her hand away and she buried her face in Sam's hair. A muffled groan fell from her lips.

"Why'd you stop?"

"You didn't fight."

"Well, it's just second base. It's not like you haven't been there before."

"Then don't move your hips."

"It was involuntary. Like a twitch."

"Babe, we're walking a very fine line here." Alex placed feather-light kisses on the back of Sam's neck. "I'm gonna have to put you in the burqa soon."

"Okay. Guess I have been torturing the shit out of you." Sam grabbed Alex's hands and held them against her stomach. "Go to sleep, BG. You're tired."

"Well, I'm kind of awake now."

"Oh. Well, tell me how you found Yogi. I remember you said you both rescued each other."

"I got him while I was living on the East Coast, before I moved back here. I met him the day of Madison's funeral."

"Oh, crap, I'm sorry. You don't have to talk about it if you don't want to."

"No, it's fine. One of our friends pulled him from a shelter because he was time stamped. You know what time stamped means?"

"They were going to put him down?"

"Yeah. I told my friend I would keep him until they found a good home for him. I figured I had nothing better to do except cry my eyes out, so might as well cry with him. After about a week, he was following me everywhere. We became inseparable. That's how we found each other. And here we are today, getting rescued all over again."

"Well, I love him."

"You know we're a package deal, right?"

"I can put up with you, if it means having him around." Sam turned and put her arms around Alex's neck. "What did I rescue you from?"

"Myself."

CHAPTER TWENTY

Alex sat back with a satisfied sigh, pleased with the design she had just finished. She'd arrived at the crack of dawn to get all her work done so she could head straight back to Sam's. At the thought of Sam, her lower belly tightened with desire. She glanced down at her faithful pooch. "I'm feeling lucky, Bear. Tonight might be the night, buddy."

Lenna poked her head in the doorway. "Hey, you busy?"

"I just finished the design for the Donovans. I think we should go with blue stone pavers, because it'll match the façade on the back of the house."

Lenna shut the door and sat in the chair in front of the desk.

Alex noted the stressed-out look on her face. "Jesus. You look like you've seen a ghost. What's going on? Is Soph okay?"

"She's fine. Were you online at all this morning?"

"No. I've been buried in this design for hours. Why?"

"Christ." Lenna passed her phone to Alex.

She looked down at the image on the screen and her stomach dropped right down to her toes. "What the fuck is this?" Dread clutched at her heart. It was a picture of Sam gazing adoringly at Alex as they danced, their lips inches apart. She remembered the exact moment. It was at Lenna's birthday party, and she'd almost kissed Sam before thinking better of it. Thank God.

"It's all over the Internet. Rumor mill says Sam must be gay."

"Where did the picture come from?"

"It was posted on a Facebook page this morning, and then it went viral."

"This was months ago! Who posted it?"

Lenna didn't reply.

"Who was it?"

"Cynthia."

Red rage filled Alex. "I can't believe she did this."

"Have you had any contact with her?"

"She keeps calling, asking why I haven't been at the bar. I finally told her I was seeing someone. She asked if it was 'that actress.'"

"You didn't say it was Sam, did you?"

"No! I just ignored the question and ended the conversation. She wasn't too happy. Wait 'til I get a hold of her." The rage receded, replaced with fear. "Oh God, Sam."

She typed a quick text. *Have you seen the picture? Are you okay?*

The reply was instant. *With Zach. Talk later.*

A chill went through her. The text seemed curt, but that was probably just her imagination. She shook it off.

"Well?" Lenna asked.

"She said we'll talk later." Alex dropped the phone on her desk and buried her face in her hands. "This is bad. What if she posts more pictures?" She rubbed her eyes and dropped her hands. "I need to go set her straight." Her lips set in a hard line.

"Calm down. Confrontation is not the answer. Can't have you popping her in the mouth." Lenna tipped her chair back and the muscle in her jaw twitched. "I'll talk to her."

"Oh, great. Let the black belt talk to her."

"I can control myself. And I can be very persuasive." Lenna gave an emphatic point. "Nobody fucks with my Thanksgiving."

* * *

Later that evening, Alex paced around her bedroom. The picture had been taken down hours ago, no doubt due to Lenna and her powers of persuasion, but the damage was done. It had been the lead story on *E! Tonight*, the hosts bandying back and forth about whether Sam Cassidy would come out of the closet, and how it would affect her career if it were true.

Alex still hadn't heard from Sam, and she was in full-blown panic mode. Her heart had been thumping in her chest for hours. Nausea ate at the pit of her stomach. Why did this have to happen? Why now? Things had been progressing fabulously. They'd both been so happy.

She seesawed back and forth between utter despair and quiet hope. Hope that Sam was okay, and that it would all just fade away and be replaced by another salacious story about some other Hollywood starlet. Despair because it could be ruinous for Sam's career. For her Oscar chances. For their chance at happiness.

Around nine, her phone rang. Finally. "Hey."

"Hey." Sam's voice sounded small. And tired.

"Are you okay?"

"I've been better."

Alex's heart ached for her and what she must be going through. "Do you want me to come over?"

"God no. There's paparazzi at the front gate. They've been here for hours, just lying in wait."

"Sam, I'm so sorry. I had no idea she took pictures."

"You know her?"

"Yeah. Unfortunately."

"How?"

Alex hesitated, hating to say it out loud, but she wouldn't lie to Sam. Couldn't lie to Sam. "I slept with her a couple of times. Before you and I met."

Sam's sigh echoed over the phone. "Oh."

A piece of Alex died. She could feel the disappointment. "I'm sorry," was all she could manage to say.

"I thought I recognized her when Jade showed me the post. Was she the one you were arguing with at the party?"

"Yeah."

"Why is she posting this now?"

"She called me last week. I told her I was seeing someone, and she got pissed. I guess I misjudged the situation. I thought she and I were on the same page. It was supposed be a casual hookup. Somehow, for her, it was something more." Alex rubbed at the sudden flare of pain behind her eyes. "I'm sorry." The words seemed woefully inadequate. She wanted to protect Sam. To hold her and tell her they would weather this storm, together.

"The *Addictions* producers called Zach."

"And?"

"They're concerned with the bad press that's surrounding me right now. They insinuated that they may drop me from consideration. Unless we fix it."

Alex held her breath. "What does 'fix it' mean?"

"It means I have to lay low."

"What does that mean for us?"

"I don't know. I...I just can't do this right now."

The dread that clutched at Alex's heart threatened to overwhelm her. "Why can't we both just lay low, together?"

"I can't...I can't...I just can't do this."

"Sam?"

"What?"

"Are you breaking up with me?"

"I'm sorry. I need time to figure things out." Sam's voice shook when she said, "I have to go. I'll talk to you later."

The call ended, and Alex's eyes filled with moisture. In a rare display of anger, she threw the phone across the room, shattering the glass screen.

* * *

The next night, Alex sat alone in the kitchen finishing her supper. Dark circles hung below her eyes. The conversation kept replaying over and over in her brain. There was no, "We'll lay low for a few weeks and everything will be fine." Or, "Don't worry, we'll get through it together."

Alex knew how important this movie was to Sam. Was she throwing Alex aside for a shot at having her dream come true?

"Alex, you better get out here!" Lenna called. "There's a story on Sam coming up."

Great. Just what she needed. More bad news. She trudged into the living room just as *E! Tonight* came back on.

The host smiled a perky smile. And Alex wanted to rip it off her face.

"Yesterday this picture broke, of Samantha Cassidy and a mystery woman, dancing at a gay club in West Hollywood. Looking very much like a couple. Rumors have been rampant, but today, we have a different story. Our own Jon Farrier caught up with everyone's favorite commander at Spago in Beverly Hills."

Alex's heart stuttered as the camera cut to a smiling Sam. On the arm of one Brian Davis.

Jon was grinning like an idiot. And Alex wanted to punch his lights out.

"Thank you, Janet. I'm standing here with Samantha Cassidy and Brian Davis. Sam, we all saw the pictures yesterday. The Internet went crazy. Can you tell us what happened?"

Sam's smile was too bright. Forced. Alex was sure Sam was putting on happy face for public consumption, but it still ripped her apart.

"Those were taken a while ago, at a birthday party for a friend of mine. We were having a great time. That's really all there was to it. It was just some innocent fun."

"And Brian, we haven't seen you with Sam for a while. Everyone thought you two had broken up."

His hair was slicked back, making him look like a snake oil salesman. Alex wanted to knee him in the groin.

This sudden uptick in violent tendencies was a little disconcerting.

"No, Jon. Rumors tend to be just that. Rumors. We've been keeping things on the down low. Enjoying the peace and quiet, out of the spotlight."

He smiled lovingly at Sam, and Alex wanted to puke. When Sam kissed him on the mouth, she nearly did. Bile rose in her throat and she swallowed thickly.

"I see. You guys are still together then?"

Brian squeezed Sam close. "Yep. Still together. And who knows, maybe we'll have a big announcement soon." He winked.

"Are we talking about a marriage proposal?" Jon asked, grinning at the camera.

"We'll see," Brian said, tongue in cheek.

The camera zoomed in on Jon. "Well, you heard it here first, on *E! Tonight*. There may be wedding bells in the future for this happy couple. Back to you, Janet."

Alex collapsed on the sofa and Sophia put an arm around her. Not since Madison had she felt this kind of pain. Would she have the strength to pick up the pieces a second time?

"I'm sure that was just for show," Lenna said.

Alex seethed, still stinging from the kiss. "She looked pretty fucking happy."

Sophia squeezed her shoulders. "I'm sure Lenna's right. She's an actress. That was for show. To get people off her back."

Alex abruptly stood and walked out of the room.

"Where you going?" Lenna called.

She picked up her keys and stormed out of the house.

"Don't do anything stupid!"

Alex needed to drown her sorrows. What was good for the goose was good for the gander, right? If Sam wanted to be with Brian, then maybe it was time to go back to her old ways. Mindless sex with beautiful women.

* * *

Alex's glassy eyes stared at an empty mug. "Give me another beer."

Monette patted her arm. "I think you've had enough."

Alex was sloppy drunk. And she didn't care. She'd arrived at the bar hours ago, hoping to go home with someone. Anyone. Trouble was, when push came to shove, she couldn't go through with it. Reminders of Sam were everywhere. The dance floor, where Alex had almost kissed her. The couch against the far wall, where they'd huddled close. The deck out back, where Alex had bared her soul.

With chin in hand, she quietly wailed, "I'm ruined. I can't even sleep with anybody else. I'll be celibate for the rest of my life."

"I'm gonna call Lenna to come get you. Where's your phone?"

"I broke it. Don't worry, I can drive. After I have another beer."

"I don't think so. Give me your keys."

With a sullen look, she handed them over. "You're no fun."

* * *

Over the next couple of days, Alex buried herself in work. What better way to clear your mind than physical labor? She left home at dawn each day and returned after sunset to collapse into bed exhausted. She'd also found that anger worked better than depression, so she was short and snippy with everyone who crossed her path. Lenna and Sophia gave her a wide berth.

On the third morning, she was at a job in Brentwood, digging holes to plant California aster. No, digging sounded too passive. She stabbed. Stabbing with a spade made her feel good. When the aster refused to come out of its pot, she cursed it. Then she stabbed and cursed some more. Nothing like f-bombing an innocent plant to release some pent-up aggression. In the middle of all this garden violence, this horticultural mayhem, her new phone buzzed.

I miss you.

This was the first she'd heard from Sam since the phone call. Alex brushed the grime from her hands and waited, a spark of hope blooming in her chest. When nothing more came through, she cursed some more and put the phone away without answering, muttering, "That's it? That's all you're gonna say? I miss you? Ha! Well good. And I'm not answering. I refuse to answer."

After a moment, she pulled the phone back out. Maybe there was more? Her head sagged forward. Nothing. Tears threatened, but she refused to let them fall.

* * *

Sam stared at her phone. Waiting. And waiting. Nothing. No reply bubble. No acknowledgment. Hours passed and still she stared. The slam of the front door interrupted her malaise.

"We brought takeout!" Jade hollered.

She and Emma strolled into the living room, where Sam was buried beneath a mound of pillows.

"Jesus Christ. Dig her out of there."

Emma began tossing pillows in the air, finally uncovering the desolate Sam. "Found her."

"All right, Captain Mopey Mope, what have you been doing all day?" Jade asked, toeing aside the pile of dirty tissues that littered the floor.

Sam was curled into a tight ball. "I texted her." Her eyes were swollen, and her nose was red from blowing.

"And?"

"She didn't reply."

"Maybe she's busy," Emma said.

"For six hours?"

"Oh."

Sam sat and pulled her legs underneath her. "What am I doing? Am I gonna risk losing her? Over a dumb part in a movie?"

"It's not a dumb part," Jade said. "It's the part you've been waiting for your entire career."

"So what?" She clutched at her breast, then beat it with a fist. "It hurts. In here." She thumped her chest a few more times. "I miss her! Everything sucks without her." She grabbed a handful of tissues and dabbed at the tears slipping from her eyes. "I can barely get out of bed in the morning. Do you know how that feels?"

Emma and Jade both remained silent.

"Do you?" She clutched and grabbed and dabbed some more. "I love her!" Sam hugged her box of tissues for comfort as more rivulets of tears streamed down her face. "Do you know how long it's been since I've held her? Since I've touched her?" She paused to blow again. Another crumpled tissue hit the floor. "Do you know how long it's been since I've heard her voice? Since I've heard her say my name?"

Emma and Jade stared back, mouths slightly open.

"Well? Do you?"

"Three days?" Emma asked in a timid voice.

Jade gave a quick nod. "It's been three days."

"Aaarrrrrgh!" Sam grabbed another tissue and blew her nose with a definitive *honk*! "Well it feels like a lot longer!"

"You know Logan's friend Steve?" Emma asked. "He stars in that HBO cop show?"

Sam sniffled. "Yeah. What about him?"

"He and his boyfriend Carter had dinner with us the other night. Every weekend they stay at each other's house. Like one weekend, they stay at Steve's, and the next weekend they stay at Carter's."

Jade shook her head. "Is this leading somewhere? I think Sam's depressed enough without hearing about some happy gay couple."

"That's just it. They're totally gay, and nobody has a clue."

Sam narrowed her eyes. "What are you saying?"

"I'm saying, they're together. They just sneak around. And if anybody sees them together, they say they're best friends."

"So?"

"I don't know why you and Alex just can't sneak around."

* * *

At three a.m., Sam's phone dinged.
I miss you too.

She jolted upright. She would have liked to have jolted awake, but she hadn't slept in three days. Her eyes remained locked on the screen. Her heart started racing.

She opened her mouth and yelled, screamed at the walls, releasing all the stress and misery of the last few days. When she was done, her shoulders slumped.

Okay. This whole thing was stupid. Probably one of the stupidest things she'd ever done. Walking away from love. From the woman of her dreams. Alex was the one, and goddamn it, she was gonna have her. So fuck 'em! Fuck. Them. All.

Well, maybe just keep things quiet. Let this shit die down for a bit, then sneak around like Emma had suggested. Obviously, everyone else did it.

She stared at her phone for a minute, then typed, *I'm an idiot. I'm the largest idiot on the planet.*

I don't know about largest. Maybe second largest.

Sam bit her lip. Was there a light at the end of this hellacious tunnel? *Do I still have a chance?*

The phone rang, and her hand shook as she answered. "Hey."

"I don't know. Do you think you deserve another chance?"

Sam detected a hint of humor in Alex's voice. "I think everyone deserves a second chance."

"What's in it for me?"

Sam jumped from the bed and strode around the room. "Well, all the purple chicken you can eat."

"Hm. That's tempting. What else?"

"Pinkie swear promises and lots of random touching."

"Keep talking."

Sam wanted to cry with joy. "I'm sure there's more. Oh, Thanksgiving at your house. There's that."

"Lenna will be happy."

"First class lounges. All the time."

"What will Brian say?"

Sam groaned. "Please tell me you knew that was all for show. Please." There was silence on the line, and Sam's heart lurched. "I had to do that. Just to throw everybody off."

After a moment, Alex sighed. "I know. I could see it in your eyes. But when you kissed him...something snapped inside. It was painful. It hurt. Even though I knew what you were doing, somehow, it still hurt."

"I'm sorry. I had to make it look real. And believe me, I did not enjoy it. He's an asshole, but he did me a favor. Although I wanted to kick him in the balls when he hinted about getting married. I mean, really kick him hard in the balls."

Alex chuckled. "I thought the exact same thing."

"Can you forgive me?"

"Of course. What about the movie?"

"I don't care. I mean, I do care, but not if it means not seeing you."

"This is important. It's your dream. It's a chance at an Oscar."

"What good is an Oscar if I have no one to share it with? If I don't have *you* to share it with?"

"I don't wanna be the reason you don't win or get nominated."

"I've been thinking. It can work. As long as I'm discreet." She paused, then added, "As long as *we're* discreet." There. She'd put her cards on the table.

"Are you saying we're still a we?" Alex asked.

Sam's heart started beating wildly inside her chest. "If you'll have me. And I know it's not fair to ask you to hide in the closet with me. And I'll understand if you say no, but I swear to God, someday, Alex Novato, I'm coming out of the closet. And when it happens, I want you to be there with me." The air stilled. Her happiness hung in the balance.

"I think I'd like that."

CHAPTER TWENTY-ONE

Sam drove like a maniac on her way home from a photo shoot on Saturday, running yellow lights and barely stopping at stop signs. She tore down her own street and yelled at the gate because it dared to open so slowly. Quick as a bunny, she sprinted through the house looking for Alex. When she couldn't find her, she threw open the French doors and stepped into the backyard. In an instant, she was in Alex's arms, their lips pressed together.

Sam pulled away and began rambling. "Can you forgive me? Please? Please forgive me. I was stupid. I had no clue how to fix it. And I didn't do a good job. And you have to forgive me."

"Yes! I forgive you."

"I should've told you we needed to lay low for just a little while, but I was scared I'd ruin my career. And I think I was mad because it was that woman who did it. And the thought of you with her made me crazy!"

"I'm so sorry about that."

"It wasn't your fault. I had no right to be mad. I just wasn't thinking clearly. Zach was worried I wouldn't get the part.

Everyone was worried. But I realized losing you was more awful than losing some part. I should've just talked to you." Confession complete, she fell into Alex's embrace again.

Alex stroked her hair and they remained in each other's arms for a minute. "I'm sorry it took me so long to answer your text. I was being a jerk."

"You had every reason to be a jerk."

"Next time we know to communicate better."

"Now we know!"

"Now we know."

They both took a breath and laughed.

Sam clutched the front of Alex's T-shirt and pulled her close. "We have some catching up to do. We haven't had a make-out session in a week."

"We are overdue."

They locked lips, and grunts of pleasure rose from both their throats.

Sam's kisses had an edge to them, a desperation, as her teeth nipped at Alex's lips.

"Ohhh," Alex moaned, "are you trying to kill me?"

"Mmhmm, I missed you so much."

Alex pulled back from her hungry mouth. "I need to talk to you."

Sam's stomach muscles clenched, and her face fell. "Oh no. Are you breaking up with me?"

"What? No! Why do you think I'm breaking up with you?"

"You look so serious."

"No, I'm not breaking up with you. But I do need to be serious." Alex bowed. "If I may have the floor."

Relief washed through Sam and she waved an arm. "The floor is yours."

Alex took a deep breath. "Sam. I...I know, the last few years, I haven't been a good person—"

Sam started to interrupt, but Alex reached over and placed a finger to her lips.

"I've slept around. I've hurt people. I've been a shit, basically." She gulped more air into her lungs. "And I know for a fact, you deserve so much better than me."

Sam wanted to shout, *that's not true!* But she held her tongue.

"That being said." Alex grinned. "I'm still...just a girl—"

"Oh no you're not—"

"Standing in front of a girl—"

"Oh no." Sam pointed at Alex. "You're gonna *Notting Hill* me."

"—asking her to love me."

"You *Notting Hill*ed me! You *Notting Hill*ed me!" Sam squealed, jumping into Alex's arms and raining kisses all over her face. "I can't believe it."

Alex beamed a thousand-watt smile. "I swear you're the most beautiful, sweetest, sexiest woman I've ever met. And you're cool funny to boot."

Sam threw her head back and laughed.

"And I am hopelessly, totally, completely, absolutely in love with you. And I figure if I play my cards right, you might love me back?"

"Yes, I do. I love you!" Sam's heart sang. "I can't believe you *Notting Hill*ed me, I'm the actress. I'm supposed to *Notting Hill* you."

"Well, I beat you to it."

Sam's hands cupped Alex's cheeks. "You know I've been in love with you since the first moment I laid eyes on you. I've been waiting for you to catch up."

Alex groaned as her arms shook with exertion. "Okay, you're getting heavy. I'm gonna put you down."

Sam stepped away. "Here, you jump into my arms."

"What? Sam, you can't."

"I can. C'mon, remember I have strong legs."

"I don't think so."

"Try me."

"Okay, you sure?"

Sam nodded, eyes squinting with determination. "Yeah, this'll be easy."

"I don't know about easy."

"Do it. Do it." Sam waved both hands, egging her on.

"Okay, here we go."

Alex jumped on Sam, who briefly caught her, but then started to backpedal. "Oh shit, oh shit, we're going down!"

They both giggled as they tumbled into the grass.

Alex rolled on top of Sam and their mouths melded together. Her tongue probed deep inside Sam's mouth.

Sam broke off the kiss. "Alex. Now now."

Alex's eyes were unfocused. "What?" She moved in to kiss Sam again.

"Now now."

"Mmm." Alex nibbled along Sam's neck, when suddenly, her lips froze. "Now now? Like—Now Now?" She leaned back with brows raised.

Sam nodded. "Now now!"

"Holy shit! Like right now now?" Alex shot up and took a few steps toward the house, then spun around and yanked Sam to her feet.

With Alex in tow, Sam bolted toward the French doors. When they reached the patio, she tugged on Alex's hand to stop them dead in their tracks. She kissed Alex so deeply both their legs trembled.

They started walking again, neither paying attention to anything except keeping their lips locked. They knocked into a lounge chair and fell onto it, never breaking the kiss.

Alex landed on her back with Sam hovering over her, and Alex's hands traveled wildly over Sam's body, sliding inside her shorts and squeezing her ass, then moving back under Sam's shirt to caress her breasts, a thumb brushing back and forth across her hardening nipples.

Sam broke off the kiss to take a breath and a whimper escaped. She stood, pulling Alex with her, and walked unsteadily toward the door.

Alex caught her from behind, wrapping strong arms around Sam's waist. She nipped and kissed the back of Sam's neck.

When they arrived at the French doors, all Sam could do was put her hands on the glass and brace herself while Alex's fingers made their way down the front of her shorts. Sam rested her forehead against the door, breathing heavily. "Remember that day I walked into this door?"

Alex whispered, "Funny, after you did that, this is exactly what I wanted to do to you."

Sam shivered in response as goose bumps dotted her arms. "I was a dork. How could you have wanted me?"

Alex's hand slid further down, her fingers slipping inside Sam's undies and continuing to reach lower. Alex's breath burned hot on the back of her neck when she said, "You were the sexiest dork I'd ever met."

When Alex's fingers hit pay dirt, Sam almost collapsed on the ground. "Oh, Jesus fucking…"

Alex smiled into her neck. "Welcome to third base, Sam."

Sam pushed off the door. "Inside, inside!"

Alex yanked her hand away and opened the door, dragging Sam inside. Once the door closed, she whipped Sam's shirt off, tossing it over a shoulder while grinning wickedly. Hooded eyes traveled slowly over Sam's body. Alex quickly removed her own shirt and tossed it aside.

Sam entered an almost trance-like state, lips parted in anticipation as she stared into darkening green eyes. All these months of wondering how Alex felt, all the wanting, all the waiting, was finally over. Maybe she should take a second to appreciate the moment. She glanced hungrily at Alex's abs, and her eyes made their way up to Alex's lips. She gave a slight shrug. *Okay, consider it appreciated.*

She took a step forward, and when her mouth slammed into Alex's, eager hands roamed over her back. Every flex of Alex's muscles registered between Sam's legs. She started to push Alex backward, trying to angle them toward the staircase, but forgot about the dog bed. They tripped over it and down in a heap they went.

"Who put the dog bed here?" Sam asked, exasperated.

"I think you did." Alex kissed Sam's breasts through her bra.

"Who puts a dog bed near the door?" Sam eyes closed in ecstasy.

"You do." Alex nibbled at the ridged peaks pushing against the lacy fabric.

Sam jumped to her feet. "Up, up! We are not doing it on a dog bed."

Alex allowed herself to be pulled to a standing position. "It's really quite comfortable. You must have paid a fortune for it."

But Sam couldn't appreciate the humor, because the wait was finally over. She frantically pulled Alex toward the stairs.

When Sam reached the first step, Alex grasped her hips from behind and impatient hands reached around, undoing the button on Sam's shorts. Alex pushed the zipper down, and Sam sagged to her knees, trying to crawl up the steps as Alex peeled them off. By the time Sam hit the landing between the two staircases, she was still on her knees and shorts-less.

Sam turned around to find Alex inching toward her. Her breath caught in her throat. She was being stalked by a hungry panther. And it was fucking hot.

Alex placed her hands on Sam's knees, spreading them apart, and settled between them, staying on the step below the landing.

Their lips met, and tongues entwined and probed while they breathed hard into each other's mouths.

Sam's only thought was the bedroom, and she broke off the kiss. "Let's go, let's go!" She struggled to get to her feet.

"Wait, wait." Alex slipped Sam's bra off, and over the shoulder it went. "You gotta give me a minute here." Her eyes glazed over with desire as both hands cupped Sam's breasts and fingers rolled erect nipples. Her lips soon followed her hands.

Sam could barely control the trembling. "Oh…oh…god… okay…okay. Jesus, take as much time as you need." All thoughts of making it to the bedroom were abandoned. No way could she get up from this spot without an orgasm. No way she could get up, period. She had been reduced to a giant puddle of want.

Sam cradled Alex's head, hands stroking through Alex's hair as Alex kissed and sucked her nipples. Her orgasm was near, and she needed to feel Alex inside her.

"Now now, Alex," Sam pleaded.

Alex pushed Sam's legs farther apart, maintaining eye contact as she sunk lower between them. She slid down a couple more steps for a better angle, taking Sam's underwear with her on the way down.

"Jesus Christ."

When Sam bit her bottom lip, Alex quivered. "Oh, that lip of yours." She softly bit the inside of Sam's thighs as her eager hands pushed Sam's legs even farther apart, opening her to Alex's loving gaze.

When Alex's tongue slid through her velvety, wet folds, a growl came from deep in Sam's throat. Her head rolled from side to side. When the tongue plunged inside, Sam swooned— her patented Alex swoon. She fell backward, lacking the strength to stay upright. "Oh…oh…oh my God." She writhed in ecstasy, hips grinding in time with each swipe of Alex's tongue.

Sam gasped with closed eyes when Alex's fingers replaced her tongue, which had gone on a seek and find mission straight to Sam's engorged clit. Alex's fingers and tongue took Sam to places she hadn't been in years, the sensations exquisitely torturous and mind-blowing. She met each thrust of Alex's fingers with a thrust of her own, pushing her hips up to take those fingers deeper. She threw her head back. The muscles in her neck strained. Her chest heaved as a tight knot of pleasure coiled low in her belly. It didn't take long. She teetered at the precipice, and then cried out as the orgasm shattered her insides, wave after pulsating wave ripping through her body. It seemed to go on and on and on, delicious pinpoints of pleasure coursing along every nerve ending, causing her to jerk and shudder until she was spent. Sam gave one last whimper and her body went limp.

Alex continued to kiss and lick, her tongue laving around Sam's sensitive clit until Sam flinched. With one last gentle kiss, Alex pulled away.

"Holy shit." Sam's body still quaked from the aftershocks, her limbs languid and heavy. When Alex removed her fingers, Sam felt the aching emptiness. She longed to feel Alex's tongue on her again, to feel the stretch from Alex's fingers as they moved inside her. But Sam was also desperate to make love to Alex, to taste her and touch her all over. The thought of Alex's body beneath her, rock hard and soft at the same time, gave Sam a second wind.

* * *

Alex kissed her way across Sam's torso, to her neck, and finally to her lips. She pulled away and grinned, her own heart still racing. "That was pretty good. Quick, but good."

"It was quick. I blame my total lack of self-control on the fact that I've been lusting after you for months now." Sam's breathing remained irregular and shallow. "Did we really have our first-time sex on the stairs?"

"We did. In my defense, you instructed me to get on with it." Alex wanted her again. Right now. The need to taste Sam's arousal, to watch Sam come undone beneath her was overpowering. She began working over Sam's neck with her lips.

"I admit, you were told to get on with it. I couldn't make it to the bedroom. How are you doing, by the way?"

Alex lifted her head and took a deep breath. "Well, if you must know, I don't think I've been this wet in my entire life, and I might have already come."

"Maybe I should check for you." Sam slid from under Alex and switched their positions. "I mean, what if you didn't come? Then I need to remedy it ASAP." Her hands traveled to the top of Alex's shorts.

"Okay. Should we go to the bedroom?" Alex's heart rammed into her ribcage as Sam fiddled with the top button of her shorts.

"I don't think I can make it to the bedroom. I kinda want you now." Sam's shaky fingers fumbled with the button. "Is this some sort of fucking trick button?"

"It is. It's the kind that slides through the hole." Alex's calmness was a miracle. "Just slide the button through the hole, Sam."

"I'm trying."

"Thank God I don't wear a belt."

Sam gave up on the button because her hands were trembling, and because she'd gotten distracted by Alex's sports bra. She licked her lips and desperately tried to pry it off.

"The bedroom is only thirty feet away."

"That seems really far." Sam cursed her fumbling fingers.

"The bed is so soft." Alex closed her eyes, savoring the sensation of Sam's hands wandering over her chest, willing her body to be patient.

Sam relented. "Okay. Let's go, let's go!" She shot to her feet, but not before finally thrusting the sports bra over her head victoriously. "Ha!" She stared at Alex's naked breasts, mumbling, "Oh shit, that's nice. Fuck...really nice." Sam pulled Alex to her feet, and they hurried to the bedroom. "Lose the shorts. Lose the shorts!" Sam called over her shoulder, dropping Alex's bra in the hallway.

Alex jogged after Sam on wobbly legs, undoing her shorts on the way. As they hit the bedroom, Alex's shorts hit the floor, tangled in her feet, and down she went. "Shit."

Sam turned. "What are you doing on the floor?"

"I obviously inherited your idiot-ness, if that's possible."

"Well get the fuck up. Now! And get into bed!"

Alex dug bossy Sam. And it was a hoot she liked to drop the f-bomb when turned on. She pounced onto the bed.

They rolled around until Sam positioned herself on top. "It's been awhile. I hope I don't forget what to do."

"Trust me, you won't have to do much." Alex's mind blew apart looking at Sam, naked, straddling her, those tantalizing breasts dangling like ripened fruit. No fantasy this time. It was real and happening now.

Sam's tongue probed deep into Alex's mouth, then she pulled away and went right to an ear, biting and licking it. She sucked the lobe, coaxing a groan from Alex. Sam's lips next charted a course to Alex's throat, nipping and biting at her pulse point. Stopping for a brief moment, Sam inhaled the scent of Alex's cologne, and her eyelids fluttered. "Remind me to buy a case of this cologne so you never run out." Her lips found their way down to Alex's breasts, teasing the nipples with her tongue before sucking them into her mouth.

"I'm ready, baby. I mean, we can dispense with the foreplay this one time. I've been waiting for months, and I want you now. Please..." Alex begged between ragged breaths.

"But I just got here." Sam voice was tinged with disappointment as she glanced up from Alex's breasts.

Alex grinned, because Sam looked adorable and sexy, but she needed her lower. "I know, baby, and you can spend an hour there, in about a minute, cause that's all it's gonna take. Trust me."

Sam slid down, hovering near Alex's hip, near her special spot. "But what about here?" Her tongue stabbed and licked the hot spot.

Alex's hips bucked. "Oh fuck. I'm about to lose it."

The corner of Sam's lips twitched, and she slid farther south.

Alex keened as Sam's tongue lapped and stroked. She panted in time with the fingers that pumped inside. The muscles in Alex's lower belly constricted and she came almost immediately. Her back arched off the bed and she grabbed Sam's head, pulling it closer, creating even more friction. She let out the loudest moan she could ever remember while having sex. She figured it was a pent-up three-month moan.

When her hips stopped jerking, and the throbbing inside stopped, Alex collapsed back onto the bed, hands still tangled in Sam's hair. Her eyes remained screwed shut as she basked in the feeling of being sated. A long time coming, but oh so worth the wait.

Sam pouted from between her legs. "I didn't even do anything. I mean, I feel kinda bad."

For a few moments, Alex reveled in the sensation of Sam's soft tongue as she continued to gently lick. But then the urgency came back—to touch Sam, caress every inch of her body.

"You did plenty. Come here." She rolled Sam onto her back and kissed her, and when Alex pulled her lips away, she stared down at the woman who'd managed to steal her heart. "You are so fucking hot."

"I barely did anything, you were so quick."

"That was just to take the edge off. We have all night."

"Oh right. We have to hit every room."

Alex pressed hot kisses along the column of Sam's neck, already feeling the heat between Sam's legs as her body responded, hips thrusting against Alex's leg.

"Where to?"

"What?"

"What's our next destination?"

Sam giggled. "I guess we could hit the spare bedroom."

Alex stood, offering her back to Sam, whose eyes widened at the prospect of naked piggybacking. She hopped onboard, wrapping herself tightly around Alex's torso, and off they went to christen room number two.

* * *

Hours later they found themselves in the kitchen, sitting on the floor. Alex leaned against the cabinets with Sam in her lap, legs wrapped around Alex's waist, a blanket around their shoulders, eating cold pizza—naked as the day they were born.

"We didn't do it in here yet," Sam said.

"We're gonna kill two birds with one stone." Alex gazed into her favorite pair of blue eyes.

"I don't know if I'd consider pizza a sexy food." Sam held a piece to Alex's lips, and she took a big bite.

Alex swallowed the pizza. "Agreed. Hard to eat pizza off a naked body." A lecherous grin split her face. "Do you have any cool whip?"

"Cool whip?"

"Yeah."

"I don't have any. Too fattening. I have to maintain my girlish figure."

"Chocolate sauce?"

"Nope."

"What do you have?"

"Lettuce." Sam giggled.

"What?"

"I just pictured myself eating lettuce off your abs. How many rooms do we have left?"

"You tell me." Alex finished the piece of pizza and found Sam's breasts located conveniently close to her lips, begging for attention. She latched onto a nipple, sucking it fully into her mouth, flicking it with her tongue.

Sam's eyes rolled to the back of her head. "Oh God, that tongue of yours." She reached for a bottle of water and took a healthy swig. "You should hydrate, BG. I think we have at least five rooms to go, maybe six."

Alex released Sam's nipple with a soft pop and tilted her head back.

Sam moved the bottle to Alex's lips, letting her take a sip. "You know you got it bad when the sight of your girlfriend taking a drink of water turns you on. Like majorly."

Alex pulled her lips away from the bottle. "Like how majorly?" She shifted Sam in her lap, creating space between them. Her long fingers slipped easily inside Sam's already slicked-up opening. "Hmm, that's pretty major."

Sam blew out a breathy and barely audible, "Oh."

"Oh, is right." Alex took Sam's hand and pressed it between her own legs, guiding Sam's fingers inside. They both gasped with pleasure.

"Oh boy. Is it kitchen time?" Sam asked.

"I think so."

"I can't believe how quickly you get me going." Sam managed to take another drink of water before putting the bottle down. They stared into each other's eyes. "Is this a contest?" she asked with a grin. "Because I will win."

Alex gave a small shake of her head. "No, not a competition. More like teamwork."

"Mmm, I like teamwork." Sam's mouth moved closer to Alex's lips, not touching, just hovering. Their gazes didn't waver.

"Stay here," Alex whispered, wanting Sam's lips close.

"Oh, Christ..." Sam quaked as Alex's thumb moved independent of her fingers, circling Sam's clit, then rubbing back and forth.

Both moaned and panted as they stumbled close to the edge of oblivion.

Alex buried her face against the top of Sam's chest, listening to the drumming of her heartbeat and willing herself to slow down, wanting to wait so they could come together. When she felt the clenching around her fingers, Alex let herself go, her lips capturing Sam's, and they kissed and groaned while their hips moved.

Soon the kiss stopped as other things took precedence, like riding out their mutual orgasms. When their bodies stopped quivering, they rested their foreheads together, eyes shut, arms wrapped tightly around each other, both breathing heavily.

"That was hot." Sam rubbed her forehead back and forth against Alex's. She brought Alex's mouth to hers. "I love you, Alex Novato," Sam whispered against kiss-bruised lips.

The kitchen was crossed off the list.

* * *

"What room is this?" Alex asked, lying face down on the blanket that had made the rounds with them.

"I live here, and I don't even know." Sam busied herself with exploring all areas of Alex's back. "I think we hit a home run."

"We grand fucking slammed that shit." Alex's eyelids fluttered and closed.

"Are you going to sleep?"

"You wore me out," she mumbled.

"What? I wore you out? Holy shit, where's my phone? Take a freaking memo. I out-sexed the sex queen."

Alex giggled.

Sam lay herself along Alex's back, from head to toe. "Didn't expect that, did you?"

"Are you gloating?"

"Yeah, a little bit."

"In my defense—"

"You're awfully defensive lately."

"In my defense, you did make me piggyback you around the house, and eight times up and down the steps. And—"

"You were supposed to increase your workouts."

"And…I did run ten miles today."

"Well, who told you to run ten miles?"

"I had no idea it was going to be now now time. Believe me, if I'd known, I would've sat on the couch all day with my feet elevated."

Sam continued to kiss every inch of Alex's back.

"Mmm." Alex sighed with contentment. "Did we hit every room?"

"I have no idea." Sam giggled. "I don't think I'll be able to look at my washing machine the same ever again. I mean, who would've thought to turn it on?"

"Brilliant, right?" Alex craned her head to peek back at Sam with half-closed eyes.

Sam slid to the side, so they could kiss. "Let's go, sleepy head. I'm gonna put you to bed." She stood and helped Alex to her feet.

Alex grabbed the blanket as Sam led them from the room. She slung it over them both and wrapped her arms around Sam from behind as they slowly walked down the hallway. "Where are we?"

"Not sure. I figure if we keep walking, we may recognize something."

They shuffled along.

"Wait, wait! Things are getting more familiar," Sam said. "Here we go. The bedroom! I'd say it's where we started, but we started on the damn steps."

"I'm sensing that's not where you expected it would happen."

They flopped down onto the mattress.

"No, I pictured a wonderful love-making session in the comfort of this bed."

"Beds are overrated."

"You overrate a lot of things." Sam moved onto her back, pulling Alex on top of her. She tipped Alex's chin up and kissed her softly.

Alex yawned. "What time is it?"

"It's only three thirty. If you want to have sex all night, we still have a couple of hours until daylight. But it looks like you don't have the stamina you thought you had."

"In my defense, we started way 'fore the sun wen' down." Her eyelashes dusted her cheeks.

"I'm busting on you. I love you."

"I love you too. Mmhmm. I might sleep for days."

Sam hitched the blanket over their shoulders. "It's okay, I'll take care of you."

CHAPTER TWENTY-TWO

Sam stared down at a sleeping Alex. The clock read six thirty a.m. She hadn't gone to sleep at all, content to hold and snuggle her girlfriend all night. An hour ago, she'd crawled out of bed and jumped in the shower to rinse off.

So here she lay, staring at the woman she loved, waiting patiently for her to wake up. Well, maybe not so patiently, because Sam kept gently touching Alex, pushing wild hair from her face, running a hand lightly down a toned forearm.

Soon one open, green eye stared back.

"Are you awake?" Sam whispered.

"No," Alex whispered back with a soft smile.

Sam snuggled closer. "I think you are." Taking a finger, she traced the smile on those lips.

"It's early. What are you doing up?"

"I couldn't sleep."

"You mean at all?" Now the other eye opened too.

"Yeah. I'm too juiced. You got me juiced."

"Oh, I got you juiced all right."

Sam giggled and kissed her lightly on the lips.

"I'll be right back." Alex disentangled herself and padded to the bathroom.

"Nice ass," Sam called after her. The shower turned on and she waited patiently for a proper good morning kiss.

It didn't take long. Within minutes, Alex crawled back into bed with the fresh, clean smell of soap clinging to her skin. She gave Sam a proper good morning kiss while her hand wandered to other places. Specifically, the place between Sam's legs.

Sam moaned, still amazed at how quickly Alex could get her aroused. "I almost forgot mornings are your favorite time."

Alex's teeth gripped the waistband of Sam's shorts and pulled them down. "Oh shit." This would never get old.

* * *

An hour later, they both basked in the afterglow of sexual satisfaction. As Sam lay on Alex's chest, her phone buzzed with a calendar reminder.

"Oh crap. I forgot about that."

"What'd you forget?"

"I was supposed to hike with Jade and Emma this morning. I wouldn't have made the plans if I'd known it was gonna be now now time."

Alex laughed and squeezed her. "Henceforth, it shall always be known as now now."

"Should I blow them off?"

"No, don't blow off your friends. I'm still wiped. I'll sleep. You go walk, then come back here, and I'll tire you out the rest of the day."

Sam gave her a quick peck on the lips. "All right. I'm gonna go shower."

* * *

When Sam parked in the lot at Brush Canyon, Jade and Emma were already there, both half-heartedly stretching in tank tops and yoga pants.

"About fucking time," Jade called.

Sam bounced over. "I'm not even gonna charge you a dollar today!" She gave a big hug and kiss to each.

Jade brightened. "Is it free-fuck day? Did I miss the memo?" After studying Sam's body language, her eyes narrowed. "Wait a second." She tapped a finger to her chin. "E, you know what we have here? We have a sexually satisfied Samantha Cassidy. I can smell her from a mile away. And I think I really can smell you. Did you take a shower?"

"Of course, I showered. Twice, actually." Sam took a quick whiff, suddenly unsure. She'd had a lot of sex.

"Oh my God!" Emma yelled. "You had sex!" Her voice echoed around the canyon.

Jade whacked her arm. "Jesus Christ, keep it down."

"Sorry." Grabbing Sam's hands, she gushed, "I'm so happy for you."

"Thanks, E." Sam shook their clasped hands.

Jade stuck her head between them. "Listen, bring it in."

Sam and Emma brought it in close, wrapping their arms around each other.

"Close your eyes," Jade said. "Let's observe a moment of silence…for Sam's cherry. I'm thinking it got popped in a major way."

Sam playfully pushed Jade. "You make it sound like I was a virgin, for God's sake."

Jade grinned. "Bet you felt like one when she got a hold of you."

Sam felt warmth bloom in her cheeks as she thought about last night.

"Look, it's jammed here today, so let's keep it quiet," Jade said. "Don't need some asshole with a cell phone recording anything."

Sam nodded. "Agreed."

"Okay," Emma said. "Maybe we need code words."

Jade's lip curled. "Since when did you develop such a boner for code words?"

"I don't have a boner. It's so we can speak freely." Emma lowered her voice. "You know, instead of sex, we say something else. It's gotta be a verb though. A verb and a noun." Emma's face scrunched up in thought. "Like talk. Talk will be the word for sex."

Jade raised her eyes to the heavens but nodded in agreement. Sam concurred. "Got it."

Emma continued to whisper. "And we can't say orgasm, so we need another word for that too."

"I can't wait to hear this one," Jade said.

"What are we gonna call it?" Sam asked.

"How about embolism?"

"Embolism? Where did you get that?" Jade asked.

"I watched *Grey's Anatomy* last night. Some dude on the show died from one."

"Great. We have talking and embolisms. Fan-fucking-tastic."

"And we can't say Alex," Emma said, "because people might know her."

"What do you want to call her?" Sam enjoyed this game. She'd enjoy a root canal right now, she was so sky high on love and lust.

Emma put a finger to her lips. "Well, I'm not sure, but something similar, because we don't want to confuse her with someone else."

"Who else would we confuse her with?" Sam asked.

"I don't know. What if we say Lex something? Like Lex Luthor."

"Lex Luthor was in *Superman*," Sam said quietly, still grinning like the village idiot. "I'm pretty sure I wouldn't be having sex with him."

"Ah, but we're not saying sex, we're saying talk." Emma winked.

"Right," Sam said with a return wink. And a point.

Jade cleared her throat. "Okay, shall we walk?"

Emma took the initiative, speaking loudly so all could hear. "So, Sam, how was your weekend?"

Sam inhaled some good old-fashioned LA smog into her lungs. "My weekend, so far, has been spectacular."

"Really? What happened?" Emma asked with all the wrong intonation.

"Well, Lex and I talked. And talked. And talked. We talked all night long. For like eight hours straight." Sam continued walking, but soon realized she was alone and glanced behind her.

Jade and Emma stood several yards away, staring at her with their mouths hanging open. They quickly caught up.

Jade grabbed Sam's arm. "You talked, for eight hours? Straight?"

Sam nodded, still grinning stupidly. "It was a *really* good talk."

Jade was incredulous. "Eight hours straight?"

"Yep."

"Did someone talk more than the other?" Emma asked.

Sam pursed her lips. "No, it was a pretty equal conversation. Although once I had three orga—uh, embolisms in a row. Like one right after the other. So I guess I dominated the conversation for a bit."

"Three embolisms in a row?" Jade cocked an eyebrow. "You're lucky to be alive."

"Who talked first?" Emma asked.

"I did. On the stairs. After we fell over the dog bed. We almost talked on the dog bed."

"Thank God for small favors," Jade said.

"Why on the stairs?" Emma asked.

"Couldn't make it to the bedr—ah, normal, um, talking room."

"Why not?"

"The conversation was too…charged. We needed to finish the talk…right away."

"Did you both talk on the stairs?" Jade asked.

"No, Lex made it to the talking room. After she fell. Taking her shor—taking her shoes off."

"How many things did you fall over?"

Sam counted on her fingers. "Well, we fell down once outside in the yard. We fell over the lounge chair on the patio, then the dog bed, and I think we might've fallen on the stairs. And she fell taking her…shoes off. We were pretty excited to talk."

"Sounds like you lost a few motor skills along the way."

"So your first talk. What did it feel like?" Emma asked.

"It was amazing, I literally felt the earth move. I swear there was shaking, like the stairs shook."

"Oh, we had a small tremor last night. Maybe that's what you felt," Jade said.

"Really?"

"No. Did Lex enjoy when you talked to her? I mean, she has a body built for talking. All hard and lean and shit. Must've felt amazing. For talking."

"Can I just tell you, I've never talked with a body like that before. It was glorious. Those biceps! And she has a six pack." Sam hesitated as two women walked past staring. "Of Pepsi. I put my lips all over…those cans. And her ass…assets. Went over those assets with a fine-tooth comb."

"So, how would you rate Lex's performance as a talker?" Jade asked.

"Off the charts. Best talk I've ever had, without question. Incredibly skillful talker. I want her to talk to me all the time now."

Jade shook her head. "Damn, just when I thought I didn't need panty liners anymore."

"And we talked all over the house too. We talked in every room."

"Every room?" Jade asked.

Sam nodded.

"You talked. In every room," Jade reiterated.

Sam nodded again. "We had pizza and a talk in the kitchen, on the floor. And don't even ask me about the laundry room."

"I'm asking."

"She put me on the washer. To talk. And then she turned it on."

"You weren't in it, were you?" Emma asked, confused.

"No, I was on top of it."

"Why would you turn it, ooh…vibrations. I get it." She winked and shot an imaginary finger gun at Sam.

Jade's brow creased. "Since you were in the laundry room, did you talk dirty? I mean talk about dirty laundry?"

"No. We didn't do that."

Jade lowered her voice. "I dated someone once who was into talking dirty. Damn, she was crude. I felt like I needed a thesaurus by the bed to keep up. There's only so many words to describe your vagina."

"Cooch, hooch, cooter, snatch, box," Emma ticked off.

"Box?" Sam asked.

"All those words are such a turn on, E. Where were you when I needed you? Oh, baby, I need you in my snatch, like right now. Get in my box, please, but after you remove my Amazon order."

Emma's eyes were glued to her phone. "Pooter, beaver, snapper…"

Sam's eyes widened. "Snapper? Yikes."

"Flossie," Emma continued.

"Flossie? Who the hell says flossie?" Jade asked.

"My mom actually called it that when I was young," Emma said. "She would ask if I washed my flossie."

"Did she tell you to floss your teeth, too? I bet that was confusing."

Emma flipped Jade the bird and turned her attention back to Sam. "Well, it sounds like you had a lot of fun talking."

"I'm telling you. It was a hot fucking talk."

"The time she talked to you three times in row. How did that happen exactly?" Jade asked.

"Well, she talked to me the first time, and I was extremely satisfied with the talk, and I was recovering, from such a great talk. She kinda stayed in the same talking position, and talked slower and softer, because you know, sometimes after you talk, you're a little sore, from talking so much."

"I lost track of who's talking to who," Emma said. "There's a shit ton of talking going on here!" The ping of a text distracted her. She read it, then held her phone at arm's length and took a selfie. "Logan's taking me to dinner tonight. It's our two-year-three-month-five-day anniversary."

"Jesus Christ," Jade mumbled. "So, Sam, your triple play. Let's have it, the big embolism. The big E."

Sam continued. "The big E was awesome." She put a hand to her throat. "It was truly a big E."

Emma finished texting. "What did you say?"

"What?"

Emma pulled her shorts down a smidge. "Jesus, I may have gained a couple of pounds, but that's kinda harsh."

"Huh?" Sam asked.

"I don't know. You said E."

"When?"

"You called me big."

"What?" Jade asked.

Emma lost it. "Who the fuck is E?"

"You're fucking E!" Jade shouted back at her.

A horrified Sam grabbed them each by an arm. "Oh my God. Bring it in." Sam nodded hello to a woman who jogged by, a woman Sam recognized. She oversaw new development for one of the networks. "Calm down. You're attracting attention."

Emma's eyes bugged out of her head. "I only gained two pounds. I don't appreciate being called the big E."

"Mother of fucking God, the big E is not you," Jade said.

Sam regretted making it free fuck day, because she'd be rolling in it right now.

"Well, who is it?" Emma demanded.

Placing her mouth next to Emma's ear, Sam softly explained, "Remember, our code word for orgasm was embolism. The big E."

Realization dawned. "Oh. Well, why didn't you say so?"

Jade glared. "We thought we did."

"Well, I was distracted." Emma huffed. "Why don't we just say talk? It's much easier." She smoothed down her tank top and they all continued walking. "So, continue, Sam."

"Well, I never imagined I could talk three times. I've never had multiple talks before. Ever."

"What was the talking technique on that third one?" Jade asked.

Sam waited for a group of chatty teenagers to pass. "Well, the third talk was more, on the inside. She found an interesting... spot. A spot I didn't know worked." Sam raised her eyebrows.

Jade positioned herself in front of Sam, walking backward as Sam walked forward. "She found the spot?"

Sam nodded, and her eyes glossed over. The third one had been a good one.

"Holy fuck." Jade hitched at her crotch. "Remind me not to wear cotton underwear on these hikes." She fell back in line. "I was with this chick once who swore she could find 'the spot.' She must have rooted around down there for hours. Finally, I was like, 'get the fuck on with it.' She must have used a whole tube of KY Jelly. I mean, you only stay moist for so long, am I right?"

"Ouch," Emma said.

"Ouch is an understatement. It was like pulling out a dry tampon. Fucking ouch is right."

Emma waited for the next group of joggers to go by before asking, "Sam, did you use any, uh, appliances?"

Jade jumped right in to add, "Well, we already covered the washing machine. What else were you hoping for, the microwave? Or maybe the hand mixer?"

Now it was Sam's turn to say, "Ouch."

"No, not that kind of appliance." Emma shifted closer. "Don't you guys use, you know, tools?"

Jade put her face in front of Emma's. "You mean like hammers, or screwdrivers?"

"Ouch," Sam mumbled again. This was getting more painful by the minute.

"No. I didn't mean those kinds of tools." Emma's hands circled her hips. "Like, you buckle it on."

"Like a belt?" Jade asked with feigned innocence.

Sam flashed back to the button episode. "Thank God she didn't have a belt on. I could barely operate a button I was so... talkative."

"No, no, like a harness thingy." Emma's frustration mounted as she struggled to think of the correct word. "Like..." Her hands made wider circles around her body.

"A harness thingy? You mean so you can hang from the ceiling? Damn, E, I'd like to be a fly on the wall in your bedroom," Jade said with fake appreciation. "What do you do up there, swinging around in your harness? Is it like, catch me if you can? Do you bang into things? Are you attached to the ceiling fan? Spinning slowly around, while Logan stands on a step stool hoping to get lucky, trying to time it just right. Figuring when to go all in, like double-dutch jump rope?"

Sam and Emma ignored Jade's rambling.

"E, do you mean a strap-on?" Sam asked.

"Right. I couldn't think of the name."

Jade put an arm around Emma. "We need to go shopping. I know a place on Sunset. We're gonna set you up with some appliances and power tools."

They strolled along in silence for a minute. "I've never talked all night," Emma said. "I mean, I might have talked three times tops in one night. And it wasn't like your triple play."

"Me neither." Jade took out her phone.

"Who you calling?" Sam asked.

"Calynn." Jade put the phone to her ear. "Voice mail." She waited for the greeting to finish, then said, "Babe, we gotta talk more," before disconnecting the call. "So if you finally…talked, that means certain things were said."

"Yes."

"Who caved?"

"She said it first."

Emma's brow furrowed in confusion. "Are we still talking about talking?"

"How did she say it?" Jade asked, ignoring Emma.

"Oh, it was so romantic. She *Notting Hill*'ed me."

Emma stopped walking. "Is that some new position for… talking? Cause that's a new one to me. It's not like twerking, is it?"

Jade groaned. "We're not talking about talking anymore."

"What are we talking about now?"

"You know, actual talking." Jade lowered her voice. "With actual words."

Emma turned to Sam, who mouthed back, "I love you."

The hundred-watt lightbulb flashed on. "Oh my God." Emma hugged her. "You guys said it? Awesome! Congrats, Sam!"

"That's what I meant when I said she *Notting Hill*'ed me, E."

"'I'm just a girl standing in front of a boy'? I love that movie," Emma said.

"Me too. Julia is hot. I met her one time at a party. She is so freaking funny," Sam said. "Is it weird to say I miss her? And it's only been like an hour?"

"Who, Julia Roberts?" Jade asked.

Sam whacked her.

Emma put an arm around Sam. "Not weird, girl. You're in love."

"I don't think I've ever been this happy." Sam wanted to raise her hands in the air and yell out her love. But her arms remained by her side. *Someday.*

* * *

Sitting in traffic on the drive home Monday night gave Alex ample time to reflect on the last forty-eight hours. She still found it hard to believe this was all happening. Would she wake up and find out it was all just a dream?

When she finally arrived home, Alex had quite the pep in her step. And it did not go unnoticed by Sophia and Lenna.

"Hey, bouncy, what's up?" Lenna asked.

Alex responded with a hug and kiss.

Lenna pulled back and held Alex at arm's length. "You're glowing. Are you pregnant?"

"Nope." Alex ignored the sarcasm and made a plate of leftovers, which she carried to the living room to eat in front of the TV. She was starving, and nothing hit the spot like Sophia's garlic mashed potatoes. As Alex raised a healthy forkful to her lips, she found Sophia, Lenna, and Yogi sitting on the couch across the way with a bowl of popcorn, staring. Alex swore she'd just left them in the kitchen, but Lenna could be quick as a cat.

"How's Sam?" Lenna asked before putting a handful of popcorn in her mouth.

"Jesus, popcorn?"

"We're gonna watch a movie tonight. So how's Sam?"

"She's awesome."

"How many times did you do it?"

Sophia pushed her shoulder into Lenna's. "How do you know they did it?"

"Look at her. She oozes sexual satisfaction. How many times?"

Alex put the fork down and began counting on one hand, then moved to the other.

"Whoa! Impressive!" Lenna bebopped over, sat next to Alex, and kissed her forehead. Next came the headlock, and an added noogie for good measure.

Alex took the sisterly abuse in stride, smiling and continuing to eat dinner.

The delight on Sophia's face was evident. "We're so happy for the both of you." She came over to join in the hug.

"So how was it?" Lenna asked.

"I'm not gonna kiss and tell." Alex raised a finger in the air. "I will say this. It was probably the most incredible weekend of my life." She kept the finger up and gave it a shake. "And, I will say one more thing. Thanksgiving? Book it, Danno, 'cause I'm not letting this one go."

Lenna whooped and high-fived both Alex and Sophia.

They all gave a start when the doorbell rang. Yogi began barking excitedly.

"Who could that be?" Lenna jumped up to answer the door. She was back in a few seconds. "Alex, it's for you."

Alex shrugged and hustled to the foyer, where she stopped short, mouth dropping open in surprise. The woman of her dreams stood before her.

"Holy shit!" She hugged Sam and lifted her off the ground. "You look hot. What are you doing here?"

Sam's grin stretched from ear to ear. "I thought I would pop in, you know, say hi."

They kissed long and hard.

"I can't believe you drove all the way here." Alex caressed Sam's cheek. "I love you."

Sam's eyes filled. "I love you, too. And I kinda missed you, so really, I had no choice."

"I feel like I haven't seen you for days, and it's kinda pathetic, because it's only been hours."

"Well, we're both pathetic."

"You're staying over, right? Did you bring your PJs?" Alex asked with raised eyebrows, pointing to Sam's backpack.

"Absolutely."

"Yummy. My bedroom is getting christened tonight! C'mon in."

Sam walked into the living room and gave Sophia a hug, and they all sat and chatted for an hour. In that time span, the photo albums came out, and Alex spent most of the hour groaning over pictures from her youth.

Lenna pointed at sixteen-year-old Alex. "Here you go, Sam, little Miss Hearteyes. And she thinks we're dorks."

Sam laughed at the picture of gawky Alex. "Honey, what's the matter with your hair?"

Alex peered over Sam's shoulder. "Well, it was a little frizzy back then." She didn't mind all the humiliation, really. Sam was here, and soon she'd be taking off her PJs.

Sophia nudged Lenna. "We're gonna head upstairs. Sam, great seeing you. I expect you'll be around a lot now."

They both hugged Sam and disappeared.

Sam turned to Alex. "What are we gonna do now?"

"Hm, I don't know. We could look at more pictures." Alex slowly pushed Sam onto her back, and began to play with her lips. "Or watch a movie." Alex gently nibbled on Sam's neck. And a wayward hand wandered under Sam's shirt and began teasing pebbled nipples.

Sam gasped. "Let's continue this in your bedroom."

Alex laughed and stood, throwing Sam's overnight bag over her shoulder. She pulled Sam off the couch and they headed for the stairs. When they arrived at the bottom step, she offered Sam her back.

"Oh no, let me." Sam turned. "Hop aboard."

"You're kidding, right?" Alex asked.

"No, I'm serious."

"We tried this the other day. You dropped me."

"Yeah, but I've been working out. I'm stronger now."

"In two days?"

"C'mon, this is different. Last time you threw yourself at me."

"Threw myself? You told me to jump."

"Get on, let's go."

"Okay, ready?" Alex gingerly hopped onto Sam's back.

"This is easy. I've got you." Sam took the first step and teetered.

"You okay, sport?" Alex asked.

"Phew, yeah. How much further?"

"To the second step? About six inches."

"No smartass, to the third step."

Alex laughed. "Put me down before you hurt yourself."

"I can do this...oh God...okay...success!" Sam boasted as she reached the second step.

"Congratulations. Only twelve more to go."

"Jesus Christ, how did you do this?"

"And you wondered why my legs were shot on Sunday morning."

Sam wheezed as she tried for another step. "I have a newfound appreciation for your stamina. Okay, I'm done. You're the official piggybacker in this relationship." She let go of Alex's legs.

Alex offered her back to Sam, who hopped aboard, and up the stairs they went. When they reached the doorway to the bedroom, Sam slid off. Alex bowed, ushering Sam into the room.

"Oh crap, I have to let Yogi out. Here's your bag, and there's the bathroom. I'll be right back."

When Alex made it back upstairs to the bedroom, she found Sam perusing the family pictures on the bookshelf. In her PJs. Alex softly closed the door. "Ah, the PJs."

Sam put a hand over her heart. "Well, I didn't wanna deny you the pleasure of taking them off."

Alex walked slowly across the room, eyes roaming over Sam, drinking in every inch. When they stood toe to toe, Alex gently caressed Sam's cheek, then dipped her head down to capture Sam's lips while one hand undid the top button of the PJs. Her mouth sank down and found the newly revealed skin, kissing it gently. Alex brought her lips back to Sam's as her eager fingers flicked open the next button, and then her mouth sought creamier pastures again as each opened button exposed more and more soft, silky flesh. When the last button came undone, Alex straightened and pushed the top off Sam's shoulders.

Sam's breathing became erratic. "How far away is their bedroom?"

"At the end of the hallway." Alex's lips and tongue headed south, leaving a hot, wet trail down Sam's body.

"I guess I have to be quiet."

"Mmm," was all Alex could manage as she sank to her knees and removed the rest of Sam's PJs.

CHAPTER TWENTY-THREE

The following weekend, Alex stood at the stove making breakfast. "Who all's coming?" She placed a western omelet on Sam's plate.

"Most of the people who were at Lenna's party. Wow, this smells delicious. Did you bring your suit? It would be nice to ogle you in a bikini again."

"I did." Alex refilled both their coffee mugs. "And is ogling okay around this group?"

"Yes. Everyone who's coming is aware of the situation. Ogle away." Sam took a bite of the omelet and her eyelashes fluttered. "This is heavenly."

"What about PDA? Do I have to behave myself?" Alex snapped a piece of bacon in half, holding a piece to Sam's lips.

Sam opened her mouth and took the offered bacon, kissing Alex's fingers before chewing. "No. Misbehave away."

"And why are we having this party?"

"Jade is calling it our 'Look who finally had sex' party."

Alex laughed. "Okay."

By three thirty, the whole gang was relaxing by the pool.

Sophia gazed around in awe. "Sam, your backyard is incredible! Did Alex design all this?"

"She did." Sam proudly wrapped an arm around Alex's waist.

"How am I gonna replace you if this writing career of yours takes off?" Lenna asked.

Sophia nudged a shoulder into hers. "If? You mean when. We all need to stay positive."

"Well, *when* my writing career takes off," Alex nodded at Sophia, "I doubt I'll be an overnight sensation. I won't be quitting right away."

Lenna's mouth turned down at the corners. "I'll miss having you around."

Alex playfully punched her in the arm. "Are you getting sentimental? Besides, I'll still be living with you, unless Sam needs a live-in landscaper at some point." She shot Sam a questioning glance.

"Oh, I'm sure I'll need one at some point. Lenna, make it happen."

"Alex, move out!" Lenna shouted.

They all laughed.

A few minutes later, Zach stood and cleared his throat. "If I could have everyone's attention."

Jade and Calynn began pouring champagne into plastic glasses and handing them out.

Alex leaned into Sam's ear. "Wow. Was us having sex that big of a deal?"

"I hope not."

After everyone had a glass, Jade stood beside Zach.

He nudged her. "Do you wanna announce it?"

"Hell yes!" Jade raised her glass. "Hear ye, hear ye!"

Sam cringed. "Jesus, is this really happening?" she whispered to Alex.

"I guess they're really excited for us."

When all eyes were on Jade, she continued, "Please raise your glasses. I have a very special announcement." She paused and looked around. "For the last three weeks, Zach and I have been hammering out a contract."

"Am I signing a prenup?" Alex asked Sam quietly.

Sam snickered. "Not that I know of."

Jade continued, "This contract is for our very own…Alex Novato." She raised her glass in Alex's direction. "Alex, you're being fucking published!"

Alex's mouth dropped open. "What?"

It took a few beats for everyone to digest the information. When it sank in, the gang screamed with excitement.

"Holy shit!" Sam shrieked and jumped into her arms.

Alex caught her, dropping her glass into the pool in the process.

Lenna and Sophia came up and wrapped their arms around Sam and Alex.

Jade pushed the foursome into the pool. Emma shoved Jade in, Calynn returned the favor, and soon everyone was splashing around and dunking each other.

More bottles were popped, and the champagne flowed freely.

Jade jumped on Alex's back, and raised a fist in the air. "I kept that shit quiet for three damn weeks!"

The gang was impressed with Jade and her weeks-long bout with discretion.

Emma clapped. "You should get an award."

"I guess there's a first time for everything." Riley fist-bumped Jade.

"You actually kept a secret? I don't believe it," Sam said.

"Believe it, Sami. I mean, it was a struggle, but I did it."

The next toast was for Jade, unlikely keeper of secrets.

Alex grabbed Sam and kissed her long and hard. When she pulled back, her eyes were filled with joyous tears. "I can't believe this is happening. I would've never gotten here without you."

"I think it would've happened someday." Sam wrapped her arms around Alex's neck. "My girlfriend. The published author. Congratulations, baby."

"Thank you, beautiful. Thank you for everything."

"It was my pleasure. And speaking of thanks, let's be thankful they weren't toasting our sex life. 'Cause that would've been weird. Even for my idiot friends."

* * *

The sun sank low on the horizon, and after many beers and much food, most of the gang relaxed on lounge chairs around the firepit.

Emma, the tipsiest of the bunch, had some advice for the new couple. "Sam, now that you guys are sexually active, you should be careful what you do in your backyard."

"What do you mean?" Sam asked. Her arms were wrapped around Alex, who lay in front of her on the chaise. The blanket they were snuggled up under hid their wayward hands.

"Well, I heard the paparazzi use drones now, with cameras, to get pictures of celebrities in compromising positions."

Riley, currently second place on the tipsy scale, chimed in, "I heard that too."

"I've never heard that," Jade said.

Emma crossed her arms. "*The National Enquirer* did a story on it last week. There were pictures and everything. They caught Angelina Jolie naked by her pool. At least, it kinda looked like her. It was a little fuzzy."

Riley pointed at Emma. "I saw it too, but I thought it looked like you."

"What? Oh, no shit?" Emma bit her bottom lip, a worried expression on her face.

Jade cackled. "It was probably you, E!"

"Very funny." Emma stuck her tongue out at Jade, then turned back to Sam. "I think you can wear, like, aluminum foil on your head. It kinda acts as a barrier, and the camera can't penetrate it."

Jade and Calynn stared at Emma with open mouths and raised brows.

"Oh boy." Sam giggled into Alex's ear. "Here we go."

"What now?" Jade asked.

"Yeah, I read it somewhere," Emma said.

"So is that what you do, E? Walk around your backyard with a tinfoil hat on your head?" Jade asked.

"I don't know. Maybe?"

Jade looked at Calynn. "Honey, I don't even have a retort."

"Give it a minute."

The minute took a second. "You wear a tinfoil hat on your head, around your backyard, in the middle of the day? In the sun? You know you cook on aluminum foil, right? So you're probably frying the shit out of your brain. Which would explain a lot."

Calynn spoke up. "Actually, E, you're confusing the tinfoil hat thing. Some people believe it blocks aliens from penetrating your brain."

A drunken Emma ruminated over this new intel for a good six seconds. "Oh, right, right. That's what it was. Never mind. I had a dream once I was kidnapped by aliens."

"And the hits keep coming," Sam mumbled in Alex's ear.

"They were probably attracted to your hat," Jade said. "Bright, shiny objects and all. Why bother with a cornfield when there's Emma in a tinfoil hat? It probably actually happened."

Emma paused. "Really? No. The dream was pretty vivid, though." She absently touched her head, probably hoping to find a tinfoil hat.

Lenna and Sophia came over to the fire, interrupting the conversation. They plopped down on a lounge chair together.

"We're taking a poll on best slow songs to dance to," Sophia said.

"Bee Gees!" Alex put a fist in the air. "To Love Somebody."

"Yeah! I love the Bee Gees!" Emma yelled. She took a running jump onto Sam and Alex's lounge chair, landing hard and knocking the wind out of them.

Jade was incredulous. "What the hell, PS10?"

"I kinda love them too," Sam admitted.

Emma snuggled in with Sam and Alex. "Sam and I are closet Bee Gees fans. We listen when you're not around, Jade." She abruptly stood and plugged her phone into the speakers. The opening notes to the song started to play. "Who's gonna dance with me?"

Alex stood. "E, I will not leave a fellow Bee Gees lover hanging."

They slow danced and sang along. Soon others joined them on the makeshift dance floor.

Sam recorded on her phone. "You guys are tone deaf!"

Yogi barked and scooted around the swaying couples.

Jade, who had disappeared briefly, returned and placed a tinfoil hat on Emma's head. "Keeping you safe, girl. Keeping you safe." Jade patted her ass.

Logan tapped Alex on the shoulder, wanting to cut in. "Why are you wearing a tinfoil hat, babe?" he asked, taking Emma into his arms.

"Because Jade loves me, and she doesn't want me kidnapped by aliens."

Alex approached Sam with a slight bow. "May I have this dance?"

Sam jumped to her feet and slid into Alex's arms. Almost everyone was singing along now.

Jade tapped away on her phone. "Jesus Christ, this song is from 1967. I'm embarrassed for all of you."

Calynn pulled Jade onto the dance floor. And then, to Jade's horror, started singing.

"Et tu, babe?" Jade asked softly.

"It's a classic, babe."

* * *

After their guests left, Sam and Alex soaked in a hot bubble bath together. Sam had her back against the tub and Alex lay in front of her. Sam's wayward hands had access to all sorts of erogenous zones.

Alex sighed with contentment and turned so they were facing each other. "I can't believe the book is getting published."

Sam stroked a hand across Alex's breasts. "I know. It's incredible."

"Did you hear anything more about the script?"

"The director they want isn't available, so everything is on hold for now."

"That's good. Maybe by the time they're ready to go, the whole Facebook thing will be a distant memory."

"Exactly." Sam captured Alex's lips with her own. Soon the kiss deepened, and Sam's fingers dipped toward Alex's hip bone.

"Oh." Alex's breath hitched as Sam's fingers traveled lower still.

Sam's tongue drove into Alex's mouth. It wasn't long before Alex was clutching at the back of her neck, hips thrusting forward as her orgasm began.

When it ended, she curled into Sam's chest, eyes sleepy with satisfaction. "I'm so happy."

"Me too."

"And it's because of you."

Sam kissed her head.

"I never felt like this before." Alex gazed into Sam's eyes. "Never."

Sam's own eyes filled with moisture. She was only human, and a small part of her had wondered how she would measure up to Madison.

"I know we haven't been together long, but…" Alex paused for a moment. "It feels so right." She grabbed Sam's hand and kissed it. "I wish I could find the words to describe it. I'm probably not doing a good job. Which is kinda silly since I'm a writer and words are my thing." Alex smiled. "Honey, are you crying?"

Sam nodded. "I can't help it. I'm a big mush." She wiped at teary eyes.

Alex pulled her down for a kiss. "I love the fact you're a big mush."

They cuddled in silence for a few minutes.

Sam sighed. "My dad used to read me a book when I was young. I made him read it to me every night."

"What was it?"

"*Guess How Much I Love You.* It was about two rabbits, little nut-brown hare and big nut-brown hare. And the little one started out by saying, 'I love you this much,' and stretching his arms out. And the big one said the same thing, stretching his arms out. And they kept going on and on, trying to top each other. Then big nut-brown hare said something like, 'I love you across the river and over the hills.' And the little one cooed, 'That's very far.' And not to be outdone, the little one gushed, 'I love you right up to the moon,' and fell asleep. The big hare whispered to him while he slept, 'I love you right up to the moon and back.'"

Sam smiled at Alex. "And that's how much I love you, right up to the moon and back."

"That's very far."

Sam kissed her head. "It is." She ran her hands down Alex's arms. "I wanna shout it out to everybody. I hate that I can't do that."

"It's okay. The people who care about us know, and that's all that matters."

"How did I end up with such a great girlfriend?"

"Guess you're just lucky."

Sam buried her nose in Alex's hair. "We're starting to prune. We should probably get out."

"I can't move right now. I'm too content."

Sam smiled. "The bed's calling us."

"But I'm so comfortable."

"C'mon, BG, let's go to bed," Sam whispered. "I still have things I wanna do to you, and it's hard in a bathtub."

"I'm up."

CHAPTER TWENTY-FOUR

Six months later

"You're making me dizzy." Sam sat at the kitchen counter reading while Alex paced back and forth.

"The review should be posted soon, don't you think?"

"Zach will tell you when it's done. Relax."

"I can't." Alex looped her arms around Sam's neck and kissed her cheek. "What are you reading?"

"My script for this week."

They both jumped when the front gate buzzed.

"Are you expecting someone?" Sam asked.

"Me? I'm not even here." Alex kissed Sam's ear. "I'm the invisible lover, remember?"

"Like *Ghost*, only better."

Alex grinned. "Maybe it's our goofy medium, aka Whoopi Goldberg."

Sam checked her phone, which was linked to the security camera outside. "Oh, it's Goofy all right. Goofy One and Goofy Two." She walked over to the intercom. "Yes?"

"You bitches clothed?" Emma shouted.

"Jesus Christ, speak into the microphone," Jade said. "And stop yelling. They may be naked, but they're not deaf."

"I always just yell at the gate. Where's the mic?"

"It's by the camera."

Sam cleared her throat. "Ahem."

Emma smiled into the camera. "Hi Sam! Jade won't let us use the code because she thinks you may be having an embolism." She giggled.

Jade leaned into view. "Yeah, get out of bed and open the gate. And get dressed, for God's sake. Well, Sam, get dressed. Alex, as you were."

"We are dressed, and we're not in bed, jackasses." Sam buzzed the gate open and unlocked the front door.

Jade and Emma barreled in moments later.

"Why aren't you in bed? Bored with each other already?" Jade asked.

Sam ignored the question. "To what do we owe the pleasure of this visit?"

"Moral support. Hey, PS10, how are you doing?" Jade sauntered over to Alex and gave her a hug and a kiss. "We thought we'd wait for the review with you. What's for lunch? We're hungry."

Alex blew out a deep breath. "Good. I need the distraction. I'll make grilled cheeses."

Sam opened her laptop. "Let's see what's happening in the world today, shall we? Hm. The new Jocelyn Brown movie opens tonight."

Jade grabbed some chips from the cabinet. "I heard it's great. She'll probably win another Oscar."

Sam clicked on the local news section and gasped. "Oh my God!"

Emma jumped up from her seat and peered at the screen. "What? I don't see anything but garage sales. Are you looking for more pillows?"

Alex turned the stovetop on. "Babe, more pillows?"

"Jesus Christ. No more pillows!" Jade said.

"I'm not looking for pillows. It's baby goats. Honey, baby goats." She turned the laptop toward Alex.

"Oh, they're cute. I like the brown one."

"That's Maynard. The black one is Maxwell. They need a home."

"Why do they need a home?" Alex asked.

"I don't know. All it says is free to a good home. They're not far from us. We should adopt them."

"Baby doll, you don't have the property for baby goats. Someday, you can get a big farm in the country and get as many goats as you want, but you can't do it right now."

Emma agreed. "Sam, you can't have baby goats. I think it's against the law or something."

"Those things will eat your cell phone if you're not careful," Jade said.

"I want them." Her pleading eyes had no effect, and her shoulders sagged with disappointment. "You guys are killjoys."

Emma thrust her chest out. "I have news."

"You're pregnant," Jade said.

"No. I just got a part in a movie."

"That's great, E!" Sam said. "What's the movie?"

"*Femme Fatale*. I'm going to play the lesbian love interest to the lead actress."

"Is there a sex scene?" Jade asked.

"Yeah. A couple of them, and they're hot. At least, in the script they were hot."

"What are you gonna do to prepare for it?"

"What do you mean?"

"I mean, are you gonna sleep with a woman to prepare for the part? For research purposes."

"I don't think so."

"You have to make it authentic. Lesbians can sense a fake orgasm a mile away."

"It's not a porno. I'm gonna have to fake it."

"Well, they can tell when you fake a fake orgasm."

Emma looked to Sam for confirmation. "Really?"

Sam played along. "Lesbian love scenes can be tricky."

Jade put an arm around Emma. "E, if you pull this off, you'll be a dyke icon forever. Every con you go to, they'll be lining up. For the rest of your life."

Emma chewed on her bottom lip. "So you think I should sleep with a woman? For research purposes?"

"Absolutely," Jade said. "Leave it to me. I'll find you someone. Now, do you know what to do down there?"

"I...I guess."

"You don't sound too sure."

"I mean, there's not a lot going on down there."

"There's plenty going on down there. Listen," Jade pointed, "you gotta be willing to go all-in. You gotta commit. Don't think you're gonna get away with just finger fucking."

Emma took a quick peek at her fingers, while Alex and Sam coughed to cover up their giggles.

"That's amateur hour right there. You gotta be willing to go downtown, is all I'm saying. And sometimes it ain't pretty downtown. Sometimes it's a little wild and woolly. Like a Chia Pet. You gotta be willing to put your goggles on, fire up the weedwhacker, and go hunting for things."

Emma sagged against the countertop. "Hunt for things?"

"And you might wanna take your ring off before you try anything. You don't wanna lose it, especially if you're going down on some Chia Pet. How you gonna explain that to Logan? 'Honey, the fifty-thousand-dollar rock you bought me is lost in some girl's cooter.'"

Emma's mouth hung open.

"Oh. And when you're done downtown, do yourself and your hypothetical lover a favor. Do a little wipe off before you come back upstairs."

"Huh?"

"Do a little cleanup." Jade waved two fingers in front of her chin. "Personally, I do it, and I prefer my partner do it, too."

Emma's forehead creased in confusion. "You mean, like with a Wet One or something?"

Jade groaned. "I don't know, E. I don't think you can do it."

Emma's chin jutted out. "I'm an actress. I can do anything."

"Oh, you'll act your way through it? Okay. Well, nobody's gonna yell 'cut' while you're down there doing something wrong. I mean, you may get a tap on the head. If you get that, you need to take your incompetence back to the other team."

Emma brooded.

Jade seemed to sense her hesitation. "Are you taking notes? You should be writing all this down."

Emma reached for her purse. "Let me get my phone."

Jade's expression turned solemn. "One more thing."

Emma pulled her phone out, fingers poised and ready.

"You may have to motorboat some nips before you make it downtown. It's a must in every lesbian sex scene."

"Motorboating? That seems like such a guy thing."

Sam struggled to keep from laughing.

"You wanna be a dyke icon or not?" Jade asked.

"Yeah."

"Then you better learn how to do it. Practice on something." Jade's eyes came to rest on Sam's ample cleavage. "Practice on Sam."

Emma took a sideways glance at Sam's chest, prompting Sam to inadvertently put an arm over her breasts. "She's not practicing on me."

"I'm not practicing on Sam."

Jade wiggled her eyebrows and pointed to her own A cups.

Phones dinged simultaneously, interrupting Jade's 'How to Become a Lesbian in Five Minutes' tutorial.

"Oh shit, the review's done," Sam said.

"Crap." Alex buried her face in Sam's neck. "Somebody read it."

Jade cleared her throat. "Okay, ready? Here we go. 'Alex Novato may be the most exciting new name in sci-fi. Her debut novel, *The Seekers*, hits the ground running and never stops. This first-time author has created a dark world filled with intelligent dialogue and compelling characters. The female main character, Taryn Kros, is a force to be reckoned with. The pacing of the novel is fantastic, and the moral and political implications of the choices Taryn must make resonate deeply. This is the first book of a trilogy and deserves a spot on your bookshelf next to the likes of Pierce Brown, Hugh Howey, and Margaret Atwood. A must-read for any science fiction fan.'"

Jade took a breath. "Wow."

Sam squealed with joy and jumped into Alex's arms. "See, baby? I told you it would be okay."

Alex twirled her around. "Holy shit, I can't believe it!"

Jade high-fived everyone. "Let's celebrate! And it just so happens I brought bubbly with me." She pulled a bottle from her bag and held it aloft.

"You just *happened* to have champagne?" Sam asked.

"I was being all positive and shit."

Alex took the bottle, popped the cork, and poured a glass for each. "Here's to a successful book." They all raised their glasses and cheered.

Jade put an arm around Alex. "I stopped by the bookstore near Monette's last week, to lay the groundwork for a possible book signing. They were excited to do something. You know, local girl makes good. The timing will be perfect now that we have a good review under our belt. I'll get back with them and set something up. Probably in the next two weeks."

Alex nodded. "Sounds good. And Monette will want to celebrate with us too. We could move from the bookstore to the bar."

Sam's eyes twinkled with excitement. "Yeah! Another party at the bar."

Jade quickly put the kibosh on that idea. "Calm down, Princess Bride. I think you've reached your quota for gay bar hopping."

Sam's face fell. "Oh c'mon." She turned hopeful eyes toward Alex. "Honey, you said a lot of straight people go to Monette's."

Alex nodded. "True, they do. But I agree with Jade. It's probably not a good idea. The Facebook thing finally died down. Let's not push our luck."

"But I have to go. I can't let you celebrate without me."

"Hon, I won't stay long, I promise."

"I'll keep you company, Sam," Emma said. "We'll watch a bunch of sappy romantic movies and listen to the Bee Gees."

"Don't forget *The Brady Bunch*," Jade said. "I hear Jan's gay. Maybe you can pick up some pointers."

While the conversation swirled around her, the wheels in Sam's head turned. There was no way on earth she was missing this party. She nibbled on her lip as an idea hatched.

Sam had a plan.

CHAPTER TWENTY-FIVE

The advertising they'd done for the signing must have worked, because a haphazard line had formed at the front of the bookstore and snaked outside. Alex fidgeted in her chair.

"Look at all those people. Do you see it?" Jade asked.

"I see it. I can't believe it's for me, though."

"Oh, it's for you, girlfriend." Michelle, the publisher's marketing director, smiled as she helped Alex arrange business cards, pens, and other trinkets related to the book.

The cashier up front had a stack of books, and red ropes lined the way to Alex.

"Water's in this cooler. If you need anything else, give me a shout." Michelle gave Alex's shoulders an affectionate squeeze. She was an attractive woman, with close-cropped dark hair and a keen sense of style. It was obvious from her furtive glances that she was digging Alex.

Alex barely noticed her. That ship had sailed long ago. "I will, thanks."

Jade took the seat next to Alex. "I'll be right here with you. You need anything else before we start?"

"Nope, I'm good." She tried to relax by taking some deep breaths.

Michelle walked to the front of the store and addressed the crowd. "Ladies and gentlemen, for those of you here for the book signing, welcome, and thank you for coming. What we're going to do is have you form a line at the first checkout counter. After buying your book, follow the ropes back to our soon-to-be famous local author, Alex Novato."

People began falling into line.

"Didn't expect this many right away." Jade's voice was barely above a whisper.

"Neither did I," Alex said. And then in the next breath, "Oh boy."

"What?"

"Lots of familiar faces."

"What does that mean?" Jade asked.

Alex leaned into Jade's ear, trying not to move her mouth. "Remember the three-way?"

It was Jade's turn to lean into Alex's ear. "No shit? Who?"

Alex leaned back in toward Jade. "The couple in front of the cashier. Short blonde with the tall blonde."

Jade faced forward, lips barely moving. "It was a couple?"

"Yep. Wanted to spice up their sex life," Alex whispered.

"Well, that's spicy all right. At least they're smiling."

"Shit, names, names…" Alex mumbled.

The two women approached the table. "Hey, Alex. So good to see you again."

"You too. How are you ladies?"

"We're great. Super excited to read your book."

"Well, thank you for buying it. Stacie, right? And Susan?" A shot in the dark.

"Yes."

Score! Alex signed the book and passed it back, breathing a sigh of relief.

Both women grinned wildly. "Maybe we'll catch you at the bar later?"

"Yeah, sure." As the couple walked away, Alex spotted another familiar face. "Oh boy."

Jade put a hand over her mouth. "Now what?"

Alex reached for a bottle of water and pretended to take a sip, effectively hiding her lips. "She liked handcuffs."

Jade's eyes widened with interest and she swayed to the side to get a better look at the line. "Who?"

"Long blond hair, red shirt."

Jade scratched an imaginary itch on her top lip. "I'm sensing a pattern here. Got a thing for blondes, do we?"

Alex moved her lips close to Jade's ear as the woman in red approached. "I don't remember her name."

"Hi, Alex. Wow, I can't believe you wrote a book," the woman said.

"Thank you so much for buying it."

"Who are we making it out to?" Jade's voice was sweet and innocent.

"Karen. Alex knows me."

"Of course she does. I was just asking." Jade smiled at her suggestively.

When Karen moved off, there was a lull in the line. Alex murmured into Jade's ear, "Freaking genius, you."

"That's my job. I will always have your back. And if it means flirting with every woman to get their name, so be it. And if she hits on me later, I expect you to have *my* back."

"I will, girl." Alex glanced at the front door. "Oh boy."

Jade panicked. "Another one?"

Alex pressed her lips together in a straight line.

"Jesus Christ. Is there anyone you haven't slept with?"

"Besides you?"

"I guess plastering your poster all over the gayborhood wasn't such a bright idea."

"I don't know. They're all buying books."

After an hour of signing, Alex flexed her hand and wiggled her fingers. Books were flying off the shelf. Nobody could have anticipated this kind of response. She couldn't wait to share it with Sam.

Jade checked the line before the next patron approached. Her face went slack. "Oh my fucking God."

"What?" Alex asked, right before the next customer in line handed Alex his book.

Jade coughed and covered her mouth. "Tweedledee and Tweedledum are in line."

Alex nodded thanks to the man in front of her and passed his signed book across the table to him. When the gentleman walked off, Alex sat back and pretended to stretch, an arm shielding her mouth. "Who?"

Jade nodded in the direction of the two "men" in line.

Alex spotted them and did a double take. "Oh my fucking God is right."

It was Sam and Emma. In drag.

Jade hissed her annoyance. "This is what happens when those two morons spend too much time together."

Alex giggled at the sight.

Sam had a big, bushy, blond mustache stuck to her upper lip, and some sort of awful wig, like a pompadour. She wore old jeans and a denim jacket over a Tractor Supply Company T-shirt. A pair of heavy-duty work boots completed the outfit.

Emma sported a black goatee and big black sideburns, Ray-Bans, black jeans, black biker boots, a long-sleeved white shirt, and a leather vest. She also wore a Harley-Davidson baseball hat with a ponytail sprouting from the back.

They approached the cashier and bought books.

"Shit, they're almost here," Alex whispered, horrified. "It's like the Village People gone bad."

"More like the Village Rednecks."

The pair made their way to the table. "Hey, little lady," the blonde drawled.

"Aaand, they're southern," Jade said.

"My name is Carl, and this here is Othello, and we think you are just the cutest." Carl sat on the table, leering at Alex.

Alex stared stupidly, trying not to laugh.

"Here now, how about you give us an aut-o-graph." Othello pushed both books toward her.

Alex put her head down and signed Carl's book, chewing on her lip to stifle the laughter. She scrawled, *Carl, I'd totally switch sides for you. Call me, Alex.*

Carl handed his phone to Jade. "Now, little lady, would you mind taking a picture?"

Carl ambled around the table and jerked Alex to her feet for a photo op.

Alex jumped as Othello slapped her ass. She jumped again as Carl's hand wandered dangerously close to the zipper on her pants.

"Well, you're all jittery like a filly, now, aren't you?" Carl crooned. "You need to be broke in, is what I'm thinking." Now it was Carl's turn to slap her ass.

Alex tried so hard not to laugh, but it was a losing battle.

Jade stood to take the photo, muttering under her breath. After she snapped the picture, Othello made his way back around the table.

Jade's eyes bugged out when she looked down at his bulging crotch. "Whatcha got there, partner? Is that a banana in your pants, or are you happy to see me?"

"You like it, honey? 'Cause I might be happy to see you." Othello licked his lips.

"Actually, no, I'm incredibly nauseated." Jade grabbed Othello by the arm, escorting him away from the table. "Now don't you knock anything over with that thing."

Carl gave one last wink to Alex. "Thank you, lovely lady. I'll be sure to get started on this book right quick. Or maybe I could interest you in some bedtime storytellin'."

"Maybe you should give me a call later, handsome," Alex replied.

"Don't mind if I do." Carl gave a short wave and hustled to join Jade and Othello.

* * *

Carl put an arm around Jade when he caught up to them. "Thank you for your hospitality, pretty lady."

"Please shut up," Jade said. To her ears, their southern drawls were like nails down a chalkboard. She led them to the back stockroom, away from the crowd. "What are you two freak boxes doing?"

Both girls guffawed.

"You should have seen your face!" Emma grabbed her sides, howling.

Sam caught her breath from the belly laughs. "Did you shit a brick? 'Cause it looked like you shit a literal brick. *And*, we're going to the bar, is what we're doing."

"In that?" Jade asked, pointing to their outfits.

"Why not? It's perfect. Nobody will recognize us."

Jade shook her head and closed her eyes.

"C'mon, it's pretty funny," Sam said. "Right, little lady?" She put an arm around Jade and bumped a hip into her.

"Just be careful. And E, what is in your pants?"

Emma clutched at her crotch. "This happens to be the prosthetic penis from *Boogie Nights*. Logan knew a guy and asked if we could borrow it."

Sam threw her shoulders back, a haughty look on her face. "It has a name."

Jade's lip curled in disgust. "You're kidding."

Emma shook her head. "Nope. It's called Big Daddy. Impressive, huh?"

"It looks like a watermelon."

Emma playfully thrust her hips back and forth. "I think it's kinda sexy."

"It looks like it was designed for Andre the Giant. You know you're only five-four, right? That thing is taller than you." Jade glanced down at Sam's pants. "And where's yours?"

"It's there."

"Where?"

"Here." Sam grabbed at her zipper.

Jade peered at Sam's crotch. Nothing remotely resembling a sexy bulge was visible. "What's in there, a peanut?"

"No! It's tube socks."

"With or without the stripe?"

"With, of course."

"What color?"

"Orange."

Jade turned her attention back to Emma and shook her head in disgust.

Emma waved a hand dismissively. "Nobody will even notice." She thrust her hips back and forth again.

Jade was sure Big Daddy would be attracting all the wrong attention. "Whatever you do, keep it away from me."

"I wanna see Alex. Can't she come back here?" Sam asked.

"She's busy. We'll see you at the bar. Now go, before you scare all the gays and lesbians away."

"How do you know we're not gay?" Emma asked. "Maybe we're gay men."

"No self-respecting gay man would be caught dead in those outfits. Unless it was Halloween. Now take Big Daddy and get the hell out of here. Go, go." Jade shooed them away.

CHAPTER TWENTY-SIX

Sam spotted Sophia at the bar talking to Monette as soon as they walked in. She swaggered over and plopped herself down on the stool next to her.

"Why, hello, beautiful lady," she said in her southern male drawl.

Sophia barely glanced at her. "Hi. I'm sorry, I'm busy right now." Sophia frowned at Monette.

Monette stared with narrowed eyes and was rewarded with a quick smile. She continued staring and finally recognized Sam. "Holy shit." She cackled. "What are you drinking, my good man?"

"Beer for me, and whatever this lovely lady wants."

Sophia turned toward Sam with annoyance. "I'm sorry, but I'm married." When she turned back, Monette giggled. "What's so funny?"

Sam snorted. Sophia clearly did not get the joke.

Sam offered a hand. "I'm Carl, ma'am, pleasure to meet you."

Sophia gazed into Carl's eyes and finally recognized Sam. "Oh my God!" she shrieked, dissolving into a fit of laughter. "What are you doing here? I thought you were forbidden to come."

"Well, I wasn't gonna miss this. So we raided the props room at work."

"We?"

Sam pointed at Emma, who sat on the other side of Sophia. "Meet Othello."

Sophia turned to the attractive, shortish man sitting next to her.

"How you doin'?" Emma's eyebrows danced up and down as she did her best Joey from *Friends* impersonation.

Sophia cackled again. "You two are nuts."

From across the room, Lenna spotted them and stormed over to tap Sam on the shoulder. "May I help you? Babe, are these two bothering you?"

"Honey, calm down." She reached for Lenna's arm to pull her close. "It's Sam and Emma."

Lenna pulled back and peered at Sam. "Holy fuck. I almost threw you down for hitting on my woman!" Lenna gave her the once-over. "Nice digs. You look like you fell off a backhoe."

Sam snickered and hugged her. "I'll take that as a compliment."

Next Lenna motioned to Emma. "Come here, you." As Emma stood to say hello, Lenna's eyes landed on her crotch. "Jesus, what do you got in there?" She seized a handful of prosthesis. "We have some gay men here tonight, so you might wanna keep your back against the wall, if you know what I mean." She shook Emma's fake junk. "Nice goatee, by the way. You look kinda sexy."

Emma blushed. "Thanks."

"Where's Alex?" Lenna asked.

"She's not here yet," Sam said. "Still signing books."

"Did she see you?"

"Oh yeah."

"Did she piss her pants?"

Sam blew out a disappointed breath. "I don't know. I haven't had a chance to talk to her. Jade tossed us out."

"You two are crazy." Lenna ordered a beer from Monette.

Emma came over to Sam and whispered, "I have to pee."

"What?" Sam pulled back. "Now?"

Emma nodded.

Sam put her hands on her hips. "Well, I guess you'll have to use the men's room."

"You have to come with me," Emma begged. "I can't go alone."

Sam took stock of the clientele at the bar. It was a mixed crowd tonight, both gay and straight, women and men. "Okay, let's go."

Both made their way to the restrooms. When they stood in front of the men's door, Sam asked, "Ready?"

Emma took a deep breath and nodded.

When they walked in it was deserted, and they both breathed a sigh of relief. There were two stalls and four urinals.

A nervous Emma latched onto Sam. "Come in with me."

"Oh Jesus. Okay." Sam locked the stall door and turned around to give Emma some privacy. As she stood minding her own business, she heard a soft whoosh. "What was that?"

"I didn't hear anything."

"I think someone's here," Sam whispered. As she strained to listen, there was a splash behind her.

"Oh shit," Emma mumbled.

"What?" Sam whispered.

"My dick fell in the toilet."

Sam's voice rose in disgust. "Oh gross."

"Darn it, now it's gonna be wet," Emma said, her voice echoing around the restroom.

Sam huffed. "Well, just pull it out."

"No. That's disgusting."

"Just pull it out, for God's sake. Then we'll dry it off and put it back in."

A snicker and a soft cough came from the other side of the door.

Sam froze. Slipping back into her alter ego, she asked, "Ah, is someone in here?"

Anonymous feet shuffled out the door.

Sam cupped a hand over her open mouth. "Oh my God. Someone was in here."

Emma was too busy staring at Big Daddy in the bottom of the bowl to care about other occupants in the men's room. "Why isn't it floating? It sunk like a battleship."

"Did you pee yet?"

"No."

Sam's toes tapped impatiently. "Okay, then the water's clean. So just pull it out."

"This is so gross. I can't believe my hand is in a toilet." Emma fished around the bowl, snatched the offending member, and threw it on the ground with a resounding splat.

"Go pee so we can get out of here." As Sam finished the sentence, the door opened, and two men came in, chatting away.

Emma flushed the toilet and hiked up her pants.

They both stared at the wet dong on the floor, which seemed to be growing right before their eyes.

Emma mouthed to Sam, "What am I gonna do?"

Sam mouthed, "Put it back," and pantomimed shoving it into her jeans.

Emma's lip curled in disgust. "It's wet," she whined in a girly voice, forgetting all about the company on the other side of the door.

Sam flinched, putting a finger to her lips and gesturing toward the men outside the stall.

Emma slapped a hand over her mouth. "Sorry," she mouthed.

Sam pulled some toilet paper off the roll, figuring she'd wrap Big Daddy to dry him off. Another guy came in, and all three began conversing.

Sam tried to shove the swaddled donger back into Emma's pants, but Emma would have none of it and pushed her hand away, knocking the wrapped woody back onto the ground.

They both gaped in horror as the toilet paper unwrapped and the fake penis rolled under the stall door, leaving a wet trail of water behind as it slowly made its way over to the sinks.

Emma peered under the stall door to see where Big Daddy's journey ended. She lifted her head, mouthing, "Oops."

The conversation on the other side of the door paused.

Sam and Emma stood stock still in the stall, praying the men would leave.

Suddenly the fake member rolled back under the door, coming to a rest at Emma's feet. "Ah…thanks," Emma said in her Othello voice.

Sam's mouth formed a large "O" as she slapped at Emma. "Shut up," she mouthed.

Emma shrugged.

It remained quiet on the other side of the stall door. Finally, the door opened and the men left.

Sam sagged with relief. "Thank God. Now put it back in, and let's get the hell out of here."

"It's soaked. It's like one of those squeegees on TV, you know, on the QVC. It sucked up all the water."

"C'mon. We'll wrap it in paper towels."

"Maybe you should pee too, so we don't have to come back."

"Good idea." Peeling her pants down, Sam went to the bathroom, making sure to keep a firm grip on the tube socks. Cotton would be a lot more absorbent than Big Daddy.

After flushing, they both vacated the stall and washed their hands.

Emma grabbed some paper towels and wrapped the donger. She inserted it back inside her pants and thrust her hips forward. "Does it look okay?" A piece of paper towel stuck out between the zipper.

Sam stood back to take it all in. "You gotta a little *Something About Mary* going on there. Fix it."

Emma readjusted things. "How about now?" A wet spot materialized on the outside of Emma's zipper.

Sam stared at the Battle of the Bulge, which now appeared ridiculously large and wet. Everybody in the county would see it. "It's fine. No one will even notice. Let's go."

As they walked out of the bathroom, two men were coming in. One gazed down at Emma's crotch, then at her face, and gave a knowing wink. She winked back, and as she walked behind Sam, she made a show of thrusting her hips back and forth, like she'd just gotten lucky. She received a nod of appreciation from the winker and the other guy slipped his phone number into her pocket.

They found a table to stand at while they waited for Alex and Jade to show. "Do you want another beer?" Sam asked.

"Yeah sure."

When Sam got back to the table, she found Emma with two scantily clad women. One already had an arm around her. "Why, hey, what do we have here?"

Emma smiled. "This here is Candi, and this is Montana."

"Howdy, ladies." Sam offered a hand to each.

Candi pressed herself suggestively against Emma, ogling her fake junk.

Jade and Alex walked through the door at that moment, much to Sam's relief. She wanted to go greet them but didn't want to abandon Emma.

The music slowed down, and Candi squealed, "I love this song!" She tugged Emma onto the dance floor.

Sam chuckled at Emma's dilemma, but the amusement didn't last long as Montana grasped her hand and yanked her toward the newly minted couple.

* * *

Jade and Alex made their way over to the bar and joined Sophia and Lenna. "Anybody see two poorly dressed, shortish, gay-looking men come in?" Jade asked.

Lenna nodded in the direction of the dance floor. "Those the gentlemen in question?"

Emma and Sam were getting their groove on with a couple of cute women. "Oh, for fuck's sake," Jade said.

Alex laughed.

Sam looked beseechingly over, begging for rescue, and Alex waved back.

"If E's not careful, she's gonna be the next one to get her cherry popped." Jade glanced at Emma's zipper and her mouth dropped open. "Is there a wet spot on the front of her jeans?" she asked no one in particular.

"Should we go get them?" Alex asked.

"Nah." Jade turned back around and asked Monette for a beer.

Soon Zach, Jessica, Jackson, and Riley arrived to show their support.

Zach pulled Jade aside. "I got your text. Where are they?"

Jade pointed to the sea of humanity slow jamming on the dance floor. She had texted him pictures from the book signing, showing both gals in all their drag king glory.

Zach spotted his sister and his face paled. "Oh God. Should we do something?"

"They look like they're having fun," Riley said.

Finally, Sam managed to extract herself from her clinging dance partner and headed over to Alex.

Alex's eyes traveled over Sam's body. "Hi, honey, nice outfit."

"I expected you to rescue me."

"I was having too much fun watching your ass in those jeans. Kinda tight, aren't they?" Sam playfully shoved her. "Monette, may I have a water please?" She stared at Alex, desire clear in her eyes.

Alex stared back and cracked up again.

"What are you laughing at?"

"You, babe. Sorry."

"I look good, don't I?"

"You look...manly. But you need to work on your walk."

"What's the matter with my walk?"

Alex whispered into Sam's ear, "You sway those sexy hips of yours too much." She pulled back and winked.

"Wanna make out?"

"Not with that caterpillar on your lip."

"Um, what's Emma doing?" Zach asked.

Jade glanced over. "Ah, swapping spit with a chick."

They all turned and stared at the show.

"We should do something, right?" Zach asked.

"Wow, they're really getting into it," Riley observed.

When they pulled apart, the wet spot had been transferred to the front of the other woman's white pants.

Alex's brows shot up. "Whoa, what happened there?"

"Did Emma just come on that girl's pants?" Riley asked.

Sam jumped in. "No. Big Daddy fell into the toilet, and we stuck him back into her jeans. It was soaked."

Zach's forehead furrowed. "Big Daddy? Who's Big Daddy?"

"E stuffed a huge fake woody down her pants to make herself look well-endowed," Jade explained. "And I guess somehow she managed to lose it in the toilet. I don't even wanna know." She took a swig of beer.

Zach's expression screamed for an intervention.

"Don't look at me. She's your sister."

"Go help her," he begged.

"Help her do what?"

Zach continued to stare at Jade.

"Jesus Christ, I don't know what you expect me to do," Jade grumbled as she walked away. When she reached the happy couple, she yanked on Emma's arm to get her attention. After a heated discussion, they left the dance floor.

When they got back to the bar, Emma flagged down Monette and asked for another beer.

Riley sidled next to her. "Why were you kissing her?"

"Research. For my next role."

Riley nodded.

Emma's goatee teetered from her chin, having come unglued from the kissing.

Riley waved a finger. "Ah, E, you gotta costume malfunction going on."

"What?"

"You're losing your facial hair, Andre the Giant dong," Jade said.

Emma touched the goatee. "Shit. Sam, do you have the glue?"

"Yeah."

"We can go back to the bathroom," Emma said.

"Oh no. I'm not going back there."

Alex came to the rescue. "Monette, can they use your office for a sec?"

Monette nodded and tossed the keys to Emma, and off they went for repairs.

* * *

When they came back, Sam searched for Alex but couldn't find her.

"Where's Alex?" she asked.

"Over there." Riley pointed across the room.

Alex was talking to an attractive woman.

"Who the hell is that?" Sam growled.

"Michelle," Jade said.

"She knows Alex is taken, right?"

"Don't get your boxers in a bunch, she knows."

Michelle held onto Alex's arm—her bicep, to be exact. *Sam's* bicep. Sam had never been the jealous type and was taken aback at her own reaction.

"Sami, you have a dollop of steam coming from your ears."

"I don't like how she's touching her."

"Since when are you jealous?"

"Since I have a super-hot girlfriend, that's when."

"Fair enough. Where's E?" Jade craned her neck in search of Emma and her appendage.

"Over by the DJ," Riley said.

Emma had a blonde on either side and was chatting them up.

Jade groaned. "Oh shit."

"What?" Sam asked.

"That's two-thirds of Alex's three-way."

"What?"

"You heard me."

"What do you think they want with E?"

"I imagine they want a three-way with Big Daddy," Jade said matter-of-factly.

"Damn. That thing is trouble." Sam tipped her beer back. "You know, I'm kinda bumming."

"Why you bumming?"

"No one wants to get in *my* pants."

"I wanna get in your pants. I mean, literally. My feet are cold, and I don't have socks on."

A woman in red bought Jade a drink, and Jade began conversing with her.

Sam lost sight of Alex and then found her surrounded by a group of women. She gnashed her teeth in frustration. All these women hitting on her girlfriend, and she was powerless to stop them. She had half a mind to go over to Alex and plant one on those luscious lips, but instead she pouted.

Finally, Alex appeared by her side. "Hey, what's the matter?"

A dejected Sam toed the ground. "You have these women falling all over you, and I can't do anything about it."

"You still have those keys?"

Sam dangled them. "Yeah."

Alex took her hand and led her to Monette's office. They slipped in, locking the door behind them.

"Hey." Alex cupped Sam's face. "I love you. I don't even notice those other women. You're the only thing that matters to me. Okay?"

Sam gave a slight nod, still thrown by the whole jealousy thing.

Alex kissed her.

Sam pulled her closer, wanting and needing a whole lot more than a kiss.

* * *

Meanwhile, back at the bar, Calynn had finally arrived.

"Babe, you are a sight for sore eyes," Jade said.

"Why?"

"Don't ask."

Emma strutted over and slammed down a fistful of small paper slips. "Check this shit out."

Calynn's eyes zeroed in on Emma's zipper. "What the hell is that?"

Jade snorted. "Oh, meet Big Daddy, the schlong who ate Hollywood." She sifted through the slips of paper on the bar. "Are these all phone numbers?"

"Yeah, bitches. I'm obviously a handsome drag king."

"You can thank your fake willy," Jade said.

A petite woman approached Emma and tapped her on the shoulder. "Would you like to dance?"

Emma was led back to the dance floor. She turned and winked at Jade and Calynn.

"That one-eyed snake has gone to her head."

* * *

By the end of the evening, most of the gang was royally trashed. Alex and Sam sexed it up on the dance floor, impersonating a happy straight couple.

Emma was at the bar with Jade, Calynn, and Zach. She bent her head down to Jade's chest and tried to motorboat her.

"What the hell are you doing?" Jade asked.

"I...I just try to motorboat you...but I couldn't find 'em," Emma said with a pained expression on her face. She glanced over at Calynn's chest, and slowly extended a hand.

Calynn glared. "Don't you fucking dare."

Emma's hands stopped in their tracks. "I think that...s...a dollar," she grumbled. "This thing is annoying!" She reached into her pants and removed Big Daddy, plopping him on the bar. "I need another beer." She raised two fingers. "Make it two. Big Daddy's thirsty."

When Monette brought the beers, Emma put Big Daddy in one of the glasses. "There you go, buddy," she said affectionately.

* * *

Sam awoke the next morning with a serious hangover. She moaned at the morning light filtering in from the windows.

Alex was asleep on her stomach. Sam lay half on her, one leg possessively slung across her hip. It took a few minutes for things to come into focus. They had partied hard last night and drank way too much. Things were fuzzy, especially how they'd made it home.

Sam ran a hand through Alex's hair, trying to smooth down the wild curls. Alex was beautiful like this, lips slightly parted, long lashes dusting her cheeks, face peaceful in repose. Sam couldn't resist the urge to touch. She bent down and lightly kissed a bare shoulder, then nibbled down Alex's arm.

A rustling nearby caught her attention, and she lifted her head. A pair of brown eyes stared back from the other side of the bed. Sam blew an errant strand of hair from her eyes and rose up to get a better view of the intruder. Across the way, a tiny mouth munched back and forth. Rubbing sleep-crusted eyes, she shook her head to clear the cobwebs and peered across the bed again.

"Huh." Sam shook Alex's shoulder. "Honey," she said softly.

"Mmm."

"Are you awake?"

"Mmm."

"Why is there a baby goat in our room?"

Alex's eyes shot open. "What?"

"There's a baby goat in our room."

Alex popped up and surveyed the room. "What the hell?" Her eyes searched out Sam for an explanation, but all Sam could do was shrug. A soft bleat floated across the bed. "Holy shit, there's a baby goat in the room."

"He's cute."

"Is that Maynard? And is he eating your mustache?"

"Yes, he is."

"Huh. I guess they really do eat anything."

"What should we do about it?"

Alex took a moment to take in the scene. "Don't know. But looking at you is making me horny. Let's have sex and we'll come back to it."

"In front of the goat? Isn't that a little weird?"

"We can feed him the rest of your outfit, keep him busy. Oh, wait, there goes the wig."

Sam's phone rang. "It's Jade." She put it on speaker and answered. "Hey, what's up?"

"Did you see *WeHo Daily* yet?"

"No, we just woke up."

"Hold on, I'll show you." Jade texted a screenshot from the website. It was a picture of Alex piggybacking Carl around the dance floor, with the headline, "Local Author with Mystery Man."

Sam hooted. "That's hysterical!"

"I thought you'd like it."

"You know what's funnier?"

"What?"

Sam texted Jade a picture of the goat in their bedroom.

"Jesus Christ."

Alex headed to the bathroom. "Ah, honey?"

"Hold on Jade. Yes, baby?"

"There's another one in here."

"Another what, babe?"

"Another baby goat. He's in the tub, sleeping. I think it's Maxwell. Obviously, I can't say no to you when I'm drunk. Might wanna take a memo."

"Let me get this straight: sometime between the bar and home, you two birds stole a pair of baby goats?" Jade said. "While riding around in a limo."

Sam nodded. "Yes, it appears we did."

Alex crawled back into bed and snuggled her.

"But, as my girlfriend likes to say, in our defense, they were free to a good home. So it's not like we committed a felony or anything."

Alex nipped her nip.

Sam giggled and pulled Alex's head closer to her breasts, inviting more activity.

"You think this is funny?" Jade asked.

"No, it's very serious." Sam laughed as Alex motorboated her.

"Was that what I think it was?"

"What did you think it was?" Sam pushed Alex's head lower and groaned when Alex arrived at her destination.

"Oh my God. Okay, okay, I deserve this. What base is she on?"

Sam's breathing became erratic. "Third."

"Touché, Sami, touché."

CHAPTER TWENTY-SEVEN

"Marie's here with the dresses."

The stylist wheeled the clothes rack in, and Sam threw the latch across the jamb to leave the door open for Jade, Emma, and Calynn, who would be joining them shortly. Sam had booked them all rooms at the Peninsula Beverly Hills.

Alex and Lenna went over to inspect the clothes, wearing their complimentary hotel robes and slippers.

"Is there a pantsuit for me?" Lenna asked.

Sam patted her on the shoulder. "I took care of it."

Alex punched her sister. "It's the Oscars, numb nuts. You should wear a dress."

"I don't do dresses."

"You're so precious."

That comment earned Alex a throwdown on the couch.

They were still wrestling when Sophia entered the room. "Really?" With hands on hips, she addressed WrestleMania. "Hey, I have an idea, let's act like we've been here before."

"It's the Academy Awards," Lenna said. "I have no clue how to act."

"You'll be fine," Sam said.

"Are you sure you don't wanna leave her here, babe? She can be all sorts of embarrassing," Alex said.

Lenna bopped her in the head with a pillow and pushed her onto the floor.

Jade burst through the door at that moment, with Emma and Calynn right behind her. "Party time, bitches!"

Emma squealed. "Wrestling match!" She ran over and pounced on the Novato sisters.

Jade folded her arms in disgust. "How about the adults start getting ready. The first graders can go last."

Jade, Sam, Sophia, and Calynn headed into the bedroom to get dressed.

After a few more minutes, the three stopped wrestling and sat with their backs against the couch.

"These robes are nice," Lenna said. "I'm sticking it in my suitcase. Do you think they'll notice?"

"Will there be room? What with all the beer you shoved in from the mini fridge," Alex said.

Emma burrowed between the sisters. "Guys, take whatever you want. They don't care."

"They don't?" Lenna asked.

"Nope. Take it all." Emma looked at the dining room table. "Where's your gift basket?"

"Lenna shoved it in Sophia's suitcase. She doesn't get out much."

Emma nodded. "I decorated a whole room with hotel stuff once."

"Really?" Lenna asked.

"Yeah. I bought a new suitcase just so I could take it all home. I've taken a comforter, sheets, curtains. I took an entire serving set once, too. Served six."

Lenna's eyes widened. "Wow. Aren't you the little klepto? Cool."

"You took all that?" Alex asked.

"Yep."

Lenna scouted the curtains.

"Don't you dare," Alex warned.

"What? We need curtains in the spare room. These are kinda nice."

"Do it." Emma nudged a shoulder into Lenna, egging her on.

"No." Alex's mouth set in a hard line. "Don't do anything that might reflect badly on Sam."

The mention of Sam's name was all it took for Lenna to be properly chastised.

A half hour later, Sam breezed into the living room with hair up, makeup on, and dressed to the nines.

Alex stared, mouth slightly agape. She was a vision, perfect and beautiful. Sam's blond curls were piled on top of her head, with feathery tendrils hanging down the side of her face. She wore a gorgeous, black, sleeveless gown with a sheer throw over her bare shoulders.

As usual, Alex's eyes stopped at the full cleavage.

Sam smirked. "See something you like?"

Alex swallowed. "Uh-huh. I kinda wanna take that gown off right now."

Sam laughed. "You'll have to wait a few hours," she teased. "Do you think you can manage?"

"I guess I'll have to."

Sam pointed to the bedroom. "All right, dorks. In you go."

Alex gave her a quick, careful kiss, not wanting to ruin her makeup job. "You're gorgeous," she whispered.

* * *

They stood around the living room an hour later, waiting for the limo. Sophia fussed with the buttons on Lenna's sleek, elegant pantsuit, while Jade, Calynn, and Emma tried to find comfortable shoes from the selection Marie had brought. Logan waited patiently nearby, handsome in his black and white tuxedo.

Sam was busy admiring her girlfriend. Marie had chosen a free-flowing silver gown for Alex. There was a slit up the side—showing off a sexy, tanned leg—and an open back. The hairstylist had straightened Alex's unruly waves so they cascaded down past her shoulders.

Sam ran a finger along Alex's arm. "You look like a goddess. We need to dress up more often."

"Well, you're breathtaking." Alex drank her in. "I can't believe you're mine."

"And I can't believe how lucky I am to have you."

Alex's eyes fluttered shut. Sam's hand had found the gap in her gown, and it slid between her legs, up, up, stopping at the dead end.

Sam chuckled at the expression on Alex's face and gave her another peck on the lips. During the last two years, occasional rumors had surfaced about Sam's love life, and how Alex was always near, but the whispers had never become full-blown accusations. It had certainly kept Jade busy, trying to explain to the press the reason for their closeness. Just a couple of friends living together for the time being was her usual line. Alex had remained steadfast in her support of Sam's career, never insisting she come clean about their relationship. But it pained Sam to keep their love and life they shared a secret. In fact, as time went on, it got harder and harder. She needed to step out of the closet, sooner rather than later. Alex deserved that.

Jade's phone buzzed. "Car's here, peeps. Let's roll. PS10, I think you have some drool coming out of your mouth."

They all filed downstairs and into the limo.

"Who's presenting Best Actress?" Emma asked, nestling back against Logan.

"Jocelyn Brown, baby," Sam replied.

Jade grabbed at her chest. "Be still my gay heart."

Emma poked around in her purse. "Anybody hungry? I have Jolly Ranchers." She pulled one out and popped it in her mouth. After a second, her face pinched with distaste and she spit it back into its wrapper. As Emma put it back in the purse, she glanced over at Sam…and winced.

"What?" Sam asked.

"Nothing." Emma snapped the purse shut. "Did you prepare a speech?"

"No, I didn't want to jinx it. And there are some strong nominees. I mean, I can't imagine I'll win."

"You were great too," Logan said. "Think positive."

"Yeah, be positive," Jade said. "But don't forget the camera is on you when they announce the winner. Watch your face. Don't look disappointed. Look gracious."

"I know."

"Don't roll your eyes."

"I wouldn't roll my eyes."

"Don't curse."

"Shut the hell up."

Alex fidgeted next to Sam.

Sam sensed her uneasiness and squeezed her hand. "You okay?"

Alex nodded.

"You'll get used to it. Stick with me, baby." Sam winked.

"What's gonna happen when we get there?" Lenna asked.

"The red carpet is gonna be a zoo, so stay close to me and Calynn," Jade said. "We'll kinda hang back while Sam, E, and Logan go first. Follow my lead, and you'll be fine. Okay, we're here. Everyone ready? Smile, people!"

* * *

The driver opened the door.

Sam exited the limo first, and the fans went wild. Emma and Logan followed to robust cheers.

Alex's heart leapt into her throat as she stepped onto the red carpet and gazed around in wonder. All the fans along the ropes clamored for Sam's attention. Alex tried to give herself a pep talk, praying she wouldn't stumble in the high heels. She walked next to Jade and Calynn, Sophia and Lenna bringing up the rear.

Sam and Emma were both pulled aside for interviews, so the going was slow. Sam's grace in these situations amazed her. An image of Sam walking into the patio door popped into her head and she smiled to herself.

Jade leaned into her ear. "What's so funny?"

"Sam was so dorky when we first met. When I see her like this, I'm always in awe."

"Let's face it, she's a huge dork. That hasn't changed."

When the interviews and photo ops finally ended, the group entered the auditorium, and took their seats in the tenth row.

* * *

Sam settled into her seat and tried to relax by taking deep, calming breaths. No biggie, right? It was just the Oscars. Ha! She wanted to puke into her handbag.

She had Alex on one side and her mom, Angela, on the other. It would be a long, torturous wait for the Best Actress award, but having loved ones on either side would hopefully keep Sam from jumping out of her skin with anticipation. What would really keep her calm would be Alex's arm around her, but PDA was off the table.

Toward the end of the evening, Jocelyn Brown appeared on stage. Alex grabbed one hand and her mom grabbed the other.

Sam shifted in her seat and jiggled her leg. All the hard work, all the years on stage and TV, all came down to this moment. All her hopes and dreams. Her stomach knotted. She bit her lip and squeezed Alex's hand.

"And the winner for Best Actress is…"

They all held their collective breath.

"Samantha Cassidy for *Addictions*."

Sam's jaw dropped open. Her heart stopped beating. She sat frozen in her seat until Alex kissed her on the cheek and her mom shrieked. It took a moment to find the strength to stand, and when she did, she turned to a tearful Angela. She knew her mom was also remembering Sam's performances as a young child, and her father.

Sam turned to Alex, and they embraced.

"Congratulations, baby. I love you so much," Alex whispered in her ear before releasing her.

Emma and Zach kissed her, and Jade bear-hugged her on her way out of the aisle.

As Sam approached the steps to the stage, she lifted her gown. Now was not the time to face plant on the top step of the Dolby Theatre. She headed toward the podium and graciously accepted the Oscar. Staring at the statue, she put a hand to her throat. This was her dream come true. She blinked back tears.

"I really didn't expect this, so I didn't prepare anything. And I know you hear that all the time, but it's totally true."

"Booyah! Drop that fucking mic, Sam," Jade yelled from the audience.

"Aaand, that's my crazy manager, Jade Ramos. Hope you guys bleeped that out. Ah, let's see." Sam took a moment to soak it all in—the cameras, the rapt audience, the icons of film and television all gazing at her. "I'd like to thank the producers at Columbia for allowing me to play this role. All my co-stars, who were terrific. I'd like to thank the crew, the awesome writers. My director, Tom Shepherd. I always love working with you. My agent, Zach Barrett. My manager, Jade Ramos. And my mom, who puts up with me every day." Sam took a breath to steady herself. "And I'd like to dedicate this to my dad. He's not with us anymore. He passed away when I was fourteen, and he was my biggest fan. He made me a homemade Oscar when I was five." Sam looked skyward. "Daddy, I won the real one now."

* * *

Alex wiped a tear from her cheek.

"And lastly, I'd like to thank the love of my life—"

Jade grabbed Alex's hand and squeezed. "Holy mother fucking shit, she's doing it."

"—who's been by my side for over two years now—"

"Holy mother fucking shit, she's coming out."

"—Alex Novato."

"And, she's out."

Sam's gaze locked on Alex. "I love you so much. I loved you the first time I laid eyes on you."

Alex mouthed back, "I love you too."

"Hot damn," Jade said with admiration.

"And while I have your attention…"

"Oh, lord Jesus, what now?" Jade asked.

"I just want to ask. Alex, will you marry me?"

Jade shook her head in disbelief. "Oh my God. Oh my fucking God."

A hush went through the auditorium, then slowly the clapping started from the back, and like a wave it took over the entire room. Cheering and shouting soon followed.

A dumbstruck Alex sat unmoving, mouth hanging open.

Jade nudged her shoulder. "Answer!"

Alex nodded. She mouthed, "Yes."

Sam laughed. "Well, she said yes, so I guess you're all invited to the wedding."

The audience went wild and rose to their feet.

"Thank you so much!" Sam pumped the Oscar in the air.

"Holy fuck, don't drop it," Jade shouted in Alex's ear. They were both laughing and wiping at the moisture on their cheeks.

Sam was ushered off stage, and the show cut to a commercial break.

* * *

"Thank you, Sam," Jocelyn said when they got backstage.

"For what?"

"Now they'll have something to talk about other than me dropping and breaking this little statue last year."

"Oh, you're welcome. I mean, coming out of the closet in front of millions of people definitely trumps a broken Oscar, don't you think?"

"Coming out? You didn't just come out. You shot the fuck out of there."

"I did, didn't I?"

"Like a goddamn cannon. Congratulations. You have balls, Cassidy. Your girl's gorgeous, by the way."

"Thanks."

Alex and Jade soon joined her backstage. She hugged Jade and turned to Alex.

"Did I give you a heart attack?"

"Hell no." Alex pulled her in for the most award-winning kiss in the history of the Oscars.

When they broke apart, Sam was alight with excitement. "I can't believe it. I can't believe I won."

"I can't believe you proposed. On stage. At the Oscars!"

"Well, I've been waiting for the right moment, and when I was standing at that podium tonight, I knew it was perfect. I love you so much, and I wanted everyone to know it. Everyone in the world."

"Well, I would say mission accomplished. Looks like we have a wedding to plan. How many people did you just invite?"

"The more the merrier, right? I have to go to the press room. I'll see you in a few."

"Okay, I'll let you go. I love you so much." Alex kissed her again.

"I love you too."

* * *

Shortly after two a.m., the limo turned into the parking lot at Monette's. The Oscar sat on the seat next to Sam. Mr. Emmy finally had his friend.

When the limo stopped, the gang filed out. Velvet ropes led to the door of the club. Word had spread that Sam and Alex would be at the bar sometime after midnight. Fans who had been in line for hours screamed, hoping to attract the attention of Hollywood's new royalty.

Sam and Alex walked hand in hand through the chaos, high-fiving people and posing for selfies. Emma and Logan followed behind.

Jade had arrived before everyone else, and when they entered the club, she handed them baseball hats embroidered with #CassiNova. Laughing, they put the hats on. The place was packed with regulars, family, friends, and Oscar winners. All wearing hats.

Sam pulled Jade in for a big hug. "The hats are perfect. Where did you get CassiNova from?"

Jade pointed to Emma. "Well, believe it or not, from E. She blurted it out a couple of years ago."

"Yeah bitches! It was *me*!" Emma took a selfie and texted it to Logan, who stood by her side.

Jade placed an arm around Emma's shoulders. "I think she levitated when she said it."

Sam giggled. "Too funny. The hats are brilliant, by the way."

"I'm trending you bitches up." Jade high-fived them both.

"I'm going to the bar. Do you want anything?" Alex asked.

"Not right now, baby, thank you."

Alex gave Sam a peck on the cheek and headed to the bar.

Sam murmured into Jade's ear, "Wow. There's a lot of people here."

"Yep, I invited everyone. Jocelyn Brown is here."

"Where?"

Jade pointed toward the bar.

Sam put a hand to her heart. Across the room, Jocelyn and Alex were chatting. "Holy shit, she's talking to my girl. And she just made Jocelyn laugh." Sam beamed with pride.

Soon Lenna joined her sister. Sam's eyes widened. "Oh no, no, no, don't put her in a headlock, not in front of Jocelyn."

She breathed a sigh of relief when Lenna simply put an arm around her baby sis.

Eventually, Alex found Sam and led her to the dance floor. "Hey, guess what?" she asked.

"What?"

"We don't have to hide anymore."

They shared a very public kiss.

Soon the whole gang joined them.

The music slowed down, and the DJ announced, "This next song is dedicated to our own CassiNova."

When the first notes played, Alex and Emma whooped and grabbed their respective partners. Jade crossed her arms and cursed.

And they all slow danced to the Bee Gees' "To Love Somebody."

Alex pulled Sam close. "This is our first public slow dance, you know."

"I'm aware."

"You know this is gonna be the song we slow dance to at our wedding, right?"

"I know. Guess how much I love you?"

"To the moon and back?"

Sam caressed Alex's cheek. "You got that right."

"Have I told you how stunning you look tonight?"

"Many times."

"Have I told you I can't wait to motorboat the shit out of you later?"

Sam giggled and pulled her closer. "Have I told you you're the best thing in my life? And now I can tell whoever I want?"

"Well, you kinda just told forty million people. So there's that." Alex lifted Sam and twirled her around. When Sam's feet were back on terra firma, Alex whispered, "I love you, Sam Cassidy."

Sam snuggled close, softly singing the rest of the song in Alex's ear. It was a perfect moment. The whole night had been perfect.

* * *

Sam and Alex awoke in their hotel room the next morning, naked and wrapped around each other.

Sam groaned. "I have a mega hangover."

Alex yawned. "You only had four beers. I lost count and cannot feel my tongue right now."

The Oscar on the table mesmerized them both.

"Can you believe it? It's really there," Sam said with reverence.

"Amazing."

She left the warmth of the bed, shrugged into a robe, and headed to the bathroom. When she came back out, someone knocked.

"I'll get it." Sam peered through the peephole and opened the door to a pajama-clad Jade, who had a stack of newspapers in her arms.

She made a beeline to the bedroom. "Check this out, bitches. Oh. You naked in that bed, PS10?"

"As the day I was born."

"Good. I've been waiting for this for a long time." Jade slipped under the covers.

Alex rolled on top of Jade.

"Whoa, you are naked."

"I said I was."

"Like, really naked. Sam, she's naked."

Sam settled on top of the covers in her bathrobe, leaning back against the headboard with a newspaper in hand. "Well, that's been your dream, right? Getting Alex naked in bed? Have at it."

Jade lay rigid beneath Alex, eyes rapidly blinking. "I think I was kidding. She's really naked."

Alex continued to lay on top of her, staring down in amusement. "Something wrong?"

"No, no. Nothing's wrong. You're just pretty naked."

"Wanna three-way?"

"Oh fuck." Jade was clearly out of her league. "You're kidding, right? Sam, she's kidding, right?"

"Nope, don't think so."

Alex continued to wait for an answer.

"Maybe next time?" Jade whimpered in a small voice.

Alex rolled off. "Chicken."

Sam laughed as she paged through the newspapers. "This is great. Look at this first one. *'Hashtag CassiNova Trending Up, Sam Cassidy Proposes to Her Girlfriend in Acceptance Speech.'* That's funny. And here, *'CassiNova, Hollywood's New Power Couple.'* With a lovely picture of us kissing by the way. And this one *'Hashtag CassiNova Forever, She Says Yes!'*"

"Oh my God, we're a hashtag. We've made it!" Alex leaned over Jade to kiss Sam.

Another knock sounded.

Sam padded into the living room and opened the door.

Emma shuffled in and cautiously navigated through the clothes littering the floor. "Somebody had a good time last night," she mumbled on her way to the bedroom.

"What the hell are on your feet?" Jade asked.

"What? These are my slippers." Emma wiggled the rabbit ears on her big, fluffy, white slippers.

"Jesus Christ, what'd you do? Stomp on Bugs Bunny?"

"Shut up. They're cute." Emma climbed into bed and slid under the covers next to Jade.

"So when's the wedding?" Jade asked.

Alex shrugged. "Honey, when are we getting married?"

"I guess next year. And now that I'm officially out of the closet and probably out of a job, we may have to do a GoFundMe campaign to pay for it," she said in jest.

"You still have the series," Emma said.

"Yeah. But movie roles may be scarce."

Jade put a finger in the air. "Hold on, Sami, I forgot to tell you."

"What?"

"At the Vanity Fair party last night, I ran into Donna Williams from Universal."

Sam perked up. Donna was a bigwig at the studio. "And?"

"Well, you know the Janis Joplin biopic that's been floating around for years?"

"The one that never seems to get made?"

"Yes, that one. They want you for it."

"Even after charging out of the closet?"

"Yep."

"You're shitting me, right?"

"No, I am not. They want you. It's gonna be a prime gig."

"Are you telling me outing myself did not destroy my career?"

"That is what I'm telling you. Congratulations, Sam, your career is not dead."

Sam and Alex exchanged a tender glance.

"I love you." Sam crawled across Emma and Jade to get to Alex. She scooched down next to her.

"Group fucking hug," Emma hollered. "Is it still a dollar? 'Cause I don't have any money."

"You don't have any bucks in those bunny shoes of yours?" Jade asked.

"Nope."

They all snuggled into each other.

"CassiNova forever!" Jade shouted.

Emma put a prideful fist in the air. "I thought of that shit."

Jade gave Emma a squeeze. "Yes, you did, Jan Brady. Yes, you did. Drop that mic, girl."

Lori and Everette

Bella Books, Inc.

Women. Books. Even Better Together.

P.O. Box 10543
Tallahassee, FL 32302

Phone: 800-729-4992
www.bellabooks.com